Among Us

R. E. Henderson

DEDICATION

I dedicate this book to my wife, daughter and family.

Prologue

Chris Wilson stood in front of his mirror, as he made sure his hair, mascara and black fingernail polish were just right. He looked himself over- dressed in a black shirt with a black pair of Tripp pants that had green chains that hung down on the side. He admired the man he had become, the man he had set out to be since he was a teenager years ago. He had a smile on his face, but the moment he heard a knock on his bedroom door the smile turned into a look of confusion.

His hands shook as he reached for the door knob and wondered who it could have been in his house. He was certain he was alone, since it was not even an hour ago that he danced around to loud music in his boxers while he cleaned the house. That was his own kind of party. Now though, it frightened him and sent goosebumps down his arms to think he wasn't alone. As he turned the knob, he felt faint, but with his eyes closed, he found what little strength he could and opened the door, only to an empty hall. He peeked around the corner where a breeze surrounded him and swayed the curtains down on the other end of the hall as well.

With ease, he stepped out into the hall and crept along the hardwood floor where he focused his thoughts on the pictures along the wall. The first picture he noticed was taken back when Chris and his best friend Michael

Gable were 17 years old at a Friday night school event where on either side of the boys was a girl whom they both loved, Angela Stutts. However, unbeknownst to the boys, from that night forward things would never be the same.

Chapter One

Most of the weekend after the photo was taken, Angela had spent her time with Chris, which for him it was his first date and the first girl who had ever showed a bit of attention to him. It was a simple date of course. They had gone to the movies and yet didn't even hold hands, but as simple as it was, it meant everything to Chris. He was sure the date was leading somewhere, but then that Monday at school everything was out of proportion.

He walked into the lunchroom in a blue and white checkered dress shirt and tan khaki pants- anxious to find both Angela and Michael, the only two people his age that he cared about. Although when he found them, he didn't expect to see Angela sitting on Michael's lap with her arms wrapped around his neck. Chris couldn't move, he was breathless, not knowing whether to run or hide, cry, or even to pick a fight with Michael. Angela caught sight of him and ran over and embraced him with the biggest hug she ever could. He lost all train of thought.

"My, Chris, are you losing weight?" She asked. He was self-conscious of his weight as was, so the question was a bit offensive, but he kept his cool and acted as if it was just a kind gesture. Deep down though, he had a funny feeling that something was going on between Michael and Angela. He was right of course, and it hurt that he was right.

Soon after, it turned into where he couldn't even hang with Michael without Angela following right beside them, or in Michael's case, his arm over her shoulder. From then on there was just something about her that Chris couldn't trust. He couldn't put his finger on why, but knew it was bad.

***

Chris laid in bed and stared up at the ceiling as he tried to sleep. The phone on the night stand beside him vibrated from a call. "Hello?" he answered. "Yeah man I'll come down out there." He threw on a jacket and tip toed down stairs as not to wake his folks. And when he opened the front door, there was Michael on the steps with a flask in his hands. "What's up man?"

"Terrible."

"Why what happened?" Chris took a seat down beside him. Michael offered him a drink of the flask. "No thanks."

"Suit yourself." He took a swig and stared off into the darkness. "It's Angela, man. So we had plans to go to the movies tonight with my brother, right? Well we pulled up to her house and Barry said, *'I wonder what Eric is doing here'.*

I walked up to her door and I could see her in the living room laying in that Eric guy's lap in her pajamas. He had his arm around her waist. Which, by now I was pretty heated, and so I banged on the door. She answered all innocent, "What's up?"

"What do you mean what's up? What's going on? I thought we were going to the movies?"

"Calm down Mikey, I can't go. I haven't seen my boyfriend in a while and luck would have it we get to see each other tonight."

"Boyfriend? Since when has this been going on? I thought I was your boyfriend."

"About a few months before I met you guys."

"You have had a boyfriend this entire time and we made love?"

"Yeah, but shhh, he doesn't know about that," Angela giggled.

"Forget you!" I screamed and walked away. She tried to call me back, but I didn't turn around. Well, not until I heard a *WHACK*! From where their neighbors were playing basketball and it went over the fence and knocked her rear end out. I couldn't help but laugh, even though, her boyfriend ran out the door after me."

"What did Barry do?"

"Oh my brother? He jumped out of the car and pushed me out of the way and faced the guy and said, "You lay one finger on my brother and I swear it will be your last. I know you're over 18, right?"

"I'm 19." I kid you not Eric shoot where he stood. He was terrified of Barry.

"19!" Barry screamed. "Okay then, I don't guess you want to go to jail, so stay away from my brother. Let's go Mickey". So we got in Barry's car and that was that, we left."

"Wow, so what happened to Angela?"

"I really don't know. Mom didn't even say she called. In all honestly, I don't even care. She broke my heart. All I know is that you and I haven't been close the last few months, and I'm sorry about that. I should've been smarter."

"It's okay man, you are here now. You want to stay the night?"

"Na man, I gotta walk around some."

"Okay, you're more than welcome to stay if you want."

"Thanks, but I guess I'll see you some time tomorrow."

"Hey, you want to go to the field and play some Shovel Rock?"

"We'll see man, night." Michael stood to walk away.

Chris though, started to head back into the house when he heard a thump and turned around to see Michael face down on the ground and grunted, "Thanks kitty!" Chris went inside and laughed as he closed the door behind him.

***

As he walked through the woods, Michael thought as much as his inebriated mind could let him think, which was mostly about his family, Chris, and of course Angela. He loved Angela to death, and he thought she loved him. She was really the first girl whom he had been with. The first girl that ever showed an interest in him, same as she did with Chris. It was then he knew why Chris felt so bad all of the time. He didn't even know Chris anymore, and really messed with him.

The moon shined through the trees which left just enough light for his breath to be seen. Sticks and fallen leaves crunched underneath Michael as he balanced himself from falling on his rear end. It didn't help that he tumbled against every branch. The liquor really took effect on him.

With a little way from Angela's house, something loud banged continuously up ahead that echoed in his ears. Sure enough, outside of the woods, a party raged on. It was one of her many parties that he was never invited to. Groups of teens had gathered around the yard with cups and bottles in their hands. "Well what's going on here?" He thought to himself as he stumbled up the front lawn. The most he could do, given he could barely hold himself up, was scream her name. But no Angela came to his calling.

Inside, the teens were all drunk as he was. Groups of guys in red and white lettermen jackets were mumbling songs in a barber shop quartet style of music. Both the dining room and living room were taken over as one big pillow while drunks who had too much would pass out where they lay. Pizza boxes, bottles, empty cups stacked all around the sound system, while broken bottles scattered around the floor. Uneaten pizza crust stuck out in random places in the cabinets.

"Hey, you tree, where is Angela?" Michael leaned toward a tall person beside him. He had thought he put his hand on the person's shoulder for stability. "Oh you are a tree. Well forget you too, piece of wood. Ok Mikey, bud, you're losing it. Let's think now. Where would Angela be? Could she be in this closet? Nope not there. Is she in her bedroom? Better not be in there with that Leric...Jeric...Seric...oh Eric, that's it. I'm drunk. Why yes, I am. To the bedroom!"

He stood outside of her door, trying to keep it all together and knocked. No answer. He knocked again and still, nothing. "Angela?" He slowly walked in. "Ange- Oh there you are!"

He found her in the bathroom, her head was face down in the toilet bowl. "Mikey what are you doing here?" She whispered so that no one else could hear her.

"I need to talk to you."

"Well close the door." She pulled herself up and washed her mouth in the sink. "What is it Mikey?"

"Ang, I love you! Why are you doing this to me?"

"I gotta go."

"No, no not that. Why are you with that...that...that poo poo head?"

"Poo poo head? I'm in love with him Mikey."

"No you are in love with me. Me Angela. YOU...LOVE...Me!"

"I do love you Mikey, but I'm in-love with Eric."

"That's a bunch of...I gotta puke." He turned around and puked. "Hey, fishy. There's a fishy in the toilet. Why is a fishy in the toilet? Are you going to murder the fishy like you murdered my heart?"

"No, you puked in my fish bowl."

"Oh...well okay then."

"I think you better leave."

"Not until you agree you will stay with me."

"Just go."

"Come home with me."

"This is my home."

"No it's not!"

"Mikey?"

"What?"

"Just go!" Angela screamed with tears in her eyes.

"One more thing before I go." He placed his hand on her shoulder blade and kissed her as passionately as he could. Her lips warm and gentle against his. "You will be missing that by the end of the night."

Now he wanted to drink more, but knew that if he did drink more he would be in trouble. He held his head up high and walked out the front door and yet no matter how high he held his head his eyes were still a bit teary. That much pride he couldn't hold.

"Well I'll be," a voice said from the shadows. "Look who it is boys. Let's have some fun."

Michael turned to his right and faced Eric and his friends who came his way. "Do you think I'm afraid of you? What makes you so 'cool' anyways? You're so lucky, you have the most beautiful girlfriend in the world. I could dream to have her in my arms...again, but all she cares about is you. You! Of all people. And you are willing to throw all of that away just to be macho and hit me? What a waste of life. Cherish it, be with her." He shook Eric's hand before he stepped down on to the sidewalk. Eric didn't know what to do, he was speechless. Angela stood on her porch and cried as Eric walked over to her and leaned against the doorway.

"What's wrong?" he asked. He put his hand on her back and tried his best to comfort her.

"Don't touch me! I think you should leave. Matter of fact, party's over! Everyone get out!" She pulled away from Eric and ran into her bedroom where she slammed the door behind her. The pictures on the wall outside her door fell and smashed on the floor.

***

Down the road, headlights slowly came up over a hill and flashed on Michael. He squinted to see who was behind the wheel.

"Get in the car." Barry ordered as he rolled down the window. Michael didn't hesitate and climbed in and fastened his seat belt. He stared up toward the sky which dawn was now on its way and didn't say a word. Barry pulled away and it was then that Michael let loose and broke down. Barry stopped the car and held on to his brother and rocked him to comfort. "It's okay bro, let it out. Let it out. I'm not going anywhere."

It took him awhile, but when he finally did calm his

nerves, they ate breakfast and watched the sun rise.

Chapter Two

Angela cried herself to sleep. She didn't know which to believe: either that she was wrong for how much she loved Eric, that she missed Michael, or for everything that she had done to cause her to feel this way. All she wanted was to be left alone and cry to figure it all out.

The sun was shining through her curtains, and the birds that chirped in the early morning that had woken her up from a deep hungover sleep. Slowly, she opened her eyes and rolled over on her back. It didn't take long before she felt vomit rise to the back of her throat. This had been going on for a week or so now, where she had woken up to sickness. It of course only happened in the morning, and has only but gotten worse. She ran to the bathroom and released what was left in her from the night before. With her head rested against the toilet bowl, she stared at the frog wallpaper that for some odd reason had got her to think of Michael and of how sweet he was and that he really cared for her. It made her vomit even more. This, she knew, was guilt and even more with her nerves shot.

Before she could even begin to go through the house and clean up everyone else's mess, she picked up the phone and called Michael. No answer. She then decided to call Chris, and thought that maybe he was with Michael.

"Hello?" He asked, as he pulled himself up and tried to make himself awake.

"Hey Hun, is Michael there?"

"Who is this?"

"Your friend Angela."

"Angela?"

"Yea it's me."

"What are you doing calling here at 7:45 in the morning?"

"I have to talk to Michael, is he around?"

"No he's not, I don't know where he is, probably at home in bed. He was here last night drunk, but he left. Look, he's really heartbroken over what happened, I don't think you need to be talking to him."

"Yeah, I know, but I just have to kiss him and see if I love him."

"If you *think* you love him, then you really don't." Chris hung up the phone without a proper goodbye. She expected that, but didn't expect the blow to feel that hard.

***

She unlocked the bedroom door as she walked out into her hallway, and hoped that nobody was passed out in front of the door. Her eyes were puffy from crying all night, and her hair looked like a bush in the wind. Too weak to walk, she scooted herself along the hardwood floor. The house was a wreak and even toilet paper hung from the willow tree in the front yard. It'll take days, if even that, to clean the mess up, but was the party worth it? She really didn't know the answer to that. She stood, looked out the front screen door, and felt the cold winter breeze. All at the same time she did not even take notice of the couch behind her.

"Sleep well?" She turned to see Eric on the couch, arms crossed with a smile on his face. "I want to know every detail of what you and that kid did."

"Just leave it alone Eric."

"Leave it alone!? Leave it alone! He made a fool of me! How should I feel, knowing my *fiancé* is messing around with a child!"

"Then leave if it hurts you that bad. He was a friend. Heck, you've messed around before."

"I never cheated on you one time, Angy! I have always been loyal to you."

"Oh yeah right, being around all your buddies. You have to be so macho, so cool. It's so cool to cheat on your girlfriend isn't it? Plus, it's not like you're ever around anyways."

"Babe, I was here last night, wasn't I?"

"Not really, I barely even saw you."

"This is so not right; you cheat and I'm the one getting the 3rd degree. You know what? You are way out of line. It's time to teach you a lesson!" He stood from the couch while he took off his belt. Angela ran toward her room as she heard Eric yell behind her, "Come here girl! I'm not playing with you!"

She crawled to the back corner of her closet where she held on to the stuffed monkey Michael had got her at the fair. The walls shook from every kick Eric made to the bedroom door to break in. There was a *THUD* as the door fell against her dresser. She held her breath as there was only silence.

After a few minutes of just listening and waiting, she felt as if she was finally alone. All she knew was that she wanted to get out of the house and run to Michael and tell him how she felt. She decided that it was safe to come out of hiding. On her hands and knees, she pushed open the door. Nothing. Still silent. She looked to her right and then to her left, nothing in her way. Slowly, she pulled herself up and walked out a little way, and let the closet door creak shut behind her. Her bedroom door lay beside her with broken pieces of the door frame still attached to the hinges.

A warm breath of air landed on the back of her neck. She screamed as hands grabbed her shoulders and threw her to the bed. She had forgotten to check her bathroom, where Eric had waited for her with patience. She felt the cold steel of Eric's knife press against her throat. "You make one more scream and I swear this bed will be filled with your blood! Do you hear me!"

Angela nodded her head slightly in agreement, where tears rolled down her cheeks. She closed her eyes, not sure what was about to happen, but she knew it was going to be bad.

Chapter Three

Chris simply walked on into Michael and Barry's house, where their front door was never locked as long as Chris could remember. He followed the distinct sounds of a video game down in Barry's bedroom in the basement, and then took a seat down on the couch beside Barry.

"Whoa, hey! Chris, man, you scared me." Barry didn't take but a second glance off his game.

"I'm good at that huh?"

"Yeah, yeah you are. What's up?"

"Nothing really, came by to hang out with you guys. Michael asleep?"

"Yeah buddy." He laughed and knew that with how bad Michael had gotten the night before, that surely wouldn't be feeling all the best today.

"How's he doing?"

"Mickey's doing okay, just tired ya know? He just made a few mistakes, we all do. But you have my permission that if you ever see him with alcohol again, to kick his rear end for me. Can you do that?"

"Maybe. I'm sure I could if needed."

"You see him as a brother don't you?"

"Of course, you guys are like a second family to me."

"Well okay then, there you go. Take up for your family, keep them safe."

"You do have a point."

"Oh I know I do. But what was you guys going to get into today?"

"Probably just play some Shovel Rock."

"Shovel Rock? What's that?"

"Come on, lets wake Michael and you'll find out." Chris wore a mischievous grin. When he had an idea, there was nothing stopping him.

They made their way into Michael's bedroom where posters of random movies, a few rock bands, and street racing cars filled up the empty spaces on the walls. Barry asked, "So do you see anything we could use to wake him up with?"

"Umm...I got it," Chris said with his eyes focused on the movie poster to the 1974 *Texas Chainsaw Massacre*. He opened the closet door and pulled out a Leatherface mask from the top shelf. "Here, this should do it."

"Not really, you got to go all the way. Be right back." Barry left the room as Chris sat down in the desk chair in front of the television. He looked around and thought of how when he very first came over to play that there were cartoon characters on the walls along with matching bed sheets. And now, look at where they have headed in life-how they used to spend all hours of the night listening to music and playing video games or having their own horror movie-a-thons. Time had really flown by.

He was so far gone in his own thoughts that he didn't even realize that Barry had returned. Barry placed his hand on Chris' shoulder and startled him back to reality. "Shh,"

Barry whispered, dressed in a torn up jumpsuit, gloves, and work boots. Chris helped him with the mask, careful not to touch the blade of the welcoming chainsaw in Barry's hands.

On the count of three, Barry yanked on a string and started up the motor. Michael jumped almost five feet off the ground and landed on the floor. He screamed as loud as could be and cried as he tried his hardest to crawl away. Chris fell on the floor where tears just rolled down his face from laughter.

"Dude! That was so cruel!" Michael tossed a pillow at Barry, but the chainsaw made its mark. A cloud of feathers floated around the room. Barry picked feathers out of his hair and said, "That was pretty good though."

***

"So where are we going anyways?" Barry asked while he was following behind Chris and Michael who each held a shovel and a box of golf ball size rocks through the corn field behind their house.

"Just by Old Spooks place," Michael replied and had on dark sunglasses.

The field was once a corn field owned by John Spooks, who disappeared 40 years ago. The corn field now lead to his abandoned house that even though it is covered in shrubbery and vines, it still looked clean and new as it was before...to a point, besides of little nicks-and-nacs here and there. Some say he comes back to visit every so often, just wanders through the woods on the other side. Others say, the last anyone ever saw of him was when he ran through town speaking gibberish of green lights and voices, and that he was committed to Christy County Mental Institution. Every story is here say and none was ever proven. He was gone.

CLANK! "Good Lord! These rocks do fly pretty far!" Barry said, watching a rock fly over his head and into the woods past the fields. He couldn't see it land, but heard it hit in the distance.

"Yep, that's the best I've done in a long time," Chris handed the shovel to Michael. No bases, no rules. The key to Shovel Rock was simply to have fun and see how far you can hit the rocks, which for the most part is a good stress reliever in most cases.

"Ok, so what's the bet?" Michael asked.

"The bet is, that you have to hit the rock through the bird house hanging on the side of the barn," Chris tossed a rock up and down ready for the pitch.

"Well alrighty then, let's give it a shot." Michael knew this was an impossible task, but he has never backed down from a bet, especially the crazy bets that were created during a Shovel Rock game. His eyes followed Chris' every move who was like a cat in an attack mode for a bird.

Chris pulled back his right arm as Michael gripped on to the shovel. His pitch was fast, but it wasn't fast enough for Michael as he took a swing and hit. The rock ricocheted off a tree and smashed dead center of the bird house.

"That was amazing!" Barry yelled and cheered along. "Let me have a whack at it."

"Okay amateur, this isn't like when you, me, and Dad played baseball in the back yard, it's a bit different. No need for fancy tricks, just hit the little punk," Michael informed him.

"Just pitch the rock show off." Barry smiled as he got himself ready.

"Children please, let's just play the game," Chris yelled from the outfield.

And the pitch. "Strike one!" Michael yelled

The second pitch was a little slower. "Strike two! Come on Barry, you got this."

"That's right, just one more. Bring it boy."

It happened in only seconds as Michael made the pitch, but in slow motion he watched Barry hit the rock and did not have time to dunk as the rock came back toward him and knocked him in the forehead. "Ouch." Was all he said as he fell to the ground on his back, unconscious.

"Mikey! Mikey, wake up! How many fingers am I holding?" Barry hovered over Michael while blood ran down the right and left side of his forehead.

"Chicken?" Michael asked.

"What? Come on I think we need to get you to the hospital." Barry tried to help him up.

"I'm good, chill bro." He pulled himself up from the ground only to sway side to side. "Whoa, I'm dizzy. Yea we better go." And then fell face first in the dirt.

"Not good. Watch him I'll be right back." Barry ran down Old Spook's dirt drive way.

Chapter Four

Chris held Michael up as Barry checked him in at the reception desk until a nurse was able to roll over a wheelchair for Michael to sit and relax. Barry and Chris followed him into the ER. Past Room 4, Michael glanced up to notice a familiar girl asleep on the bed. "Whoa guys, hang on a second!" He yelled and grabbed on to the doorframe to stop from moving. "What in the world?"

They all look in on Angela with a swollen bruised face and gauze wrapped around her head and right eye.

"Come on, let's get you fixed up." The nurse said.

"No, no I got to see her," Michael tried to pull himself out of the chair.

"Mikey sit down," Barry held on to his shoulders. "It's okay. Chris will you go in with her? Is that okay Mikey?"

"Yeah, sure," Michael nodded in agreement as they wheel him to Room 8.

***

The closer Chris got to Angela he tried not to pay any notice to the IV in her arm and the breathing tube in her nose. It just didn't seem right, well neither did a rock to Michael's head, but with a teenager it was all fun and games until someone got hurt- then it was hilarious. But, he pulled up a chair and took a seat down next to her. All he could do is stare and wonder what happened to her.

He leaned back in the chair and looked out of the window at the clouds floating by and daydreamed about what it would be like to fly with the birds and swoop through the clouds. A boy could only dream, but his dream interrupted with an almost silent, raspy voice. "Chris?" He looks down at her bright blue eyes staring up at him. "Yeah it's me. How are you doing?"

"Please, grab my hand?" She asked in a friendly way. Chris intertwined his fingers with hers as softly as he could. She turned her head and bawled. He was a bit startled and nervous as could be, and moved to the bed beside her as he rubbed the back of her neck. "I can't believe he did it."

"Who? Did what?"

"...Eric."

"Eric did this to you?"

"Yes...he...oh my!" Angela wept. "He-"

"Shh shh shh." He looked down at the floor. "I'm so, so sorry."

"Hold me Chris, just please, hold me." She calmed down as Chris wrapped his arms around her. Her body shook softly. "Please don't tell Mikey."

"...What?"

"Please don't tell Mikey. There's no telling what he would do."

"You're right." He looked out the window once more, not knowing what to think, but guilty and happy at the same time for holding her.

***

Four rooms down, Michael was placed on a bed. At the same time, the doctor walked in to the room behind him from an x-ray.

"So Doc, what's the damage?" Barry asked.

"Well the good news is there is no damage, except for one little stitch. The fainting was from anxiety. What does a boy his age have anxiety for?"

"Girls," Michael moaned, fighting a muscle relaxer the doctor had given him.

"Well that'll do it. I'll get his paperwork ready to be checked out. You're free to go. Get some rest Mike."

"Yeah, yeah, you too Doc." Michael said while the doctor left the room. "Hey Barry?"

"Yeah Mikey?"

"Thanks."

"No prob little brother."

***

Michael wheeled himself, still a tad drunk from the meds, down to Room 4, while he waited for Barry to sign the last of the paperwork. He stopped in the doorway and glared with envy at Chris and Angela.

"Well looky here, what do you think you are doing?" Michael rolled over to the side of the bed.

Chris sat up and looks over at Michael, "Shhh, she's finally calmed down and back to sleep."

"So how long we're you going to keep it a secret that you two were sleeping together?"

"What are you talking about? Mikey, man are you okay?"

"No, my best friend is sleeping with my girlfriend. How do you think I feel?! Look at you, you are still holding her hand."

"She asked me to, man, I promise. She needed comfort."

"Oh well forget you then," Michael said and sped out of the room. Barry watched the action from the door way.

"Barry what's wrong with him?" Chris asked.

"Don't worry about it, it's just the pills is all. He won't even remember us being here by the time we get home. You coming?"

"No, I think I'll stay here awhile."

Barry looked at the poor girl on the bed and knew it was bad. "Look, Chris, I'll treat you as my brother 'because I do consider you one, so think about what you are doing here. Really, really think about it before you make the same mistakes Mickey did."

"Okay Barry, I'll do that." He watched Barry walk away, thinking to himself, *'Is this really worth it? Is she really worth it? If I stay with her will she cheat on me like Mikey? No, no, not after what happened. Would I lose my best friend over a girl? How long will she and I even last? Does she even like me? This is all just too crazy, I'm thinking about this way too much.'*

Chapter Five

Angela had her little visit in the hospital for the rest of the week and some odd days after that, to which she slowly recovered. Each day, Chris visited her after school. She appreciated him dropping by, and yet at the same time she waited for Michael every second that she was there. A part of her knew it wouldn't happen, that she and Michael would never be together again, and yet another side of her didn't want to hurt Chris. Chris had been a really good friend to her, even though she worried that he wanted more than what she was looking for.

***

While at school, Chris tried his best for Michael to even talk to him. The moment he had even the slightest glimpse of Chris, he vanished the other way. Michael was done with Chris, and had nothing to do with him anymore. Their friendship was through even though, Chris wanted both his best friend and his first crush at the same time, but he couldn't fathom that he couldn't have both.

***

As he walked up the sidewalk, Chris noticed two men in suits walk out of Angela's house. A black Buick was parked along the curb. "Good afternoon," one of the men said to Chris before he stepped into the passenger side of the car. His eyes caught Angela on the porch swing as the men sped off.

"Hey there, I have something for you," Chris, sat down next to her. She stared off into space and wiped tears that were in her eyes as Chris brought her back to reality. He set his backpack down on the porch, reached inside and pulled out a cross necklace. She didn't seem to care as he put it on her.

"Thanks Chris." There was nothing but worry in her voice.

"You're welcome. I thought you might like that….So who were those guys? M.I.B.? Just curious."

"Oh, no, those were detectives on my case. They are trying to find Eric and arrest his behind, but he can't be found. So, as of now I don't know what to do. There is going to be a cruiser sitting outside every night until they find him. They know about you, so don't worry, they aren't going to interrogate you or anything."

"Wow that's crazy." Chris thought to himself, *'What did I get myself into?'*

Angela reached in her pocket and pulled out her ringing cell phone. When she saw who was on the ID and quickly answered it with a smile. "Hey Mikey, what's up?"

"What in the world happened to you!?" Michael asked from the other end of the line, angry.

"What do you mean?"

"What do I mean!? The Feds were here to investigate

me! I'm supposedly a witness to what ever happened. I was drunk that night, if my parents found out I'm dead!"

"Michael please stop, you don't understand. Come over and we will talk."

"Is *he* there?"

"He who?"

"Your husband, Eric. Or better yet, your new boyfriend, Chris."

"He's not my boyfriend."

"Oh, so you just sleep with him, whatever then."

"Mikey! Please come over and I'll tell you."

"Forget that, no."

"Fine! Eric beat me! There, now you know!" Angela screamed into the phone, hit END and threw it out into the yard. She leaned back against the swing next to Chris, who was completely stunned. She buried her face in her hands and sobbed. Chris put his hand on her neck and began to rub behind her ears. She shrugged his hand away and dashed to her bedroom.

Caught off guard, he picked up her cell phone and sat down on the couch in her living room.

***

Once Michael heard the silence from the other end of the phone he knew the call had ended. He didn't move an inch. The strength in his body left him completely as he fell off the porch swing on to the floor. Guilt ridden of what he had said, he vomited up his dinner into the bushes beside him. Slowly, he pulled himself up and made his way inside feeling faint.

He managed to make his way downstairs and into the basement where he collapsed on Barry's couch. His mind wandered back and forth on why he was even being considered a witness, and then it dawned on him-the handshake. If he didn't show up that night to win her back, then that wouldn't have happened. If only he had only listened to Barry, but then his body said to forget what everyone told him at the time, and then for him to get drunk and act. On the other hand, another voice said, "*See Mikey, look where alcohol gets you?*"

Here came the rest of his meal; he rolled off the couch and crawled to the tiny trash can beside the entertainment center and vomited up what was left in his stomach. Barry stepped downstairs to find Michael on his knees. "Hey, hey man you okay?"

"I am now." Mikey wiped his mouth.

"Here let me help you up." Barry laid him back down on the couch. "You got a hold of her didn't you?"

"How can you tell?"

Barry dropped down in the recliner by him. "Love sick."

"Eh it's more than that, about the detectives too. Just everything. Barry, listen, she was beat."

"No way! Mickey...did you?"

"No! Lord no! They say I'm a witness. Somehow."

"Well if there has to be a trial, I'll be there by your side."

"You don't think there will be one, will there?"

"With something like that, I'm sure there will be. But I can guarantee it will be local, nothing national. Do you understand?"

"Yeah I think so. And I'm scared of what Mom and Dad will do."

"Don't worry about it bro. Everything's going to be okay. Here, let's play some hockey on the PlayStation and keep your mind from it."

***

Chris knocked on Angela's door every so often to try and convince her to come out. Later that evening, her parents tried to bring her a plate of food, but she still didn't come out. They were are all concerned for her, not knowing what is going on in the bedroom. Soon, thoughts were created of that she had committed suicide, or that Eric had found his way in for a second helping, or even worst-killing her. This really worried them even more than they already were. It had been five hours since they had even heard a peep from Angela. Her dad couldn't handle it anymore and knocked down her door. Angela laid on the bed with her head phones on and in a deep sleep. It was a sure relief that she was okay.

She rolled over and when she woke up and saw her parents and Chris in the door way she screamed. Her door laid in the floor...again. "What are you all doing?!" She yelled.

"We didn't hear from you, we were worried." Her mother said.

"I'm fine, can you please get out?"

"Sure honey, I'm sorry about your door. I'll fix it." Her father said.

She rolled over with her back towards them. Once her parents disappeared from the room, Chris sat beside her and softly kissed her on the shoulder.

"Hey." she said without emotion.

"Hi, how are you?"

"I'm okay. Sorry I ran out on you like that. Everything just built up on me all at once. I'm just losing it."

"It's okay, you got me." He gently rubbed her back.

"I have to be honest with you Chris, I love you to death, but I'm not *in* love with you. You understand?"

"You're *in* love with Michael."

"That's right. You need someone better than me. I don't want to hurt you, you are a great friend believe me. I appreciate all that you have done for me, really. Your necklace is on the dresser, you should take it when you leave. Religion is not my thing. With all that's going on, I just don't believe."

"I really don't know what to say...I guess I better go."

"That's okay, I'm really sorry."

"So when are you coming back to school?"

"I don't know..."

"Okay, well good night then." Chris took the necklace and walked out, devastated.

She laid there thinking as she held back tears from

realizing she did the same thing to Chris that she had done to Michael. All she kept asking herself was, *"What's wrong with me?"*

Chapter Six

Chris walked all the way to his home. He took the same route Michael walked-except he wasn't intoxicated. Although, he did feel the same heartache and knew that if he didn't make things right with Michael then he would be alone for good.

"God please help me, I don't know what I've done wrong, or what's even going on. Please help me find the right path to take. I'm lost God, help my find my way home," Chris prayed out loud as he stared up at the sky.

Snow fell lightly as he felt the first flakes against his forehead. All he could do was cry and stick his hands in his pockets. He felt the necklace cold and alone- meaningless. With no use for it, he tossed it into the woods.

The second he got home he tried to call Michael, but there was no answer. Feeling sick to his stomach he didn't know if it was from hunger or from his nerves being shot. He tried to eat some cheese and crackers, but even just the site of food made him feel even more sick. So, he settled with a bowl of ice cream and fell asleep watching the 1985 version of *Fright Night.* Nothing was better than the classics.

***

He woke in the middle of the night with an empty ice cream bowl on his stomach, there wasn't anything on the TV except a white snowy screen. Chris turned off the TV and laid the bowl on his night stand. He then glanced over at the clock: 2:32 a.m. and rolled back over and fell back asleep.

At 3:15, he woke up again, drenched with a cold sweat, his heart pounded and breathed heavy. He ran to the window and opened it for fresh air. *"What in the world kind of nightmare was that?"* He asked himself.

It started out like any other dream, he of course didn't know that it was a dream, but he felt like he was really there and it was reality. He walked through the snow covered woods, wearing nothing but house shoes, his pajamas, and a robe. There wasn't a single light around besides the moon up above. All around him, he felt unseen eyes that stared directly at him that watched his every move. Frightened, he closed his eyes as he heard a high pitched scream of a woman in the distance. A hand grabbed ahold of his face, and yet he tried to run, except snakes wrapped around his ankles to where he couldn't move.

He opened his eyes to see the woman floating above him in mid-air. She stared down at him for a couple of seconds, then floated toward him in a swift ghost like manor. He recognized her as Angela in a white gown. Her face was innocent, but when she smiled she showed sharp wooden teeth as sharp as knives. She opened her arms and said in an evil voice, "You will be next!"

Chris didn't have time to react before she burst into flames, twirling around and around and screamed in both pain and laughter.

It was then when Chris woke up. Though he doesn't go back to sleep right away, he laid there until he did. But, by the time he merely dozed off, the alarm clock rang its annoying ring at 7 a.m.

Chapter Seven

After he arrived at school, Chris stood at the entrance of the cafeteria, looking around for Michael. He noticed him sitting in the middle of the group of the street racing teens. Michael looked up at Chris and grabbed his bag before he headed out the side door.

This sort of thing had been going on with Chris and Michael for the past week. Where ever they had seen each other, they departed in two different directions. In the lunch line it was more difficult to run, so they sucked it up and stood in complete silence. Today though, Chris followed Michael around all day to try and even get at least one word in with him.

***

After school he dropped by Michael's house and knocked on the front door but got no answer. He walked on in and could hear laughter down in Barry's bedroom. He opened the door where a cloud of smoke passed by his head. One person coughed while another person laughed at the same time. Barry and Michael sat on the couch, while a friend of theirs' named Screw laid on the floor.

"Whoa fat boy, get out of here, this stuff isn't for little boys," Screw said as he looked up at Chris. Both Barry and Michael turn to Chris.

Michael, coughed up smoke and stood up, "Who, what? Yea, fatty, get out of my house." Chris doesn't move, not knowing what to do- just stood there and watched Screw roll around laughing.

"Mickey can I talk to you for a minute?" Chris asked. He crossed his arms, and they knew that he was being serious.

"No! Get out!"

"Whatever Mickey, I guess you just don't want to know that Angela loves you. She doesn't give a flying flip about me, she wants you. So have a good life. I tried to make things right with you," Chris walked back up the stairs all at the same time listening to even more laughter behind him as he closed the door and headed to the kitchen.

As he grabbed a Diet Coke from the fridge, he heard a voice behind him, "You're still here?"

"Yeah Michael, I am. Just wanted a diet coke before I left." Chris turned and faced Michael with blood shot eyes and leaned against the fridge.

"Why didn't you get a drink from your girlfriend?"

"I don't have a girlfriend. I would if she wasn't so out of her mind in love with you."

"Whatever Chris, that girl will say anything. Just leave me alone will you?"

"No Michael, I'm serious. Are you willing to throw away your best friend over a girl? I can understand if you don't want her, but why push me away?"

"Look, you just don't even know what it's like to be in

love with someone who treats you like you're her savior and then throw you out on the curb."

"Oh I don't? Why do you think I came here then? What do you think I had to talk about? That was it, she did the same to me because she wants you! Look, be with her or don't be with her that's your choice, but don't come looking for me for your 'pal'. From this day forward we are through!" Chris slammed the back door as he left Michael to stand alone.

Michael caught himself from falling over, completely stunned. He grabbed a glass from the counter and threw it at the door where it smashed and left the Coke that was inside to drip down the walls.

Barry heard the glass break from down stairs and ran up to Michael. "Hey you alright?"

"Just leave me alone okay, I've got to think about some stuff."

"What about?" Barry asked, taking a seat at the dining room table.

"I don't know really all what's going on. Chris says that Angela doesn't even like him, she loves me. After what happened, I don't know if I even want it anymore. Until everything with the law settles, I'm afraid to even talk to her. I don't know what to do Barry."

"Well Chris obviously still wants to be your friend if he was man enough to face you today after what had happened. I can honestly say I'm proud of him for that. Angela though, if that is something that you want then, I know I said stay away, but she if she really cares then just be very extra careful."

"I've got to go."

"Whoa no, hold on a little while. You're way too high for that, don't even think about leaving this house. Go on upstairs and sleep it off alright?"

"Yeah."

"I mean it Mikey."

Chapter Eight

Chris woke up the next morning cuddled up with his stuffed monkey just in time for the sunrise. He didn't want to leave his spot in the bed where the sun shined straight into the window at a perfect angle that made it in a way romantic. He would've spent the rest of his weekend up in his room, but there had to be something to do. Not having Michael around, he was at a loss of entertainment and joy. So, he pulled himself out of the bed, put the monkey on the top shelf of his bookshelf where it was before hand, and headed downstairs for breakfast.

His parents sat at the table with his dad reading the paper as his mother cut up fruit. He couldn't remember when the last time was that they had all eaten around the table together, but seeing them like they were was a different pace for him. I guess that times were changing.

"Well good morning," his dad said and set down the paper.

"Good morning dad, mom," He gave them both a hug and sat on the opposite end. His mother takes her plate of cut up fruit over to the kitchen counter, nibbling on them as she threw some eggs in a skillet. "Hey didn't you say that if I gave you my desktop computer you'd buy me a laptop?"

Chris didn't know why he just thought about that, but that was something his dad had told him months ago when Chris started school.

"Well yeah, but I thought you said you didn't want one?"

"I changed my mind."

"Ok yeah, when do you want to go looking for one?"

"Well Christmas is coming up, I can wait until then."

"Na, it'll be okay, you want to go after breakfast?"

"Are you okay with that?"

"Well yeah. I told you I'd get you one."

"Sure, lets go."

***

After he spent an hour or so in the computers, as Chris tried to explain to his dad that you needed the internet for WI-FI to work, he picked out what he thought would be a perfect computer for himself. Chris was cheap, the more expensive something was, the worst in value it was to him; which is the same way he looked on restaurants and the way he looked on movies. He never looked for what the critics have rated the movie or how many stars the movie has, but more along what the plot was and how old it was. The older the better.

While the employees personalized his computer, he headed over to the horror DVD section, taking his time to really pick out something worthwhile. "Nothing better than a horror movie," he said out loud not even realizing it.

"Here, have you seen this?" A boy came up to him and

asked while he handed him a copy of *Book of Shadows: Blair Witch 2*. The boy was dressed in a black hooded sweatshirt and baggy black pants with red stripes and chains on the side. The pants were known as TRIPP pants. His hair was short and spiked as well as dyed purple and black which matched his black fingernails and eye shadow.

"No I haven't seen it. I've seen the first one though. It was amazing."

"Yeah I know, so you'll like this one," the boy says while looking at Chris. Something about this boy caught Chris' eye that he couldn't tell if it was his dark clothing, or that the boy was evil and pulling him in to take his soul. He just couldn't put his finger on it. "What?"

"Na...nothing," Chris says nervously, "Thanks for the movie."

"No problem. Well see you around."

It dawned on Chris why he was feeling the way he was, it was the feeling like he knew the boy from somewhere, and yet he did know where. "Hey wait a second."

"What's up?" The boy turned around.

"What's your name?"

"David, David Lowery." He held out his hand. "I just moved in your neighborhood like a week ago, I'm surprised you didn't notice the moving van and all."

"Sorry, I noticed it, it just didn't dawn on me that it was you." He shook David's hand.

"Na man, it's cool. Sometimes I like to be unnoticed. But hey I've got to get going, my mom told me I shouldn't drive this far. What can I say, the only way I'm going to learn the roads is by driving them. What are you doing later?"

"I'm just going to be hanging out at the house, why?"

"Would you care if I dropped by?"

"No go right ahead."

"Alright. It was nice to meet you...?"

"Oh Chris, Chris Wilson. Nice meeting you too." David walked away.

Chris had a funny feeling that the meeting was meant to be; that he knew from that moment what he's been longing for- a dark style of living.

***

As he sat on his futon bed searching the internet, Chris waited on David. The sun had set over an hour ago where snow had begun to fall once again. He put off watching *Blair Witch 2* and was going to wait on David to watch it together. Instead, he set up his surround sound and watched the original first. With the surround sound it gave him the feeling of actually being in the woods and hearing the footsteps beside him.

Going on 8 o'clock, he heard someone knock on the front door. He ran downstairs at a quiet pace not to wake his parents, whom have already gone to bed for the night, and opened the door to David. "Hey man, come on in."

They head upstairs to Chris' room. "Watching *the Blair Witch Project,* I see." David laid down his shoulder bag next to the futon. "This is a really cool place, kinda dull and orange. Why orange?"

" 'Because it makes the walls cool under the black light."

"Yeah I guess so."

"You know you can sit down right?"

"No, I thought I'd stand the entire night," he chuckled. "I'm only kidding. I'm just going to stand a bit and get the nervous out of my system."

"Why are you nervous?"

"It's just being in someone else's room again, feels weird. I mean come on, do I look friendly to you?"

"Well to me you do, even though I don't even know you, but I must trust you if I'm letting you stay the night."

"You have a point. You get the internet up here?" David looked toward the laptop on Chris' lap.

"Yeah, wireless."

"That's cool, but man electronics, they will be the death of humans one day."

"How so?"

"Have you seen *the Terminator* movies?"

"Yeah I have them."

"Ok then, there is my prime example. What are you searching for anyways?"

"I'm just doing my research on what a Goth is."

"Goth...why Goth?"

"Well...you are Goth aren't you?"

"No I don't consider myself anything except a soldier of God. Are you religious?"

"I'm a Christian yes. So, how come you picked me out of all people to be your friend. I'm not dark like you."

"Well that's just it, I wasn't always 'dark'. I see a lot of you in me. Let me tell you a story. So, when I was around 13 or 14 I started realizing how lost I was. I knew right off the bat I was different than everyone at my high school. So, I was at home one night studying the bible and Isaiah 9:2 popped out at me, 'Those who live in darkness have seen a great light'.

So, I kept trying to figure out what that meant and I just couldn't seem to find it. But it finally hit me, I was searching on line for horror movies and a lot of freaks in dark clothes own a lot of these websites. So, freak, outcast, whatever you may call them, I felt was me. I was an outcast as it was. I changed my ways and look at me now, happy as ever. Sure I look depressed, but I'm not at all. I do stay away from people and I do hide a lot, but that's only 'cause I like being in my own little world. Nothing 'dark' about it."

"So, you don't worship the devil, or do drugs and go out and kill people?"

"No, none of that's even remotely cool. Sure, I kill people but that's only in my stories. I wouldn't have the guts to kill someone in real life."

"So, why are you a fan of horror movies?"

"Well, look at it this way, wouldn't you rather know what you are fighting against before the battle, or...be completely unprepared when the battle begins?"

"Hmm, I guess I'd want to know."

"Okay my point. So, this movie is almost over, so do you want to go ahead and watch the sequel?"

"Sure, why not." Chris pulled himself off the futon and walked over to the entertainment center. He heard a song on a ring-tone he has heard before, but cannot place where he heard it before.

"Hello?" David answered the call. "Hey sis! How are you? You're coming here when? Oh yeah I can't wait to see you…Love you too, bye-bye."

David hung up his phone and put it back in his pocket, looked at Chris and said, "Well I don't believe it."

"Don't believe what?"

"My sister is coming to town. I haven't seen her since…well since dad died."

"I'm sorry to hear that."

"Naa no worries. I want you to meet my sis though, she's just like me."

"You've never seen me around girls yet. I freeze up the first time I meet someone."

"She's the same way. It's not like I'm hooking you up or anything."

"That's true. Sounds cool to me." And yet, he didn't sound too enthused to meet a new girl, he still loved Angela and a small part didn't want to move on. "So, tell me again why I'm going to love this movie?"

"Because it's a great movie, said and done."

"Ok, I'll take your word for it," Chris pressed play. They watch the movie and a few more movies after that before Chris fell asleep on the couch and David on a blanket on the floor.

Chapter Nine

The next morning, Chris woke up and didn't see David on the floor. He suspected that David must have left in the middle of the night or even earlier. It reminded him of himself when he was 7 or 8 when he would leave Michael's house during the night as he attempted to spend the night. Michael did the same thing, believing Chris' house was haunted-mainly because Chris had fun in making him believe it. Thinking of those old times made Chris giggle to himself, but deep down he knew those moments wouldn't happen again.

He sat up and took a look around the room as he gave out a strong yawn. His bedroom door was left open, David walked in wearing the same clothes as the night before.

"Hey, you're awake," David said with a box of donuts. "Do you know you snore louder than a train?"

"No I didn't. Guess I blocked out that memory. Did you know you sleep on your back and don't even move an inch?"

"Yeah that's uh...that's what I've been told. So it's Sunday, the weather is chilly and nice I might add; what are you doing today?"

"I haven't really given it much thought."

"Well what do you usually do?"

"Shovel Rock on most Sundays."

"Shovel Rock? That sounds fun actually, but I got

something else in mind. Come on."

"Wait a second, where are we going?"

"Have you ever been hiking?"

"Umm yeah of course."

"Well okay then, let's go."

"Alright, talk to my folks. I've got to get dressed."

"Okay," David said before taking a bite into a jelly donut.

***

"Tell me about yourself," Mr. Wilson said from his recliner across from David.

"Well I was born over Transylvania of all places in the back of my dad's plane. But I was raised in Lexington, Kentucky."

"You were born *on* a plane? That's wild."

"Yeah I came faster than they were expecting."

"How come you moved from Kentucky to here?"

"Well to make a long story short, I used to play hockey all the time when I was younger and Dad never missed a game even when he wasn't flying. I knew something was wrong the one game he didn't show and when I got home my mom and sister were crying, holding his flight jacket.

Dad's plane went down the second the puck hit the ice. He always made sure our family was set with money in his accounts, so we moved here to be closer to my mom's family. My sister stayed up there with dad's family, but she's visiting soon. And in case you are wondering, I'm 18 and I drive and I don't drink or smoke. Those seem to be big issues."

"You seem like a pretty good kid to me. I have a lot of trust in people. Not my place to judge anyone. I'm sorry to hear about your dad. I think I read about that crash, didn't it happen not long ago?"

"Yeah, landed in a chicken coop. He just had to make his special scrambled eggs before he went," David burst out laughing.

***

David's laughter was heard upstairs while Chris dressed. He buttoned his jeans just as someone knocked on his door. "Come in," he pulled on a black skull shirt. "Oh hey, mom."

"Hey I want you to be careful out there today, okay?"

"Yeah mom, I should be okay."

"You're only 17, a year ago we would've said no, but your father insists you get out there and have some fun. Now you don't know this boy, so at the sign of any trouble-"

"Mom, I got it okay? Nothing is going to happen. Just to keep you happy, I'll keep my knife on me, deal? I'll even keep the Army National Guard on speed dial, or even the Mafia on speaker phone. Which by the way I could do that if I had my own phone."

"You're too young and Lord you are just like your father."

"Why does everyone keep telling me that?!"

***

The ride up the Smoky Mountains both Chris and David were quiet. David mostly thought about his father as Chris thought about Angela. Out of Knoxville and into Sevierville, the snow fell thicker as it laid on the ground. "Are we going to be able to make it back in to town?" Chris looked out from the window.

"Oh yeah definitely, I've never been stuck in snow before with this jeep." From a two hour drive, they end up at a graveyard near the top of the mountain.

"I've never known this graveyard to be here before," Chris closed the passenger side door.

"Not many people have, I wanted to get some shots in today."

"Shots?"

"Photos, pics, snap shots, ya know?"

"Oh, right. You do photography?"

"You got it. Your passion is movies, mine's photography. Art is art in my book. Come here I want to show you something," David made his way in to the graveyard. The wind blew his trench coat behind him. He led Chris near the back and under a pine tree. From behind the tree views a magnificent over look of the town of Pigeon Forge below. Chris gazed into the horizon and only paying attention to the clicking of David's camera.

"Is that...?" Chris turned around to see a headstone

facing the town.

"Yep, that's my dad. We had him placed here for the view where he could feel he's flying up in the sky forever."

"Wow that's really amazing."

"Yeah, yeah it is," David kneeled down at the grave. "I love you dad."

David kissed two fingers and placed them on the headstone. He stood and took one last picture and turned to Chris. "You hungry?"

"Is that a fat joke?" Chris smiled. David smiled also, shaking his head with amazement.

<u>Chapter Ten</u>

3:15 a.m. Chris awoken from yet another nightmare, one where Michael had died in a car accident. Chris' body went numb as if he was in the car himself. He opened his window for fresh air, but for a short time lost his breath, sweat poured down his forehead. He did not sleep the rest of the night and left for school thirty minutes earlier than normal.

He found Michael with the street racers. Like as before, Michael noticed him and tried to run, but this time Chris caught up and grabbed on to his shoulder. "What do you want?!" Michael yelled

"Why don't you even want to flipping talk to me anymore?" Chris yelled back standing almost three feet from him.

"You stole my girlfriend, what do you expect?!"

"How many times do I have to tell you that I didn't steal her, she wanted you the entire time."

"Did you sleep with her?"

"What?"

"Did you sleep with her?!"

"No I didn't, Michael."

"Well then if she wanted me, then where is she now huh? Huh?" Michael asked with his arms crossed, his back propped against the wall behind them.

Chris opened his mouth to explain, but was

interrupted by the loud P.A. system echoing through the halls as it comes to life. "Would Michael Gabel and Chris Wilson please report to the office?"

***

While they walked into the main office it was like they walked into a pit of death. There was always a cold feeling and every one of the administrators drooped at their desks with depressed looks on their faces. Not one time did any of the students see a smile from any of them. As Michael and Chris walk by, they stare at them as if they have done something terribly wrong, which didn't help in making them think they did do something.

Entering in Principal Wilcox's office, Chris noticed the same detectives that were leaving Angela's house days before, and now they stood behind Principal Wilcox's desk. Wilcox, in his leather chair, motioned for the boys to sit. They do and both grip the arms of the chairs.

"Boys, this is Detective Marshall and this is Detective Acuff, they would like to ask you a couple of questions," Wilcox broke the silence.

Giving them a chance to breath, Detective Marshall laid down a photograph in front of them. "Now boys, do you recognize the girl in this picture?"

"That's Angela," Chris said.

"Angela who?" Detective Acuff asked.

"Angela Stutts," Michael said.

"How do you two know her?" Marshall asked.

"We both dated her," Michael looked over at Chris.

"How long ago was this?"

"A couple of months and we broke up not too long ago."

"What about you?" Marshall turned to Chris.

"I...uh...I uh didn't really date her, we just hung out."

"Well which one of you is Michael Gabel?" Acuff moved toward the desk.

"That would be me." Michael sat up straight in his chair.

"Where were you on Saturday night?" Acuff asked Michael directly.

"I was...hanging with my brother all night."

"What about you?" Acuff turned to Chris.

"Best Buy with my parents and then a friend, David, spent the night." Michael looked over at Chris and gave him a look that asked who David was.

"Okay Principal Wilcox, I need you to get on the phone with their parents and confirm these inquiries."

"Michael, I want you to read something for me will you?" asked Marshall.

"Sure."

"Okay, Detective Acuff, the letter." Marshall turned back to Michael. "Now Michael, I want you to read this out loud, is that okay?"

"Okay," Michael shook as he took hold of the sheet of paper from Detective Acuff. He began to read but stopped as he turned the paper over as he realized it was upside down. *"Dear Michael, I'm writing this to you to tell you that I do love you with all of my heart. I didn't see it before but I clearly see it now. You and Chris both mean the world to me in ways that nobody else can. I hate this with a passion that with everything that has been going on, you and him have lost sight with each other. A lot of it is my fault. I've messed up everything we all have together. I take complete and total blame for that. I love you all dearly and I'm sorry for all of the trouble and pain I have caused you. Loves and kisses, Angela."*

There was a silence in the room, both Michael and Chris tear up. They look at each other and then down at their feet.

"Boys, do you understand what that was?" Detective Marshall asked. The boys shake their heads. "This morning sometime around 3:15 a.m., Miss Angela Stutts, was found in her bathtub, both her wrists were slit. She committed suicide. This letter was taped to the bathroom door. She's gone boys, no more Angela. Now, we want to know what happened to cause her to do this, and why are you two involved? Let's start from the beginning, tell me everything."

Michael began his story with the concert. Back and forth, they each tell their sides as best as they could. They both were nervous, but they made it through in just a couple of hours. Detective Marshall sat on the edge of the desk, listening intently while Detective Acuff took notes.

<u>Chapter Eleven</u>

As Chris arrived at the funeral, he noticed Michael standing away from the group of people that stood in a circle around Angela's grave all at the same time her mother breaking down and her father holding up her mother. Chris walked up and stood next to Michael and ignored the evil looks Angela's father sent the boys way.

"Hey." Chris broke the tension between the two boys.

"Hey."

"Why are you way up here?"

"They don't want us down there."

"Who don't?"

"Her family."

"They don't think we caused this do they?"

"I'm afraid so. And that's what we get for loving someone."

"Hey listen, I know things have been different between us, but..."

"Don't. Just don't alright? Just because Angela's gone doesn't change the fact that we aren't friends anymore."

"Well do you think it's possible that one day we will again?"

"I don't know Chris. All I know is that I want to go home, smoke, and just forget about all this. Bad enough I'm in pain, and this rain is keeping me wet and that doesn't help." Michael walked down the hill as the crowd broke. Chris leaned against the pine tree and watched Angela's coffin lowered into the ground.

***

Michael had done just as he said he would, stepped inside the house and headed straight down to the basement all the while he took off his jacket and loosened his tie. He tossed his jacket over the couch and kicked his shoes to a corner of the room. He then flopped down on the couch as he grabbed a bong from the coffee table onto his lap. He smoked a little bit, laid his head back and tried to sleep.

Each time he began to doze off, his eyes opened watched tiny green bunnies jumping around on marshmallows and Angela standing in a different spot of the room. Closer and closer she moved toward him. She was dead and her body was dressed in what she was buried in; her skin was pale as her eyes were black as coal. The blood from her wrists dripped down to her fingertips, dropped and disappeared before touching the floor.

She opened her mouth to speak, but all he heard was Barry screaming, "Michael…Michael…Michael wake up."

Michael did wake up and opened his eyes to the room spinning around him. Barry hovered over him and grabbed the bong from Michael's hand. "Dude, did you smoke the entire bag?"

"Yeah I did," Michael stared, at the television while watching it spin around and around and yet the entertainment center stood still and balanced in its place.

Barry bent down on his knee and looked straight at Michael. "Alright, look, we have a problem here. Not just me, and not just you, it's both of us. We really need to quit this stuff. It's getting bad."

"I don't care right now, alright? I watched the first girl I ever loved be put in the ground, who killed herself over me. How do you expect me to feel?"

"Mickey she didn't kill herself over you."

"Yes she did, you didn't read the letter."

"No I didn't, I tried when the detectives came here looking for you. They said it was evidence and withheld it from me and mom and dad."

"That doesn't make me feel any better."

"Well man I'm sorry, but I really don't know what to tell you. All I know is we don't need this anymore." Barry tossed the bong behind him to the wall as it shattered into pieces. The last bit of smoke faded in the air.

Michael held back tears and said, "I think you are right."

Chapter Twelve

Chris walked up to his bedroom and changed clothes as soon as he got home. He laid down on his bed and attempted to watch the 1980 version of *Friday the 13th*. Toward the end of the movie where Alice was in the boat, a knock came from Chris' bedroom door. He paused the movie and didn't really want to get up and calls out, "Come in!"

"Hey buddy, how are you?" David walked in.

"I'm doing okay, just watching a movie."

"You up for some company?"

"Sure, I guess."

"Good, there's someone I'd like you to meet." David leaned out of the way for his surprise guest to enter. Chris' eyes bulged at the beautiful girl who walked into the room, her hair was pure black down to her shoulders, blue and black Tripp pants. She wore a blue corset over a black fishnet shirt. "Chris, I would like you to meet my sister, Becky."

"Hi," She walked toward Chris.

"Ha...ha...hi," Chris stuttered with his hands in his pockets, even though he was laying down. He couldn't think of what else to say, but for some reason pictured the look on his parents face when she walked through the front door and wondered what they had thought of her.

"Well go ahead, shake her hand," David insisted with

a mischievous grin.

Chris pulled his hand out of his pocket and raised it towards Becky.

"Oh come on David, you know I don't shake hands. I hug," Becky surprised Chris as she wrapped her arms around his neck and squeezed tight. "So what are you watching?"

She sat down beside him, calm as if she had known him forever. The room had an awkward silence and David loved every minute of it. He smiled a cheesy smile as he took a seat down by his sister.

"*Friday the 13th*," Chris broke the silence as he tried to make eye contact with her.

"That's a good movie. So David tells me you want to write books for a living. Is that so?"

"Yeah I haven't sat down and wrote in a while though." He can't remember if he ever mentioned that to David or not about him wanting to write books. But it was still a good conversation starter.

"We all should write one together, seriously we should."

"She's right, what do you say Chris?" David asked.

"Sure, sounds like fun."

***

They spend the day watching movies and talking, having a good time on into the night. Despite everything that had been going on in Chris' life recently, he could truly say that this evening had been a happy one for him. Nervous with Becky there, yes, but happy.

David checked his phone, "Well guys, I'd hate to cut it short but we're going to have to go. You have school tomorrow don't you Chris?"

"Yeah, yeah you're right," Chris said and then he turned to Becky. "Well it was nice meeting you."

"It was a pleasure meeting you too," Becky gave Chris a hug and headed toward the door.

"You take care buddy." David shook his hand. "Have a good night."

"Thanks, good night." He walked his friends to the front door, before heading upstairs to bed.

Chapter Thirteen

David leaned back from his desk to the bedroom door that opened to his left. It was a relief to be given a break from what he was doing, and he took the headphones off of his head and placed them on the desk.

Becky walked in and sat down on the edge of his bed, which was pushed against the wall with only the mattresses on the floor. "Hey little bro, what's happening?"

"Nothing really, just listening to music and looking up new music for my iPod."

"New bands? Geez you have a ton of CDs as it is."

"Yeah I know, I just can't get enough music."

"Well I can't argue with that. So how are you doing?"

"I've been doing okay. Having Chris as my friend has really kept me sane. You know?"

"Yeah, yeah I do know. He reminds me of you. You were so cute when you were shy. Especially the time my friend Samantha came over, you wouldn't come out of your room for nothing."

"Well she intrigued me ha-ha. Did you notice he gives you the same looks I gave her?"

"Well I can see why he does, I'm deathly beautiful, but enough of that, everyone knows. It's good to see you and Mom are doing well."

"Yeah, I'm still worried about her. She hardly eats and

all she ever does is work and then sleeps on the couch."

"She's just got to have time. I know she'll come out of it."

"Boy I hope so, it's hard to see her that way. Do you remember last Christmas when you, me, Mom and Dad rented that cabin in the mountains?"

"Yeah that was when you and Dad cut down the tree and were attacked by raccoons."

"Ha-ha, yeah, but I was meaning that was the time that I had really seen Mom the happiest."

"I agree. Though that was the last time we saw Grandma also. You know the last thing she said to me before she passed was that she wanted me to take out my piercing."

"Why didn't you?"

"Grandma was a big joker so I didn't know if she was serious or not."

"Yeah that was Grandma though. I still remember how every time I was around her she smelt like Wintergreen chewing gum."

"Or how the smallest things would scare her?"

"Ha, yeah, I'm surprised we never gave her a heart attack."

"Na, that woman was strong."

"I guess that's where Dad got it from. There was this time he took me into the sky, I'll never forget it, the scenery and everything was beautiful. Dad turned to me and said that the only things that ever made him feel free were God, family, and the sky. Not a second after that we began falling. And Dad never once gave up on us, he had control of the plane in no time."

"Ohh Lord, why didn't you and him say anything about that?"

"Dad said it was a fluke, that stuff like that happens all of the time. He didn't say how it would be if we were really falling, but I think he was just being 'cool'."

"That sounds like Dad. The world could be on fire and he'll say that at least we have marshmallows for roasting," Becky wiped tears from her eyes.

"Hey come on now, be strong." David walked over and sat down beside her and held her as she cried.

"Why did he have to die, David? Why did he have to die?"

"I don't know Beck, I really do not know," David held Becky's head against his chest. He could feel her tears seep through his shirt. His eyes were heavy and soon Becky fell asleep crying. Not long after, David fell asleep as well as he held her in his arms. They both dreamt of their father and happier times.

Chapter Fourteen

David was the first to wake the next morning. His left arm was around Becky's shoulders with her arm around his stomach. It was the first time in a long time that David had a good night's sleep. He woke up feeling both peaceful and relaxed. As he slid out of bed he did not want to wake Becky, which was a shock that her snoring didn't wake her own self up. He covered her back up and dressed for the day and headed down the stairs.

The television in the living room was on from where their mom had fallen asleep on the couch again. In the floor next to her were her pills for stress and anxiety. The tv remote balanced on top of the bottles. David turned off the tv and headed in to the kitchen. Each pan that he grabbed from underneath the stove, he checked around the corner to see if the clanking of the pots and pans had woken his mother. She laid perfectly still on the sofa with drool dripping to the floor. Now he knew were Becky got it from.

Bacon, omelets, and hash browns were done with biscuits in the oven. David slipped out the back door and walked around to the front to pick up the newspaper from the driveway. He came back in and sat at the dining room table after taking the biscuits out and placing them on top of the stove to cool. As he skimmed through the paper at job ads a security guard company caught his eye.

"You look so much like your father," David's mother said from the door way. She hugged David and kissed him on the forehead. "Good morning sweetie. Something smells good, what have you been cooking?"

"Oh just your standard breakfast." David poured his mom a glass of orange juice. "You're looking good today."

"Well thank you, I feel good too." She looked over at a picture on the wall of David and Becky when they were children. "My, my you kids are certainly grown up."

"Yeah mom we have, we try our best, ya know?"

"Well you're still my babies."

"I may be a baby but you're still an old broad." He smiled.

"Watch it boy." She sat down at the table. "What, are you reading the paper now?"

"Actually I was looking for a job."

"A job? Well how come? You still live here and have it made."

"I know, I just...well I dreamed about Dad last night and I just feel it's time for me to grow up and start helping you out."

"Well you are 18 now, so I really can't argue with you with what you want to do. I do appreciate the offer."

"What did you do now?" Becky walked in still in her pajamas.

"Your brother didn't do anything, he's just going to be a working man now."

"Oh a working man is he? David I hate to tell you, that suit you're wearing is much too nice for a job of your standards."

"You know what, I didn't spend hours slaving over this hot stove this morning for you to just gallop on in here and mouth off to me, sister." David said with a grin and placed his hands on his hips while he impersonated his mother.

"Now children, settle down. I don't want to have to put you both over my knees," Their mother sipped on her juice and then turned to Becky. "Good morning Becky."

"Good morning Mom, how are you doing today?"

David set the table and brought over the food.

"I feel great, I dreamed of him last night."

"Him? You mean Dad?"

"Yes I did. I woke up having the feeling everything is alright."

"So did I, but Mom it is alright."

"I know sweetie."

Becky turned to David. "Umm waiter, this food looks rather distasteful, could you remake it? And make it better this time."

"Yeah only if you get your behind up and cook it yourself," David sat back down. "Now who wants to say grace?"

"Grace? Wow we haven't done that since Grandpa passed." Becky said.

"I know, so don't you think now would be a good time to start again?"

"I think it's a lovely idea. David how about you do the honors?"

"Okay." Their heads bow. "Lord, we thank you for this

day and keeping our family safe together. We ask that you bless this food in that which we are about to partake in. Please give us the strength to carry on our day in your name. Amen."

"That was very nice," Becky said.

"Thanks." David picked up his fork. He looked over at his mother who had her head down not even moving. "Mom you okay?"

"Excuse me for a minute." She teared up as she headed back to the living room.

"Okay what just happened?" Becky asked.

"I don't know, but let's find out." They follow their mother to the couch. "Whoa hey mom, what's wrong?"

"Praying made me feel happy. Is it okay to be happy?"

"Yes mom it's very good to be happy. How come you feel bad about that?" David asked.

"Because of your father passing. I just feel guilty about it."

"Well mom, remember God is with us always. He's with us now as we speak, and Dad is with him also, looking down on us. You know he wants all of us to be happy," Becky said.

"You're right Becky, you are so right," Their mom wiped the tears from her eyes. "I'm sorry I keep doing this. Come on lets finish our breakfast."

Chapter Fifteen

Michael walked in through the front door and threw his bookbag down on the floor by the coat rack. His eyes were puffy and droopy from crying most of the night from nightmares. His nightmares were both about Angela and his body's need for drugs.

It was the most quiet the Gable's household has ever been in the past year or so. No loud music coming from the basement, no hyperactive Michael running back and forth upstairs. All the two brothers wanted to do now was just sleep. It was going to keep each other from giving into temptations. They weren't in the mood for anything, even video games had lost its spark and adolescent charm.

He headed down stairs and found Barry asleep on the couch, but instead of waking him he then headed back upstairs himself and climbed into bed. He had hoped he could sleep without having nightmares. The last one he had woke him giving him the feeling as if she was staring down at him. In time he hoped it would pass.

***

"Hey come on in, David's not here. He's out looking for a job." Becky held the door open for Chris. "How was school today?"

"Is it okay me being here without him? And it was

good, kind of boring."

"Oh sure, we're friends now right? And yeah school is like that."

"Ye...yes," Chris smiled.

Becky closed the door behind them and yelled toward the kitchen, "Hey mom, come here and meet some body."

"Well hello," Mrs. Lowery said while she dried her hands on a dish towel. "Who might you be?"

"Chris Wilson, I live up the street," Chris gripped the insides of his pockets.

"Well Mr. Wilson, are you here to take my daughter on a date?"

"Na...no, no ma'am." He felt his face blush.

"You're not? Well why not?" Becky smiled down over him.

"I um...umm..."

"I'm just messing with you Chris. Come on, let's go upstairs and watch a movie or something." Becky guided Chris upstairs. She could feel his sweaty palms as she held his hand, which she thought was a pretty cute thing of him.

"So is this David's room?" Chris stared into a room with dark purple walls, dark blue carpet, a dresser, computer desk and bed.

"Yep that's David's. He has always been so spacious and dull, but you got to love him. This is my room though for now- the guest room." He followed her to the bedroom at the end of the hall. The walls were painted white, light blue carpet, king size bed, and cedar dresser with framed pictures of the family on top.

"Relaxing."

"You think so? Eh, there could be work done. Come on take a seat." Becky took a flop down on the bed. "Oh come on, I don't bite...well not hard at least."

He set at the foot of the bed and leaned against a bed post, all while staring at the floor.

"What are you so shy for?" She couldn't help but smile at him.

"I'm just this way around beautiful girls, I don't know why."

"You think I'm beautiful?"

He realized what he had just said, because he had said it without thinking and looked up at her with a face so red you'd think he was sun burnt. "I...uhm..."

She laughed. "Chris it's okay, I think it's really cute and honored you think I'm beautiful. You're okay with me, really. I know you are nervous right now, but hey David was the exact same way. And look how he turned out."

"Is that a good or bad thing?"

"Ha-ha! It's a good thing. At times I couldn't get that boy to shut up around my friends once he realized that all you've got to do is just talk and be yourself. All it takes is confidence."

"Yeah, did he tell you about what happened a few weeks ago?" She shook her head and he went through the story of Michael, Angela, and himself.

"Oh wow that's horrible, yeah I can see why you are afraid to get close to a girl now."

"What, are you wanting me to get close?"

"Do you want to be?"

"I don't know...I just met you. I..."

"Chris?"

"Yeah?"

"I'm messing with you. I wouldn't jump into a relationship that fast anyways not knowing you either. I'll be honest I do think you are cute, but that's beside the point."

"You do, huh?"

"Yes I do. Hey, you brought it up."

"Yeah I guess I did, but I'm not lying though, I do think you are beautiful."

"Uh huh sure," She grinned. "So do you have any of your stories you've wrote in your bag?"

"Huh?" He looked down realizing his hands were gripped on to his shoulder bag that laid on his lap. "Oh yeah, I do actually."

He handed her a notebook and waited patiently as she read some of his stories. "Chris these are really good, honest. I like 'em."

"Thank you. I haven't really wrote anything in a while, but it's what I do for fun."

"Let's do it."

"Wait, what?"

"Write a story silly."

"Ohhh, I thought you meant...never mind."

"Kids, ha-ha."

***

Together, they wrote for a couple of hours. Chris would write one page and Becky would write the other-back and forth they went. They were really into it when they heard the front door burst open downstairs, "I got the job! Hey everybody I got the job!"

"What job?" Their mother asked. David glanced to his right to see Chris and Becky walk down the stairs.

"I applied for a security guard job and they accepted me!"

"Congratulations!" Becky gave her brother the biggest hug.

"Yeah man that's awesome," Chris joined in.

"Wow, you better be careful." Their mother was concerned.

"Yeah I will, they said I start this coming Monday at 3 p.m."

"I'm proud of you son. Come on kids let's eat. Dinner's ready."

David and Becky look at each other both wondering the same thing, *Mom cooked?*

***

"Mom's cooking was really different tonight, don't you think?" Becky asked David, while closing his bedroom door behind her. He looked up from reading the story that Chris and Becky had started while he sat in the middle of the floor. Chris sat in front of him as he leaned against the bed.

"Oh yeah, even more delicious than it ever has been. I don't know what she did, but wow!" David put down one sheet of paper and picked up another. Becky fell down on the bed behind Chris. David read the final page and continued, "Ok I'm done, that was a really awesome story so far. Do you mind if I write some too?"

"Go for it. I think that would be neat," Chris encouraged.

"Awesome. It'll give me something to do at work. From what they say I'll be working alone in the evening, so I've got to do something. What do you guys want to do?"

"I don't know, do you have anything in mind?" Becky asked.

"Well do you still have our old board games?" David rolled on the floor to turn music on from his computer.

"I think I've just got Monopoly, but I'll be right back." She left the room.

David smiled toward Chris, "I've got the game in my closet, I'm just sending her off on a goose chase."

"You're mean, but that's funny." Chris laughed.

"She likes you ya know?"

"What? That was so random."

"Yeah I know ha-ha. But yeah she does, I can tell these things."

"I don't know what to do."

"Don't do anything, you'll know when the time is right."

Chris didn't know what to think, but he liked it that someone as beautiful as Becky liked him.

<u>Chapter Sixteen</u>

Hours upon hours, Barry and Michael played guitar games on the PlayStation. With their hands cramped up, Michael paused the game. "Smoke break? Just kidding."

"Oh you're funny, but do you smell that?"

"Smell what? I don't smell anything. Are you on something? Cheater."

"No and that's my point. This basement smells like fresh air. It's different."

"Yeah really, I guess I haven't noticed it. Not used to being this clean for a change."

"It's still hard at times I know that, but in the end it'll be worth it."

"Man I really hope so. The other day, Mr. Worthington came into the auto shop ranking of weed. I couldn't help but drool."

"Yeah I know, that's like with the guys, once they found out I was practically putting myself through rehab, they stopped coming over or even calling. I can't complain though, I know what they were all about and just isn't worth it. Speaking of friends, how are you and Chris?"

"I have noticed they haven't been around, I was wondering about that. But, I just pass him in the halls and we nod our heads. That's about it. Nothing big."

"Have you thought about us getting together for Shovel Rock?"

"No I didn't really plan on it. Right now I don't think I can deal with much happiness in my life. Not for a while at least."

"Maybe you should just give him a call at least. You know deep down you want him back."

"I don't know, I'll think on it." Michael took a drink of water.

***

David sat down at his desk in the guard shack at work as he finished up a round. His rounds were once an hour and consisted of checking outer doors around his post to make sure they were secure, and that there wasn't any thefts or property damage. Each round took him 20 minutes to do, if that. He took his time and gave himself 40 minutes of leisure time in the guard shack to watch camera monitors.

He took off his security guard cap and placed it on the desk. The chair squeaked underneath him as he took a seat. Updating his shift report, he glanced at his reflection in the monitor wearing a light blue button up shirt and black pants with blue stripes down the sides. A part of him wished he didn't get the job, but another part was thankful because of the need to want to help his mother. He checked his watch, 10 p.m., last hour until his shift ended.

A gust of wind pushed the door open and slammed it against the wall. Papers on the desk fly to the other end of the shack. David swore he closed the door completely. He jumped and grabbed the door handle, took a quick glance outside before closing the door. A faint voice whispered to him, "David...David." The voice was so familiar, he couldn't place his finger on it.

"Very funny guys," He said out loud, thinking it was kids from the neighboring houses playing a prank on him. He leaned down to pick up the pages from the floor and heard the voice again, but it was louder this time. It then dawned on him who the voice was coming from. "Dad?"

He looked around but he was alone. How could he be hearing these voices? Was it possible he heard his father speaking to him from the grave? His eyes teared up. "David...I love you son."

David bolted outside, "Dad! Dad, where are you?!" Nobody was around. Up in the sky a triangular form of lights hover above the guard shack then zoom away so fast that it left not a single sound.

"I love you too Dad." He moped back inside and left the door open. Sitting softly down in the chair he cried from confusion, his body was numb. Everything happened so quickly, he didn't know if it was real or not.

Forty five minutes later, David's relief came on site. "David why is the door...Are you okay? You don't look so good."

"Yeah...yeah I'm fine. Look I'm going to go on home okay? Nothing to pass down." His eyes were blood shot, and he sat motionless in the chair with a blank facial expression.

"Sure David go home and get some rest. You've done a good job this week. Take care buddy."

On the drive home, David couldn't help but occasionally glance up at the sky every now and again to look for more lights in the shape of a triangle. But they never came.

***

Walking into a quiet house, David expected to see his mother on the couch with the television on, but she wasn't there. He peeked in her bedroom upstairs where she was sound asleep in her bed for a change, which he hoped she would have a much-needed good night's sleep. After changing into his pajamas, Becky walked in. "Hey little brother, how was work?"

He grabbed her in a hug and cried. "David, sweetie what's wrong?" she asked and wrapped her arms around him.

"I can't be sure, but I think I heard Dad tonight."

"I hear him too David, all of the time."

"You do?"

"Of course, his spirit is with us wherever we go."

"No, no I mean I really heard him. And then I saw a U.F.O. I think. I know how crazy that might sound, but it's true."

"A U.F.O.? Are you sure?"

"Yeah, yeah I'm sure. But that I'm not worried about. How come I'm hearing Dad's voice?"

"I don't know, what did he say?"

"He said he loved me, and then that's when I saw the U.F.O."

"Maybe that's God's way of telling you that Dad is in Heaven flying with the angels."

"Yeah, you're probably right. I just don't know what to think about it."

"Shhh, don't even think okay, just go on to sleep." Becky covered up David, and kissed him on the forehead. He was fast asleep before she was out the door.

<u>Chapter Seventeen</u>

They were in the middle of class change when Chris made his way outside to the walkway from the cafeteria to the library. He reached to open the door, when it automatically opened by itself and he ran into an old friend.

"Whoa hey Michael."

"Hey Chris."

"How have you been?"

"I've had better days. Excuse me, I've got to go to class."

"Hang on a second. After school today can you meet me at the Shovel Rock field?"

"We'll see." Michael walked on by towards his next class.

...

Throughout the day Michael did a lot of what he does not normally do: think. With the turning point of his life, a change from the drugs, he knew it was right to make amends with Chris. It was going to be an awkward moment, Michael surely knew that, but in time they would find their friendship they once had before. Neither of the two knew if their friendship would be as strong in the long run, but it did not hurt to try.

As he walked up to the field, Michael could hear the distinct echo of rock against metal, along with voices of laughter. Old memories unfolded, releasing his inner child that was buried deep in his heart. He came upon an unrecognizable Jeep parked just feet from the gate entrance, the gate that of which they had to jump many times to enter the Shovel Rock field.

He climbed over the fence and there stood Chris with the shovel waiting to take a swing from a pitch that was from someone Michael had not seen before. The guy looked like one of the freaks his street buddies and himself made fun of, but the woman in left field taking pictures was gorgeous despite the freakish outfit of hers. He sat on the top bar.

CLANK and the rock sours into the open field. Chris' best hit in a long time. David was ready for the next pitch, glanced towards Michael's way. "I think we have company."

Chris turned around and the second he saw that it was Michael, a cheesy grin formed upon his face. "Hey, man."

"Hey." Michael replied back, took a double take at David and Becky.

"Hey guys, could you give us a minute?" Chris asked to David and Becky. "There's an abandoned house not too far from here if you guys want to check it out."

"Yeah sure, take your time." David said.

"But not too long." Becky gave Chris a kiss on the lips

behind David's back. She then followed behind David into the woods.

"So…" Michael broke the awkward silence.

"So…, let's talk."

"Who were they?"

"That was David Lowery and his sister Becky Lowery. My new neighbors. They moved in a little while before-well a little while before Angela…passed. I guess that's the term you are supposed to use."

"I guess you're one of *them* now huh?"

"One of *them*? Oh you mean Goths? Satanists? *What*? That sort of thing? Na none of that. Fashion sense really. We're all just normal people who dress in black, that's all."

"Well that's cool…I guess. So what did you want to talk about?"

"I want to apologize for the way things have been going on this past year. I miss you man. David and Becky are great friends and all, but they don't share the memories you and I have."

"You don't have to apologize; I treated you like dirt, when you were the one who made the first move in fixing us. And yes I missed you too, especially when I needed a friend trying to break my addictions. Which I might add that I'm clean and sober."

"I can tell, you look like…well like *you* again. I'm proud to hear that from you. So what about Barry?"

"Oh yeah, clean too."

"Wow, that's good! Congrats to you both."

"Thanks man. You've changed allot ya know. You're

more open and outgoing it seems. Less afraid."

"Yeah, yeah I really am. David and Becky really helped me find myself. Especially Becky, bless her heart."

"Word man, word. Is she your girlfriend?"

"You can say that yeah, but let's stick to the matter at hand...SHOVEL ROCK!!!" Chris screamed, which gave the cue for David and Becky to return to the field.

They all laughed and played Shovel Rock until sundown. It was a fresh start to summer break.

...

Chris rode home with David and Becky. Becky sat in the back seat and stared at Chris the entire way.

"Okay, I've got to ask. Call me obvious, but are you two seeing each other or something? If not, Chris, my sister has been staring at you the way I would stare at a cookie."

"Awe is little brother jealous? It took you this long to figure it out?"

"Yeah man we kinda are. Do you accept?" Chris asked.

A serious look fell on David's face, hands gripping the steering wheel. Slowly they veered off to the side of the road. David's eyes never left from the distance ahead. Though he left a moment of silence, David casually put his hand on Chris' shoulder and smiled. "Of course it's okay. Come here and give me a hug. I'd rather you date her than some sleezeball."

"Thanks man."

"Yeah, thanks you jerk." Becky said, her breathing was heavy from the suspense of David's silence.

"Jerk? What, me? Who?"

"Yes, *you*. You jerk. You had us scared there for a minute that you were going psycho on us."

"Now would I ever do such a thing like that?"

"There's really no telling." A gigantic smile was on Chris' face.

"Welll...yeah, you're right ha-ha. Let's go huh? I got to get you guys home before work."

"What you work tonight?" Becky asked.

"Yep, they gave me the 11 to 7 shift. It's all good."

...

Michael sat on the leather couch downstairs and watched Barry walk back and forth packing his things in a box. He slumped down, holding back tears of his brother leaving.

"Hey, you okay little brother?"

"I don't want you to go man."

"How come?"

" Because we just started to get close again and now this. What am I going to do without you?"

"Mickey, you're only four hours away from me. You can visit anytime you want. You're going to be driving in a few months anyways right?"

"Yeah."

"Okay then, don't worry. You're still my brother and I

love you. You are never going to lose me. I promise."

Michael ran to his brother and wrapped his arms around his shoulders. "I love you too Barr."

Chapter Eighteen

"Boy you better not be sleeping yet." Becky climbed in through Chris' bedroom window.

"No ma'am, me is just laying here watching *Dreamcatcher.* How in the world did you get up here anyways?"

"Ladder. And great pick of a movie."

Becky laid down beside Chris and gave him a passionate kiss.

"What was that for?"

"Just 'cause. I'm glad David knows about us. I honestly didn't know how he would react."

"How come?"

"He just protects his family, like dad did. Ya know?"

"Yeah, he's a good man."

"You are too you know?"

"Yeahhhh, I guess I am. So does your mom and David know that you are here alone?"

"Nope, I'm a grown woman. It shouldn't matter."

"Oh, a woman huh?"

"Yes a woman ha-ha."

"Na, I don't believe it."

"What that I'm a woman?"

"Yep, I have no idea. I could be wrong, but who knows."

"Well I guess I'm going to have to prove it to you

then." She pulled herself closer in to him.

Chris, panicked and pushed her back a little bit, his eyes closed for a second trying to catch his breath. "Wait, wait, wait. We can't do this. I was only flirting. I didn't think we'd-"

"What why?"

"It's not right, babe. It just feels…funny."

"It's supposed to feel that way."

"No not that. I don't know, *something* is telling me to wait. I'm sorry."

"Wow." Becky sighed. "I've never been rejected before."

"I'm sorry…I just…"

"No, don't." She stood. "I've got to go."

"Don't, you just want to stay and watch the movie with me?"

"No. Not tonight." She headed out the window. "I'll see you."

Becky didn't know what to think. She couldn't understand why Chris had turned her down. Everything happened so fast. She didn't know if she wanted to cry or be angry, but something was guiding her to let it go and do the right thing by leaving.

She walked on home, her mother on the couch again watching home movies. David's 3rd birthday party played on the screen: her father held her while he had a party cone on top of his head. She heard her mother sniffling from crying in the dark.

"Mom, you okay?"

"Yes dear, sorry I didn't hear you come in. Come here and sit next to me." Her mother peeped over the edge of the couch.

"How are you doing mom?"

"I'm going okay." She turned to the screen. "You and David have grown up so much. I'm proud of you two."

"Thanks mom." Becky could not get the image of Chris' face knowing he was distraught from her actions. "Why are you watching these again?"

" Because I love 'em. Seeing your father relaxes me. Are you okay, you don't look so good?"

"I'm okay mom, just been thinking. How would you feel if I went back to Kentucky to finish school?"

"I think that would be wonderful dear."

"Do you not need me here though to help? Would you be able to survive?"

"Yes baby, I would be fine. You wanting to leave doesn't have anything to do with a certain neighbor boy does it?"

"No...well...kinda. I just don't want to hurt him mom. He's so...fragile. Young I mean."

"I understand. As long as you know you are doing the right thing, then everything is going to be okay."

"I think so also. I just want some time to really find myself again."

"Yeah but running away all of the time you won't."

"I know mom."

"It's your decision, dear. You're a grown woman now,

I have to let you go sometime."

"Thanks mom."

"So when are you planning on leaving?"

"I don't know. I'm thinking tomorrow, maybe."

"Well just remember, your room upstairs will always be yours." Her mother's eyes never left the tv screen.

...

David is set for the night: book, coffee, and iPod. His first night on 3rd shift and the night *should* go by fast. He turned off the overhead light in the office, that left only the light from the desk lamp; the perfect dimness to read a good scary story. As he reached toward the top drawer to get out a shift report, he missed and opened the bottom drawer instead.

"Well, well, well what do we have here old man? No wonder you make it through your shift each night." David reached inside the drawer and pulled out a bottle of whiskey and DVD of old black and white cop movies. "Hmm, I wonder..."

He twisted off the plastic lid of the bottle; strong scent burned his nose and took a sip. Immediately the whiskey burned his stomach and he gagged. "Whew, forgive me Father. That was a rush, but no thanks. I don't want to do that again."

He placed the bottle back in its original place. The shack was quiet as warm summer air in blew in through the crack at the bottom of the door. David glanced down at a shadow of foot prints move past the door.

BANG! Something slammed against the door. "Help me! Somebody help me!"

David jumped from his seat and swung open the door. A bald, heavy set man in blue overalls fell inside, landing in the desk chair that rolled to the corner of the shack.

"Sir! Sir, are you okay?!"

"They're after me!"

"Who? Who's after you?"

"I...I...I don't know, they just are!"

"Okay, just stay here. I'll go check it out."

"No! No! Don't go out there!"

"It's my job, I have to."

"Please, don't! They'll kill you with the light!"

"The light?" David stared down at the man. "Sir?"

The man's eyes wouldn't leave the bottom of the door. David turned to see what the man was looking at, but there was nothing except a fog seeping through the crack.

"They found me." The man gave up and let the fog seep in through his eyes, mouth and ears. When he opened his eyes they were a bright green light. "Stay away David, just stay away and let us do what we have come here to do. Stay away."

The man exploded in the seat with a shower of green slime.

"What the crap!" David screamed, covered in slime as he ran out of the shack into the parking lot. No fog or lights in sight. He vomited in a visitor's parking spot.

A figure emerged out of the shadows in a black hood and vanished around the side of the building. On instinct, David ran in the opposite direction, but he could *feel* eyes follow him. Cloth of the robe flew past him and skimmed his arms and neck.

Half way down the road, David could see blue lights from a police cruiser that pulled over a vehicle. He headed in that direction, considered screaming for help, but *something* grabbed ahold of his throat. He scratched and tugged to break free from *its* grip. Nothing had a hold of him; whatever happened, it was gone now.

Overhead in the clouds above, Dave heard an airplane flying by. The plane was so low that he could hear vibrations from the engines; a low hum. A bright green light beamed down around him.

'*They'll kill you with the light.*' David thought to himself as he remembered the man's warnings only minutes ago.

"Help me!" David screamed out. The police man dropped his ticket book and ran to David's aide. David only saw darkness as he passed out to the ground.

He awoke to his body feeling as if it had been lying on ice. His eyes a blur, ears concentrated on constant beeps of a heart monitor. A tube was wrapped around his forearm, connected to an IV. The room was cold against his naked body. Bright lights circle all around him.

"No! No! No!" his eyes focus on men in black suits. Two of the men wore distinct name tags: Marshall and Acuff.

David's body twitched and woke him from a sleep where his head laid rested on the security desk. His right hand gripped on the whiskey bottle. He breathes in heavy, heart pounded in his chest as he tried to figure out what was going on. The clock on the wall only read that he had been on duty for five minutes.

"That's some strong stuff." David said to himself as he put the bottle back in the drawer. He glanced around the walls, free of green slime.

Throughout the rest of the night he kept a close eye over his shoulder for anything and anyone who could possibly be following him. Nothing.

...

David pulled up to his house in the early morning hours. His sister's hatch back was open, boxes stacked in the back. He walked inside and heard his mother and Becky laughing upstairs.

"Hey, what's going on?" David leaned against the door way of Becky's bedroom.

"Good morning baby." His mother said with a smile. She kissed him on the cheek as she walked by him with a box in her arms.

"Morning mom." David turned to Becky. "Are you leaving Beck?"

"Yeah, I've decided that you all don't need me here. Mom's doing great, and you're doing great also. I just need to finish school and do something with my life."

"I'm proud of you sis, but don't you think it's a bit soon? And we DO need you. I'm going to miss talking with you at night."

"I know little brother. It'll be hard at first, but we got to grow up sometime. Plus that's why we have cell phones and emails. I won't be completely off grid."

"Have you told Chris yet?"

"No...no, I haven't."

"Beck..."

"I know David, okay? I know. I can't face him. I know that he loves me, but it's just something I have to do."

"Yeah he'll sure be heartbroken, but I'll see that he understands. Do you need any help with packing?" David didn't understand his own self, but he knew not to question his sister's unique ways.

"No," Becky wiped a tear from her eye. "Go on and get some sleep, you don't look so good. Tired?"

"Yeah I had a messed up night. Are you going to be here when I wake up?"

"It all depends really on how fast we get done packing."

"Well okay then. Just in case, give me a hug goodbye now sis. I love you to death, and you drive safe."

"I love you too. You keep an eye on Chris for me. Would you?"

"You got it."

Chapter Nineteen

It took David forever to fall asleep. When he did, he would see the green eyes from the man in the shack exploding and it would wake him in a cold sweat. After a few hours he decided to fully get up from bed.

He made his way down stairs and Becky had already left. David glanced out his back window up towards Chris' house, whom sat outside on the back porch with a book. He knew what had to be done.

"Hey, buddy."

"Hey, David. What's up?"

"We need to talk."

"Uh oh, that's not a good opening line."

"No, it's not man. Look, umm, Becky's gone. She moved back to Kentucky."

"What...?"

"I'm sorry man. It came as a shock for me also. Here, she left this for you." David handed him a letter. Chris took it with trembling hands; sweat formed on his forehead as he unfolded the sheet of paper.

Chris read aloud, *"My dear Chris, as much as I wanted to see you one last time, I couldn't muster it. I have to say goodbye, but not without saying I DO love you. You have given a smile to our family, and I do see you as part of my family and a brother to me. I would love for you to write or even call me if you fancy the time for it. You are young and have your whole life ahead of you; be with someone who will love you as much as I have. For me, I must finish school and begin my life. Take care and keep your faith in God. With love, Becky."*

He folded the letter in silence then placed it on the window sill. David doesn't breathe and watched Chris' every move; waited for him to break down. Chris wiped a tear from his eye, keeping what's left of his self-esteem strong. "So, that's it huh?"

"Yeah man, I believe so..."

"Will you pray with me?"

"Pray? Of course I will." David kneeled down on his knees. They pray as the night goes on.

Chris leaned up toward the sky. "Lord, I'm ready for you to take my life in your hands."

He burst into tears, David grabbed him and held him around the neck.

"God is here." David said. "God is here."

"I know, I feel him. Does it always feel this good to *love* God?"

"Always Chris."

Chris' phone rang out loud.

He smiled and answered his phone. "And God works in mysterious ways.- Hello?"

"Hey man, you busy?" Michael asked from the other end of the line.

"No man, I'm good."

"That's cool. Hey, you and David and Becky want to

come over for Barry's going away party? He leaves tonight."

"Sure man, we'll be there. See ya." Chris hung up. David gave him a confused look. "You busy tonight?"

"No, why?"

"You want to go to a party?"

"Sure, why not."

"Awesome."

...

The Gabel's front yard was packed bumper to bumper of cars. David parked across the street off to the side of the road. Chris stepped out from the passenger seat and heard music playing from inside the house.

David glanced at the group of kids on the porch with drinks in their hands who watched the boys get out of the car. "Okay, I know that look. It was a bad idea us coming here."

"What look?"

"The 'Hey it's a bunch of freaks look. Let's bash their faces in' look. I think I'm going to go."

"Are you sure man? I'm sure nothing will happen."

"Yeah, I'm sure." David's eyes never leave the group. "If you need a ride later just give me a call."

"Okay man, see ya."

David was back in the car and gone before Chris even knew it.

The aroma of the house was pure smoke and alcohol. Chris had to force his way through the front door. Loud music already caused his ears to ring. He found Michael alone outside on a porch swing; soda in one hand and a cigarette in the other.

"I thought you quit?" Chris took a seat next to him.

"I did, I'm just twirling this one around, contemplating on whether or not I want to smoke it or not."

"Oh."

"Yeah. Oh."

"How are you doing?"

"Stressed man. After today, things are going to be really different. I don't know how I'm going to do it. It's taking all of my strength now not to take a swig of beer. You have no idea how hard that is."

"No, I don't, but you have David and I to help you."

"I know..."

"Well here's what you need to do; you need to be the outgoing, fearless Michael I grew up with. Let's seeee. Oh! You see that girl dancing alone right over there?"

"Umm, yeah, what about her?"

"You my friend are going to ask her to dance. If she won't, you will dance your heart out anyways."

"God, I can't believe I'm doing this." Michael said. He took off his shirt and tied it to around his head like a ninja headband. Though he doesn't ask her to dance, she danced along with him anyways.

Chris watched from the swing, laughing at how crazy Michael's dancing was, which I don't think you could call his moves *dancing*. Picture a wild man jumping in and out of a fire and that's what Michael looked like. He was having fun, and that's all that mattered.

For some reason, Chris felt as if somewhere behind him, eyes were locked on his back. He turned around, the hairs on the back of his neck and arms stood up with goosebumps. The gate to the Shovel Rock field opened and closed in the wind; lock and key broke off of the chain. Vaguely, he saw two green lights, almost if they were eyes peering through the bushes. They never blinked and were gone without Chris realizing it.

Michael gave Barry one final hug before he stepped back to let his brother leave. Barry climbed in his car and waved goodbye as he drove off.

"Well this year has certainly been different." Michael said, taking a seat next to Chris on the top steps.

"You can say that again."

"I'm happy for Barry going on to school, but for me? This is where I'll be; right here. I can see it now, I'll be building and fixing cars the rest of my life."

"There's nothing wrong with that if you are happy though."

"Gee, thanks for the support."

"No really, who says you aren't making it in life by doing that? At least you are doing what you want. God gave you that talent so use it."

"Wow, that's a change, you've never mentioned God like that before. But thanks though. And no offense, but leave the religion mumbo jumbo out of it, okay?"

"How come?"

"Because Chris, I don't believe in God or even heaven and hell. We are just food for worms, that's all. You can believe all you want, but not me. I just don't see the point. But enough of the religion talk, where were your friends tonight?"

"I'm not sure what happened with David, he left after we got here. But Becky...broke up with me tonight and moved away."

"What? Are you serious?"

"Yeah, it stinks too 'cause I really did love her. These are supposed to be the best years of our lives, and look at all that we've gone through this past year. I'm not saying I regret what good has happened, but I just want some quiet for a little while. Get through this last year of high school, drama free."

"Ha, like that'll happen, but yeah I know what you mean. We're seniors now, when it seems like yesterday we were blowing up army men action figures with rubbing alcohol in my bedroom. All I know is when we graduate, I want to take some time off and chillax at the beach."

"The beach sounds pretty good to me."

"Ohhh yeah it does. Come on lets go help my folks clean up from the party."

"Ha, sure why not."

Chapter Twenty

"How's he doing?" Becky asked on the other end of the phone.

"He's doing okay, I think, keeping strong as best he could. I can tell he's bothered though because it's written all over his face."

"Well, good that he's okay."

"Beck," David continued. "Why *did* you leave from here?"

David, leaning back in his desk chair, stared at his computer monitor.

"To finish school."

"No, I know that's not true. Your letter didn't sound like you at all. You mentioned God for one thing; and for someone who doesn't even *believe* in God that's a big step. You know?"

"He freaked me out David, that's never happened before. I don't know, maybe it was just too much for me; meaning that Dad's dead, Mom's better, and you are working (which is a shocker). And I was falling head over heels for Chris. So maybe I was just afraid of losing him."

"And yet you left and lost him anyways. Beck, you're not making any sense to me. What's wrong with you?"

"If you only just knew."

"You're right, and I'm asking you to talk to me."

"Now is not the time."

David tossed his phone on the desk with silence on the other end. He exhaled from frustration, looked up at a framed picture of his dad and himself standing next to his father's plane. "Oh Dad, if only you could hear me. Please help us."

To take his mind off of everything, he typed in U.F.O.s on his computer. Blocked. He tried ALIENS. Blocked. And now E.T. Blocked. "What's going on? This is really weird."

He gave up and shut down his computer without thinking of anything.

...

David walked into the library the very next morning. He glanced at the computer room to his right, full of the weekend preteen gamers who spend their hours on free online games. Across from the front desk, he used the data base computers to search for any books on the information he needed.

"Can I help you with anything?" a voice asked from behind David.

He turned around expecting to see an older lady with gray hair in a bun and glasses pushed down to the tip of her nose- but sure was not suspecting to see a young college intern. The older lady librarian sat behind the front desk glaring towards the two with a prejudged look that said *'You look evil to me. Be warned, I bite.'*

"Yes I can't seem to find any books on aliens or U.F.O.s."

"Let me see." The intern stepped around him to the computer. "Well, I'm sorry to tell you that we do not have any book of that matter in our system or in any other of our districts. It seems they were all discarded and removed from our files."

"Why is that?"

"I do not know sir, but you are more than welcome to use our internet of course."

He looked at the kids, all computers used except for one. "Ah, no thanks. I'll pass for now. Thank you for your help."

"You're welcome. Thank you for coming in and drop by anytime. We close at 6 weekdays and 8 on the weekends. Have a nice day."

Though he spent his day on the search for anything, anything that could give him some insight on alien life forms, he came up with not a clue. Each and every book store, used or new had not a single book left in stock- fiction or even nonfiction. Even video stores were all checked out of science fiction films. He was at a dead end.

"Hey Michael, is Chris around?" David asked as he used his phone for the first time since getting off the phone with Becky.

"Yeah, hang on." Before he handed the phone over. "Oh hey, wait a second; how come you didn't come to the party?"

"I didn't feel comfortable, too many people I didn't know. It's an anxiety issue. Understand?"

"Yeah, sort of. We're just cleaning up now. Nobody here if you want to drop by. It's cool with me."

"Umm, yeah be there in a few." This took David by surprise.

Chapter Twenty-One

"You thinking about Becky?" Michael asked. He put some more dishes in the sink for Chris who stood staring out of the window with the water running.

"Oh no man, I was staring up at the Shovel Rock field. I saw something weird up their earlier- kind of like green glowing eyes. Have you ever seen anything like that up there?"

"No I haven't. The only time I've been up there alone was when I used to do donuts with mom's car. Or when I set up the haunted trail last Halloween."

"Hmm, maybe I was just seeing things then. I know I need a really good night's sleep though."

"Go on ahead man, I can get the rest don't worry about it."

"Ah man, that's okay. I'll stay. It's been forever since I've spent the night anyways."

"That would be cool. I thought David was coming over also, but I haven't heard from him in a couple of hours." Michael said. A knock came from the door. "Well, perfect timing I think. Hold on, let me get the door."

Michael threw down a trash bag full of soda cans and opened the door- David stood waiting.

"Sorry I'm late, I was having dinner with my mom and her shrink."

"It's fine. We were just talking about you. Wait what-a shrink?"

"Oh yeah can you believe it?" David asked. "Anyways, how was the party?"

"It was pretty good; lots and lots of temptations, but Chris helped me through 'em."

"That's my boy. Hey do you have the internet? There's something I need to check out."

"Yeahhhh, follow me."

"Mikey you're out of dishwashing liquid now!" Chris yelled out. He turned around as Michael and David entered the room. "Oh hey David, what's up? How's it going?"

Chris tossed the empty dishwashing liquid bottle into the trash all the way across the other side of the room.

"Can't complain, had a good dinner with mom."

"And her shrink," Michael added as he started up the computer.

"Yes he's right, the guy's a shrink." David said.

"That could get interesting." Chris said.

"How so?"

"They could start dating and...yeah."

"I think they are...but that's okay. He's a really good guy, so I can't complain. I will say that he helped me through a dream I had the other night."

"What kind of dream?"

"Eh, to sum it up, I was abducted by aliens."

"Wow, what an awesome dream! I would've challenged the aliens to a guitar off. That would've been sweet." Michael stared at the monitor.

"Only you would think of something like that." David said. "But no it felt so real. I could have sworn it *was.*"

"That's weird because I thought I saw green glowing eyes in the Shovel Rock field earlier." Chris pulled a chair up next to Michael.

"Maybe we should check it out after I check this thing out on the internet." David switched seats with Michael.

"What are you checking out? If my dad catches me on…umm sites again then I'm in deep trouble." Michael asked.

"What king of si-? Never mind. When I was on the internet earlier, no matter what I searched it blocked each and every site that had to do with aliens and U.F.O.s and such. It did the same thing at the library as well as at my house. Either it's a coincidence or something odd is up. Not to mention EVERY book was checked out. Sooo, I'm going to see if it does it with your all's computer also."

"Okay so what if my computer does block all the sites? Or…yeah, yeah that's right."

"I haven't thought that fully through yet; I'm freaked about it if anything. Well, here goes nothing."

David began the search with a simple topic- 'Aliens'. Nothing but a blank page. Next search- 'U.F.O'. Again, nothing. Third times a charm, he types in 'sightings'. It brings up a list of the paranormal, demons, everything except the extraterrestrial.

"See what I mean?" David asked.

"That's so creepy." Chris replied. "I've got chills down my neck."

"What about sci-fi movies?" Michael asked.

David typed it in. "No search found."

"Hmmm, interesting."

"You guys ready to check out the field?" Chris asked.

"I can't believe we are doing this." Chris said. He walked in the middle of David and Michael. They each had flashlights and a certain weapon for protection: Michael- a hockey stick, Chris- an ax, and David- a crowbar.

"I guess if we do see anything, Michael will high stick 'em, or maybe hook 'em." David said.

"Hey it was all I could find." Michael replied with their laughter.

Besides the flashlights, the moon is the only light that surrounds them. Nature sounds of the night echo all around. The night was soothing to say the least of the current events.

David broke the silence with whispered horror movie themes.

"Dude! Don't do that right now!" Michael screamed out.

"Whaaaat?"

"You know what, just…no."

"Okay…sorry." There was an awkward silence. "So do you guys believe me about the aliens?"

"Of course we do." Chris answered him. "We believe in the weird side of the world that no one else believes in. Especially what skeptics would say is impossible."

"Okay good. For a while there I thought I was going

crazy."

"David think about it, is there anybody that's truly sane? To someone 'crazy' they could be sane, and *we* are the 'crazy' ones."

"That's very true, I mean it was just odd that I couldn't find a single thing today. It was as if the government was trying to make people forget that there was such a thing."

"I agree with you there, but sorry to change the subject; we are here where I saw the eyes. And of course, nothing. I don't see anything. You guys?"

"I don't either, but it does look like the chain has melted off." David bent down to take a look.

"Yeah it does." Chris picked up a clump of metal from the ground. A bang of a shutter slammed shut from the wind. The boys shined their flashlights in the direction of the bang toward Old Spook's house. "Shall we check it out?"

"Sounds good to me, this night just keeps getting more interesting by the second." David implied.

They had to step through overgrown knee-high grass and shrubbery. All the windows were dusted over. A rain gutter hung from a single nail from the roof that rocked back and forth in the wind. Shattered roofing tiles lay on the ground, broken in pieces. Paint chips from the house lay along the trim of the house. A tree had grown out through the front porch, blocking any way in through the front door- roots had cracked the sidewalk down to a cracked asphalt driveway.

"Sooo, how are we supposed to get in then?" Michael

asked.

"There's a lock on the outside of the garage." David said. He used the crowbar and broke the lock from the door. "I'd step back, there's no telling will happen when I open this. All kinds of creatures could run out, especially raccoons, snakes, squirrels, you name it."

David twisted the handle and opened the door; however, it fell off its hinges to the asphalt. The windows shattering in a cloud of dust.

"I did not see that coming!" Michael smiled. "But that was awesome."

"Termites?" Chris asked, he wiped dust from his shirt.

"Possibly, or just aged wood." David shined his light in to the garage. "Hellloooo, anyone here?"

No answer, but I'm sure if someone did answer they would not still be standing there. They watched and waited for *something* to happen. Anything.

Chris covered his mouth and followed David inside who walked in like it was nothing. The walls and floor was nothing but layers of dust. Old man Spooks had kept his garage neat and tidy. Everything was neatly placed on the shelves.

"He drove in style I could tell you that." David ran his hand along an old original Ford Model-T. "There is so much money just sitting right here in this place."

"Wouldn't you think that if he was missing, the cops would confiscate all of this and put it in storage somewhere?"

"Na, they just forgot about him after a while and just

condemn the house like it was a heap of trash. Ha, now a rich heap of trash."

"Yeah really. Man it'd be crazy if we get inside the rest of the house and there sleeps a bear and his baby. Or even a deer on his couch. As well as the raccoons you mentioned in the refrigerator."

"I can already see that, like there's going to be spiders galore and definitely cockroaches. And yes, rats."

"Well David, there's a door on the other side of the T. Only one way to find out if it's open."

"How about you take the honors? I don't feel like dodging attacking doors anymore."

"No problem." Chris said. He braced himself to take a swing with the ax. Half way into the swing he stopped. "Hang on."

He reached toward the door knobbed and turned. It opened with ease.

"Huh." Chris said. "That was easy."

Behind the door was a stairwell that lead upstairs- 10 steps. With one step on the bottom step, Chris heard it creak under his weight. "Oh this cannot be safe...let's go."

He lead the way, though David held back to make sure that Chris made his way up to the top safe. Which he did and opened another door at the top of the stairs.

"Hey what's up there?" David asked. He leaned against a wobbly hand rail.

"A house! Come on up."

David eased his way up, not really thinking how much more Chris weighed and made it up easy. He of course made it, and closed the door behind him with the sound of crashing boards against each other.

Astonished, Chris asked, "What was that?"

David opened the door about a foot then closed it back. He looked at Chris and answered his question, "Stairs fell."

"Oh, great. How do we get out now?"

"Umm look at your hands."

"Ohhh yeah, an ax. Ha-ha. So where do we go to first?"

Straight ahead was three feet of strawberry pattern wallpaper that was once white but now faded brown. To the left was a faded lime green colored kitchen: a tile countertop, floor, wallpaper, cabinets, and even a lime green refrigerator and dishes. Not to mention the cracked leather upholstered dining room table and chairs also lime green.

Now if they were to head right, they would be making their way to the living room, and yet another door to a single bedroom. It was a small, but yet spacious house.

"Well there is sure a badly horrible smell coming from the kitchen, so I don't want to go in there. And I mean bad. More than likely that's where all the rats are. I'll take my chances with the living room."

"You don't think that smell is *him* do you?"

"Who? Old Spooks? Oh no, that has to be decayed food, or dead animal. Either way umm nope, not going in there."

"Yeah, you're probably right." Chris said, walking

toward the living room. He faced toward the back left corner of the room at a brown couch. Behind the couch is a hutch that is filled with airplane replicas. From the left of the hutch is the front door. In front of the couch is a small round television on four legs. A six foot white wall faced the left of the couch that was covered with a triangular emblem burned into the wall with seven triangles with in it. "That's artsy huh?"

"What is?" David asked. He had to turn away from the airplane replicas due to memories of his father.

"This triangle thing on the wall."

"Oh that's weird." David was silent for a moment. "Yet, I feel I've seen that somewhere before."

"I think it's cool." Chris opened the door to the bedroom. "Hey, check this out. I think I found out why he is so neat and tidy."

Navy pictures hung all over the walls of Old Spooks in uniform next to a plane, and some of group photos. The right side of the bed faced the door, while the back was against the wall to the left. He walked in the room and turned right, that he assumed was an empty area. A dresser was in the way and he walked right into it. "Son of a biscuit eater!"

"Did you just say 'son of a biscuit eater'?"

"Yes I did, and you would too if you walked into a dresser."

Between the dresser and bed was a desk and a walk in closet. The closet was full of military memorabilia, neatly organized from size and color. Books and papers on the desk were also neatly organized.

"Hey David, isn't this the kind of plane your Dad flew?"

The photos were the first thing David went to. Anything about his father made him interested. "Oh wow...that...that...that IS his plane!"

"Really?"

"Yes! That's my Dad's plane! How is this possible?"

"Maybe Old Spooks sold it a long time and your dad ended up buying it."

"Possib-" David began to say, though he stopped midsentence and stared at the items in the closet with a blank expression.

"What is it?"

"His flight jacket."

"Who, your dad's?"

"Yeah." David grabbed the jacket carefully. He looked at it and held it tight to his chest. Before Chris knew it, David was on the ground in tears.

"Hey man, it's okay." Chris kneeled down next to his friend. He wrapped his arm around David in comfort.

"Can we go? I can't be here anymore."

"Sure man, come on." Chris helped David up to his feet.

"Is that a journal?" David looked down at an open book on the center of the desk.

Chris picked it up, blew dust off of the crisp paper and read somewhat of what he could see. "Yeah it is."

"Bring it with us."

"Shew, what took you guys so long? I thought about calling the police." Michael waited outside standing guard.

"We had to find a way out. The stairs broke so we had to jump from the top of what used to be the stairs down to the basement." Chris said. David kept quiet, his mind was in a whole other world.

"What are you crazy?!"

"Yeah I believe so."

"Well I knew that. But more importantly, did you find anything good?"

"Just a journal. And a flight jacket."

"A journal? Really?"

"Hey you never know what could be in it."

"Good point."

Chapter Twenty-Two

David and Chris had left the second they got back to Michael's house.

Michael closed the back door behind him and reached for the ringing telephone on the counter. "Hello?"

"Is Mike there?" A voice asked from the other end of the line- a girl shy and obviously nervous.

"This is him."

"Hey...uh, how are you doing? Excuse me for being nervous, I'm a little scared right now."

"I'm doing fine. Who's this?" He reached over the counter and grabbed a can of soda, took a drink.

"It's Brittany...you know, Angela's friend? And am I interrupting you or anything?"

"No, no you're okay. What's up?"

"Nothing really, I just wanted to talk. Is that okay?"

"Yeah sure. Why do you want to talk to me of all people?"

"I know it's awkward because of Angie and all, I was...you were on my mind and I guess I was just wondering how you were doing."

"Oh...yeah that's fine. Sure it still hurts at times, but things have gotten better. How have you been?"

"I've been better...are you doing anything tonight?"

"I didn't have any plans."

"This is weird, but umm...would you like to get out for

a while? Just hang out?"

Michael was caught off guard and surely did not expect this at all.

"Oh yeah sure! Thing is, I don't drive yet."

"That's okay. I can be there and pick you up in a few minutes."

"Okay that works with me."

"Okay good!" She sounded cheerful from the other end of the line.

As he paced back and forth in his bedroom, Michael glanced at the time every few seconds. He thought to himself, *"Why am I so nervous? I shouldn't be this nervous; it's not like it's a date or anything. Is this a date? No, no it's just two people going out and hanging, no harm in that, right? But what if she thinks it's a date? Oh lord, what if by the end of the night I think it's a date and want to kiss her? Should I kiss her? No, bad to kiss on the first date, no kissing. No wait, it's not a date, so no kissing anyways. Okay Mikey, be cool, you didn't act this way around Angela. Around Angela you were cool, you were the man, you were the Studmaster. Then again, you're a naïve boy, you always knew she was bad, a bad, bad girl. Brittany, now she's a good girl. Or is she? She is Angela's friend after all. You never know how that group of girls was. Never mind, never mind. I guess I'll just have to see how this night turns out. Who knows I could end up drunk in a forest again. Ugh bad memories."*

He stopped to the sound of a car door slamming and

then a few seconds later, a knock at the front door. With his knees buckling, he tried to make his way to his bedroom door, only to slip on a sock and fall flat to the floor on his stomach. Once he was up, he shocked Brittany by opening the door so fast that it took her by surprise. The air from inside the house blew her hair, which to Michael he watched as if it was in a slow motion romantic comedy movie with cheesy background music.

"Ha-ha are you okay?" Brittany asked.

Michael stood with a dead stare, drool almost dripping from the edge of his mouth. "Huh? What? Sorry I was in a daze. Wow you look...amazing."

"Oops, shouldn't have said that. This isn't a date Mikey, but wow. Wow look at her. I-"

"Well hello to you too." She laughed. "Thank you. So are you ready to go?"

"Yes ma'am, lets boogie."

"Ice skating? Really?"

"What you don't like it? Or is it that you can't skate?"

"Oh no I can skate. Just haven't done it in years."

"Well guess what? We're going ice skating."

"Yes dear."

Brittany turned to Michael and gave him a look that said *'What did you just say to me?'*

"Oh crap. Sorry." Michael quickly said.

"It was funny Mike, take a breath. And I thought I was nervous."

"Hey, I'm not...okay maybe I am nervous just a little

bit."

"Well don't be. We need this night out." Brittany parked the car. "And besides, it's not like we're on a date or anything and I'm expecting a kiss."

"Or are you?"

"Ha-ha right, right." They both closed the car doors and headed on inside. "I'm going to head to the ladies room, go ahead and rent us some skates."

"Are you sure this isn't a date? If I'm already buying the entertainment."

She did not say a word, only left him with a smile as she walked in the restroom.

Michael waited until she returned, by a fireplace with a hot cocoa machine on the side. All of a sudden he felt arms wrap around his stomach.

"Guess who?"

"My boyfriend?"

"What?"

"What?"

"What?"

"Got you."

"Crazy ha-ha."

They put on the skates and walked in to the rink. The air was suddenly cooler than by the fire.

"Do you want to go first? Or would you like me to go and get used to the ice so that you'd have someone to fall onto if you lose your balance?"

"Smooth Michael. If I wasn't for sure, I'd think you were putting the moves on me."

"Sorry, I'm just in a strange relaxed good mood."

"Same here, it's a natural kind of feeling. And hey I didn't say I was complaining about the moves now did I?"

"Nope."

"Okay then."

Michael skated out first, almost natural he skated like he had never stopped before. Brittany followed on behind. He held out his hand and she held on.

"This is really nice, I'm glad I called you up tonight."

"Yeah it really is. I still don't see why of all people, you called me. That was really random."

"Now who's the one complaining?"

"Oh no I'm not complaining, not complaining one bit. Just curious really."

"Do I really have to have a reason? You were just on my mind and since...well since...you know, you and I haven't really spoken. Though of course we didn't talk much then either, but we would've become friends sooner or later- especially if you and she were to get married and I was her Maid of Honor."

"Yeahhhh, I don't think that would've happened. Not you and I becoming friends, but her and I marrying. You do know that her heart was for Eric right?

"Umm no it wasn't. You don't know how much she hated him, as hard as that was to believe. She was just afraid of him is all. If he wasn't around, you'd be right there."

"You know the ironic thing about that? Now Eric is gone, and I still can't have her."

"Do you even know what happened to him?"

"Nope, nobody does. He just disappeared."

"That's really strange. And speaking of strange, this has certainly been a really strange year for all of us if I don't mind saying so myself."

"Yeah no kidding. So forgetting the past year, what do you have planned after high school?"

"Law school definitely."

"That's really cool, good luck with that. As of me, I think I'm going to open up a garage. I love working on cars. Yeah who would've thought of that."

"Hey you're a really cool guy, I could see you doing something like that. What I can say about you is what Angela did you to you about Eric wasn't right. You're worth more than that Mike. You don't run with the 'wrong' crowd anymore. I mean you are growing up and I saw that in you the past year."

"Well thank you. From really getting to know you tonight, I don't see the wild girl from the crowd that hung around Angela, I see a really amazing woman who is very sweet and caring."

"Thank you Mike, nobody has said that about me before. Yeah I was a wild one, but nobody has ever complimented me for the good. Sadly this is my first date with a decent guy."

"Well forget those guys, you are on a date with me."

"Hey wait, we're calling it a date now. Is that what this is?"

"I really believe so." He held out his hand. She took it

gladly.

"Then I'm happy about that.

They skated until closing time, talking of high school memories and making memories of their own. Michael wanted to say that he has been the happiest he has been since Angela, but what hit him the worst was that he realized that he wasn't happy back then. So now, yes-Michael was happy and that was something new to him. The entire night he did not even think about harmful substances such as drugs and alcohol, which made him feel even way more better. Brittany did something good to him that Angela never did.

Most importantly, he liked someone that liked him back and is not with someone else at the same time. He really did make changes in his life, and better choices for himself. A small part of him believed there was a chance for him in life yet.

Brittany walked Michael up to his front door. The lights in the house are off, minus the porch lights. His parents must still be out of town.

"So I had a great time tonight." Michael stood with his hands in his pockets.

"Mmmmme too, it was wonderful. Thank you for going with me."

"It was my pleasure darling." He pulled out his hands and wrapped his arms around her, pulling her close. She laid her head against his chest, taking in the quiet of the summer and the warmth of his body.

"Hey Mike?"

"Yeah?"

"Do you smell that?"

"Hey I didn't do it I swear...okay maybe when we were skating."

"No no...ew...not that. I mean something is burning, like...plastic."

"Ew, yeah I do smell that. Where's it coming from?" He ran into the house. No sound of the fire alarm, nor smoke, or even fire. Out through the back door he could see flashing lights and a huge burning fire toward the Old Spook house. "Ohhh crap!"

Michael ran towards the direction of the fire, Brittany followed behind.

"Well, well, well, what a surprise to see you Mr. Gable." Detective Acuff turned to the sounds of two pairs of feet running toward him.

"What in the world happened?!" Michael yelled out and caught the attention of the fire fighters.

"I don't know, you tell us?" Detective Marshall asked, guiding David over, handcuffed.

"Dude, I swear I don't know what happened!" David yelled.

"Whoa what-? I don't know either, I was out on a date all night." Michael nodded toward Brittany.

"Yeah, yeah he was. See, blisters from ice skating." Brittany pointed to her ankles.

"Right, we believe you dear, but this guy-" Detective

Marshall pointed to David. "Has no record, file, or even a social security number. Can anyone explain that to me?"

"David? Is that true?" Chris asked as he walked up the driveway followed by his parents.

"It can't be, I have a birth certificate and a social security card since I was a kid. It doesn't make any sense." Tears formed in David's eyes.

"I'll be honest, there could be a technical mistake somewhere. But then again, I could be wrong. We just don't know. So until we do know, we're going to have to take Mr. Lowery in." Detective Acuff said.

Detective Marshall stepped in. "Mr. Wilson, did you and your accomplice here perform a Breaking and Entering to Stanley Spook's residence earlier today?"

"Well yeah...we just...you wouldn't understand why." Chris dropped his head to the ground.

"Look at me son, look at me. You have committed a very serious crime here. Now we don't know if it has anything to do with the fire or not, but we will have to take you in also for questioning. For all we have now, we can't keep you overnight. At the moment, you are not under arrest, we just need to make a statement. Do you understand?" Detective Acuff said.

"Yes sir." Chris looked at Michael who was just as confused as he was.

"Okay then, let's go boys." Detective Marshall motioned them to his cruiser.

Michael walked over to Mr. and Mrs. Wilson. "I had no clue about this until they did it, honestly."

"It's okay Mikey, but is there anything else we should know?" Mr. Weaver asked with his arms crossed.

"No not that I know of."

"Okay. You kids have a good night." The Wilsons walked down the driveway.

"What was that all about?" Brittany asked as she wrapped her arms around Michael's waist. They each stare at the flaming house, feeling the heat cover them.

"I don't know honey I really don't know. How long do you have before you have to go home?"

"Eh, I have a couple more hours. Why?"

"Feel like watching a movie? I don't want to be alone right now."

"Yeah sure, let's go."

3:15 a.m., Michael jumped up from the living room couch as he clutched onto a throw blanket. The same dream that awoken him many nights before since Angela's death, awoken him now from a deep sleep. He wiped sweat from his forehead and yelled out, "Brittany! Honey, are you still here?"

No sounds; only the kitchen light was still on, that shined toward the living room.

He leaned over to wipe the sleep from his eyelids, noticed a letter on the coffee table between two cups of coffee and a half eaten bowl of kettle popcorn.

"My dear little Mikey, thank you so much for this night of wonder. Sorry I didn't stay longer, I had to head on home. You fell asleep in my arms, so cute. Though I didn't

get the chance to kiss you on the lips good night, I did kiss your forehead. Have a good night sweetheart. Much love, Brittany."

Michael folded the letter, placed it into his back pocket and placed the dirty dishes in the sink. He looked out the window toward the orange glowing embers that was once Old Spook's house. Only the tree that grew from the front porch was left standing-charred, but standing. He shook his head in disbelief, turned and looked at the clock on the stove. 3:27.

A breeze skimmed across the back of his neck. The back door opened as he turned in that direction. He closed the door and locked it shut, glanced up at the reflection of Angela's corpse in the square window on the door. With a quick turn, he looked upon...nothing.

"Angela?" he asked to the empty air. His heart pounded with fear.

Footsteps creaked on the floor boards over his head that were in his bedroom. He grabbed the first thing in arms reach, (besides the dog leash on the key holder), a butter knife. Not much he could do with a butter knife, but at least it gave him the feel of having somewhat of a protection.

Up the stairs he ran, careful not to fall upstairs as he did as a child- while he turned on every light along the way. No monsters in Barry's room, no monster in the bathroom, closet, under the beds, nor in Michael's room.

With a sigh of relief, he sat down on his bed and tossed the butter knife on to the nightstand. He then fluffed up his pillow, not in the mood to turn out the lights for the rest of the night, he dressed for bed. On his way to lie down, a hand that felt like a claw gripped the back of his head. He reached around to grab a hold of the claw-like hand that's got a hold on him while screaming in pain- only to grab on to a thin bony forearm covered in a thick slimy substance. His fingernails punctured the thin layers of skin of the arm, hoping to break free of its hold. There was no veins he could feel, only pure coldness. He surely did not want to see what creature was behind him.

He kicked his feet against the floor, and tried his hardest to break free. Piece by piece his hair was being ripped out of his head. The grip of the claw would not loosen up, neither would it grow tighter either. Another claw attached hold onto his neck, picked him up in the air and tossed him into the hallway. Michael slid on his stomach, not feeling the carpet burn against his stomach and face. The lights around the house flicker on and off until complete darkness. Each bulb began to glow a bright green light.

Faint, he laid face down on the carpet trying as hard as he could to keep the vomit down. He could not hear anything except an echoing breeze. The front door slammed open with the sounds of five pairs of muddy feet squishing on the hardwood floor. Michael wanted to get up and run, escape, but the pain he felt, held him down from being so weak.

The claw-like hands grab ahold of his ankles and tosses him over the banister and dangles him in midair. He stared down at the floor underneath with five figures staring back at him with green glowing eyes. Each of them simultaneously raise their hands in the air, claw hands, and point at the wall beside Michael. An emblem of a triangle with seven triangles inside the main triangle, burned into the wall. Their eyes grow brighter until green lasers shoot out at Michael, with each hit burned a hole through his shirt and into his skin.

He couldn't scream- not a single bit of strength left in him. Blood ran from his eyes, ears, down the corners of his mouth, and dripped to the floor in a small puddle. The lasers stopped and the creatures stare in a silent eerie stare as if watching him slowly die. He slowly raised his head to see the creature that held him, only to get a quick glimpse before the creature let go. And he fell toward the ground. The last thing he saw before hitting the ground was the emblem in the wall glowing a bright green, growing brighter and brighter.

Chapter Twenty-Three

Michael stared up at the triangle from the floor, waiting on his heart to take its last breath of life. He couldn't feel a single bit of pain his body- only a chill of shock. He could only hear dead silence, his sight faded to black. With a loud scream, he woke with something shaking him.

"Mikey! Mikey wake up!" his father screamed, standing a foot away from him.

Michael opened his eyes and grabbed a hold of the banister as he fell from standing up.

"You were sleepwalking son."

He ran past his father, down the stairs and onto the front porch. The cold, fresh morning air felt refreshing to Michael as he took in deep breaths, preventing hyperventilation. "Please don't touch me dad. I need some space alright?"

"Are you okay?"

"Yeah I guess, I just had the most outrageously messed up dream. I umm...I...don't know. Can you get me a glass of water?" Michael took a seat down on the top steps. Every time he closed his eyes for no longer than three seconds he'd see the eyes of the creatures as if they were burned into his memory. He glanced back toward the open front door, up at the banister- no marks, no busted light bulbs, no strange triangle on the wall. Thank God it was only a dream.

"Here you go." His father stepped into view, holding out a glass of water. "Are you going to school today?"

"Yeah I kind of have to. What time is it?"

"Time for you to shower if you don't want to miss the bus."

Michael hated so much that he had to ride the bus to school, especially with only a couple of months shy of graduation. Slumped down in his seat, he tried to avoid being seen from his fellow classmates who each stood by their own cars, chatting before class. He made his way from the back of the bus, through a mob of loud obnoxious middle schoolers and their drooling over the older mature high school girls in short shorts.

"Kill me now." Michael said to a group of teens who stood under the entrance ramp as he got off the bus.

He made his way inside and headed straight to the soda machine. As he reached inside to get his drink, he felt eyes on him- not deadly like the nightmare, but a chemistry that gave him the feeling of wanting to smile.

Sure enough, there stood Brittany across the room looking at her man. They made eye contact and smile as they walk slowly toward each other like in a romantic movie. Each of them ignored the snickers of the so called 'popular' crowd whispering lines as *"No way, is that Brittany Bohanan?"* *"Oh my, is he really walking to* her?" Or better yet from Brittany's former friends, *"Aww she's so beautiful, what does she see in* him?"

To ag it on, Michael picked her up and twirled her

around and kissed her as he brought her down- not even caring how much gossip he has just started. In that second, he almost forgot his nightmare.

"Well good morning." Brittany held her arms around his neck.

"Good morning, how was your night?"

"You tell me, you were there till you fell asleep ha-ha."

"Wonderful then." He smiled. "Did you sleep well when you got home?"

"Better than I have before, what about you? And when you woke up on the couch, did you get my note?"

"Yes I got the note, thank you. I loved it. And no I didn't sleep well, I uh slept walked because of a nightmare and woke up standing at the top of my stairs."

"Oh honey, what did you dream?"

"I have no idea what it was about." He lied.

Brittany placed her hand on Michael's forehead. "Hmm, no fever. Now don't you be falling asleep in school today, you hear?"

"Ha, yeah I hear that. I'll just sleep on the bus or something."

"On the bus? You know you can ride with me right?"

"Are you sure?"

"Of course, you are *my* man now, you know?"

"No I didn't know. What would tell me that I am?"

"By this." she pulled his head down to hers and kissed his lips, hoping her knees didn't fall beneath her.

"Michael Gable, please report to the principal's office.

Michael Gable, please report to the principal's office." The loud speaker echoed out through the hallways.

"Oh come on it was just a kiss!" Michael yelled out to the empty air.

"I'll see you in homeroom, you better get in there before they send our cop Shades after your rear end."

"Ha, true."

"Well, here's a kiss for good luck."

"Mmm, can't I just skip the office and stay here kissing you?"

"I wish."

"Ugh."

"Good morning Mr. Gable. Principal Wilcox will see you in just a moment." the receptionist welcomed Michael into the office. Michael sat down in a wooden chair next to the closed door of the principal's office. Even this early the office staff are running around like chickens with their heads off.

Wilcox's door opened with a force to cause loose papers from the counter to fly off to the floor. "Gable, get in here son. This won't take long. You have to be in class soon. I won't keep you from that. Have a seat."

"So how's your day sir?"

"Ha! Hectic as usual. It's a Monday, always the worst." He sat down. "Okay, so, you are not in trouble...yet, but there's still a problem. You are just a smudge away from having enough credits to graduate. Problem is, you failed three classes last semester which you have two choices:

after school classes to bring up the credits...or retake your senior year. I know you can do this Michael, you're a bright student."

"Well this wasn't the way I wanted to end out my high school days. Man, I thought I was doing well last semester...then again I had a lot going on. But I turned it all around, you know?"

"Yes Michael I really know, and I'm sorry about that. What are you going to do? Either choice you make, I *know* you can make it work."

"Well...I guess it's after school classes for me then."

"Okay, I'll get them set up."

"Okay." Michael stood up. "So I'm not in trouble for the kiss right?"

"What?"

"Nothing, nothing. Thank you sir, have a good day."

...

"So get this, I have to take after school classes so I can graduate." Michael said to Brittany,

"What? Are you serious?"

"Yeah, Wilcox said all I have to do is make up for the classes I failed last semester."

"That's good, you should do it."

"Oh yeah, I'm definitely going to go for it. Whether or not I pass is the question."

"You'll pass I'm sure, and I'll help you through it all."

"Thanks. Shew, this is going to be rough, but I surely

need it." He laid his head down on her legs as they sat in the floor in gym class. Brittany played with his hair.

"Hey guys, what's up?" Chris asked walking in the door with his hands on his shoulder bag.

"Well hey Jail Bird, they let you out I see." Michael stated, not moving from Brittany's lap.

"I wasn't even arrested, but arrested or not it didn't go too well with my folks. They said since we were causing illegal activities that I'm grounded. For how long? I don't know. Knowing them, probably a weekend."

"Besides the trust issue, so what? They are doing you good; I mean think about it, you are almost 18 and you got lucky. They could've tried you as an adult."

"Well...yeah. Why so parenting right now? You were fine the other night, what happened?"

"I've had a rough night, and I found this morning that I may not graduate. Do I have confidence in myself to bring up the failed credits? No, but my baby will help me with that."

"Oh man, I'm so sorry."

"Yeah...well you're in such a cheerful mood, what did the detectives say?"

"Nothing on my behalf, just looking for info on David. It's like his family and himself don't even exist. Nothing can be found of them anywhere, except of their own words."

"That's fishy."

"Oh I know, but I don't know what the authorities are going to do with them. They said they couldn't give us any information on the case until what the courts decide. Whether they released him or not, I don't know."

"You're not in danger are you? How could anyone get away with living without a record?" Brittany asked.

"As far as I know- no I'm not in any danger. The detectives said they'd be in touch if anything was to come up. On the safe side though, my parents did put up a restraining order on him because of the whole situation."

"That doesn't surprise me, Chris. And I don't blame them one bit. Look, I know we've been friends for a long time and even now starting to get back on track after a long break up, but man I couldn't trust those kids. I mean look at what Becky did to you, and now what David did. You aren't what you used to be, they've changed you."

"A good or bad change? And his dad did just die, so that played a factor in how they acted."

"That's not an excuse for how controlling he was to you. I never knew him, though I really tried to get to know him, and even I could see that. You shouldn't be taking up for this guy, look at how lucky you are not to be in prison for the fire or whatever excuse the detectives could come up with to say you were an accomplice- which THAT could be the good or bad change in you. Good 'cause you are more open, and at the same time bad 'cause of the breaking and entering. You would've never done that without his influences. No hard feelings, I'm just being honest with you. You just don't deserve any of this."

"Thanks man." Chris let the loops of his Tripp pants hit the floor.

"No problem man. And okay I've got to ask, what's with the whole Goth look? I mean, why are you still on that path when you are putting yourself out as a target for trouble?"

"It's just a lifestyle that's just me, I guess you can say. Not trouble, or even Goth, but being unique and showing that I don't have to be like 'the norm' to show who I am. David wasn't the reason for my wearing darker clothes, he was just someone I knew I could share it with and feel accepted."

"But doing what someone else is doing, isn't that beating the purpose of being unique?" Brittany asked.

"Good point, well at least I know now I can do it alone." Chris said.

...

Chris sat in the passenger seat of his dad's car when they turned onto their street. He looked toward David's house as they drove by. A realtor had already hammered in a "For Sale" sign on the front lawn while a moving van backed down the driveway.

"They really are gone, huh dad?"

"Chris, I wouldn't worry too much about them."

"Well yeah, I know that. It just seems so...surreal. One minute we're hanging out, having fun and then the next we're being hauled off to jail because of a fire. Sure it comes down to that, though it wasn't just about the fire, but still. I just wasn't expecting it, even worst knowing I wasn't doing anything wrong."

"Your mother and I know you didn't do anything wrong. We're not grounding you, we are just keeping you safe. And you're right, life has allot of unexpected situations and growing up is all a part of learning how to deal with them."

"It just hurts that this all had to happen, right when I was beginning to be happy with myself and then it's all right back to the way things were before."

"I know how you feel, I went through the same thing at your age, but just wait, you can get your license and then get behind the wheel of your first car- nothing says freedom more than that; things will change. Right now, yeah you wouldn't be that happy, but you take your first road trip out of state, and you'll know what I'm talking about."

"I feel that way when I talk to God. When I pray it's like all my pain and fears are lifted from my shoulders. And at night, I feel like I'm flying. Do you ever feel that way?"

"Every morning when I wake up and your mother is the first person I see. And at night when we lay down to sleep. There's not a day that goes by, that I don't thank God for that. He has really sent me an angel."

"Man, why so gushy?"

"Because I know that when you find the right girl that's your soulmate, you too will feel like I do."

They had pulled into the driveway and stepped out and walked to his bedroom. He dropped his back pack and glanced around the room at the white walls with Field Day ribbons from elementary school, bands, glow in the dark stars on the ceiling, *Star Wars* figurines stood on top of his dresser, and his way too small hockey stick that leaned in the corner next to the closet. It was hard to believe that this was his childhood, when as now his interests were changed to movies and books. He felt lost.

Under his bed, he pulled out a cardboard box and dumped its contents onto the bed. He noticed a disposable camera that he did not remember having and placed it on top of the dresser and swiped off the figurines in to the box. Un-tacked from the walls, he also let the ribbons fall in, and then neatly rolled up the posters and placed them in the box as well. He felt it was now time to make some changes.

Not knowing where to start, he was starting off with a clean slate so to speak. Taking time to think, he sat down at his desk and just looked around the room reminiscing on the past year. There was so much inside that he wanted to get out, wanted to set his mind free- just forget everything. He opened the top desk and pulled out a blank notebook and a pen and just started writing, and wrote on through the night not even knowing *what* he was writing. He just wrote.

...

"Hey Brittany, come on in." A man dried off a coffee mug behind the counter of Dunzy's Coffee Shop. "How's things going?"

"Good, good, how about yourself?" She sat down at her usual spot next to the fire place.

"Well, looks like you have a new friend with you this time around. And you know me, constant work."

"That's so true. And nope, not a friend, but my boyfriend." Brittany turned to Michael. "Michael, this is Charlie Dunzy. Mr. Dunzy, this is my boyfriend Michael Gable."

"Please to meet you." Charlie reached out his hand. "You sure have a good girl as your girlfriend."

"Thank you thank you." Michael shook his hand. His eyes wandered around the room, taking in how wonderful the coffee shop was.

"What can I get for you?" Charlie asked.

"I'm not sure."

"Come on back here and I'll let you try some stuff and you can choose what you like."

"Are you sure?"

"Oh yes, that's how I learned about coffee drinks."

Michael turned to Brittany whom was getting her school books out and placing them on the table in front of her. She turned to Michael, "What are you looking at me for? You don't have to ask me, go right ahead and have some fun."

It only took a few minutes of being behind the counter of Dunzy's Coffee shop before Michael realized what his passion was- coffee. He intently watched how coffee was made, brewed, mixed, and served. He fell in love with everything that had to do with it, and even helped Charlie with customers. Michael was hooked.

The evening drew on. Michael leaned against the counter, out of breath but still smiled. He hadn't even lifted a book when they came there to study in the first place, at the moment he didn't care about studying, books, or school. With the aroma of coffee, he was in his own little heaven.

"You did very well tonight Michael, I certainly needed the help and you pulled me through. Are you sure you you've never done this before?" Charlie asked as he took off his apron.

"Nope, this was my first time. And I have to say that in doing so I had so much fun. I'd love to do this every single night. Are you looking for any help?"

"Unfortunately, this is the last night Dunzy's coffee shop will be open in Knoxville. My brother and I are moving to Christy, Tennessee and opening up a new shop."

"Oh...that's not far from here though."

"No it isn't. I tell you what, you kids are graduating here soon, so when you are out, I'll have a spot open for you there. How does that sound?"

An instant joy, Michael hugged Charlie. "Thank you! You don't know how much this means to me."

Chapter Twenty-Four

During his game, Michael stopped periodically to work on homework. He just couldn't seem to focus tonight at all, but he knew that it needed to be done and that it's due the next morning. There was only a month away from graduation and he still couldn't seem to motivate himself to finish. The closing of Dunzy's Coffee Shop left him once again discontent. And his time with Brittany didn't last long either, because of his 'laziness,' she had left him in the cold. Michael just didn't care.

With a sigh of relief, he finished the level he was on and turned off the gaming system. Time to get serious now. He took his books and sat down at the kitchen table. About to begin work when a knock came from the front door. Since he was so far into the game he didn't notice the red and blue flashing lights through the windows.

"Oh what now?" Michael's mind wanders as he opened the door to two officers standing side by side.

"Is this the Gable residence?" one of the officers asked- his eyes not leaving Michael's.

"Yes sir. What seems to be the problem?"

"Sir, you need to come with us."

...

Earlier that evening, Barry left a grocery store pushing

a buggy. He stocked up on food for the next couple of weeks. Then as he filled his trunk, returned the buggy and climbed into his car he reversed and drove off into the sunset. He arrived back at his apartment just as night filled the sky.

"Here let me help you with that." A lovely voice said, reaching around to grab bags from the trunk.

Caught off guard, Barry turned to the voice. "Thank you, I appreciate that."

"You don't remember me do you?"

He studied the name tag on her waitress uniform, 'Nancy', but he couldn't for the life of him remember her.

"You look very familiar, but I just can't place you. I'm sorry."

"It's okay. Just think back to high school." She smiled. "Hang on."

She dug through her purse and pulled out a pair of reading glasses and put them on; and then tied her hair into a pony tail. It then dawned on Barry who she was.

"No way! Wow! Yeah, I really didn't recognize you. Excuse me while I take this shoe out of my mouth."

"Ha-ha. It's okay, really- happens a lot. Shall I help you with all of this into your apartment?"

"You shall if you'd like."

As he put down the groceries on the counter top, Barry asked, "So probably a stupid question, do you live around here?"

"Yep, just down the hall. We passed as you were

moving in and I knew you didn't recognize me. So I'm sure when I saw you with groceries and I offered to help it through you off, huh?"

"You really did. From all that has went on this past year I wouldn't doubt that it would be my luck that someone would mug me of my groceries."

"Ha-ha you don't have to worry about that around here. I've been here awhile now, and NOTHING happens." She noticed Barry fidgeting a little bit. "What are you nervous about Barry?"

"Me? Nervous?"

"Umm yeah! Again, what are you nervous about? You were the king of our school and had it all and all the girls wanted you- or had you. No need for you to be around little ole' me."

Barry blushed. "Okay, don't take this the wrong way, but you're...gorgeous. And I didn't see it back then and I'm sorry about that."

"No, no, it's okay. Back then guys wouldn't take a second glance my way. We've all changed since school. Well, some a little more than others, but that's life."

"Oh yeah, I know. I've had a run in with Eric Hedlund a few months ago, and believe me, he's just as bad, if not worst as he was then. The guy's still stuck in the past and still wearing his letterman jacket and was dating a high school girl none the less."

"Wow I could imagine. He was a little bit off back then also. But hey, I'm going to take a shower, just got off work. It was good seeing you." She smiled.

"It was good seeing you too." She started to the door. "Hey wait, what are you doing for the rest of the night?"

"I don't know, probably what I do every night after work: relax, grab a bite to eat, and read. Why?"

"Would you like to go out to dinner with me?"

"I'd be honored." She closed the door behind her.

Barry rushed to put up the groceries and took a quick shower himself. He combed his hair that of which he hasn't done in years, threw on a nice shirt and blazer jacket along with a hint of cologne. Nothing would stop the butterflies fluttering in his stomach. This was certainly a new feeling for him. He was always a calm guy when it came to dating. Being popular was second hand to him. The moment he laid eyes on Nancy, his whole world turned upside down so to speak. He knew in that very moment, he wanted to be with this girl. Something about her made him feel complete; possibly from knowing her from before and knowing that she was one of the good ones. Either way, he was ready for what God had in store for him.

He paced back and forth in the kitchen, holding onto a glass of water that he has yet to take a drink of. Someone knocked on the door and startled Barry. He jumped and spilled the water all over his jacket, set the glass down and opened the door to Nancy.

"Wow, you look amazing." she said, dressed in a yellow sundress, blond hair flowing freely, and flip-flops. Barry got a scent of her vanilla perfume.

"Well thank you, you look pretty beautiful yourself.

Are you ready to go?"

"Yes sir."

He took off his jacket and threw it across the room. Not really knowing the area too well, he let Nancy choose which she suggested a deli.

They took their time eating and catching up. The most fun either one of them has had in a long time.

Afterwards, he walked her to her door. "I had a great time tonight."

"So did I." He meant it. "Would you like to go out again?"

"Hmm...I don't know. Maaaaybe." She smiled, playing with him.

"Okay, I've got to go." He turned with his head down.

They both laughed and embraced in a hug, relaxed in each other's arms. After a moment, she stepped back. "Okay, I've got to head off to bed. I'm falling asleep right here with you. You have a good night."

"Hey, you too." He waited until she was inside. Still pumped and excited from his date, he didn't want to go home just yet. He needed a drive, take in the area and feel the warm air through his open windows. He was free.

Down the road, he heard a band playing at a bar. A few cold ones would be an amazing end to the amazing night, but he resisted the temptation and drove on. As hard as that was for him to do, he knew it was the *right* thing to do. He didn't want to fall back and lose what he had going for him now. Though he could still taste the beer he used to drink, making his mouth water. His head throbbed from where he resisted.

One drink wouldn't hurt, right? He made a U-turn and sped into the parking lot. The throbbing worsened the closer he walked to the door. Something came over him-some kind of *feeling* that something was wrong with Michael. Against the pain, he picked up his phone and called home. No answer. The bar didn't seem so important anymore, so he headed back toward Knoxville.

Driving along a back road, the pain in his head had disappeared. All there was, was nothing but the sounds of the radio, and trees swaying past. He reached down to skip the song on the CD he was listening to. All of a sudden static blasted from the speakers- all the lights on the console flashed on and off before going completely dead. Confused, he didn't think to look at the road. His eyes were off the road for only a second, and he lost control of the wheel. The last he saw was the trees coming toward him.

...

Michael couldn't understand why the cops were taking him down a long back road. His parents weren't home, so he checked his phone to see if they called, forgetting his phone was on silent. He noticed a missed call from Barry. He tried to call back, but it went straight to voicemail.

"Hey bro, call me back- something's going on. I love you." He ended the call, looking up to see yet more flashing lights from emergency vehicles, and the rear end of Barry's car upside down in a ditch. The back doors of the cruiser was locked, keeping him from frantically trying to get out before the cruiser even came to a stop.

"Let me out!" Michael screamed.

"Easy, easy son!" the driver said as Michael kicked at the door. The passenger casually opened Michael's door as if there was nothing the matter, of course he was knocked to the ground as Michael jumped out and ran full speed to Barry's car.

"Barry! Barry!" He ran through a crowd of puzzled emergency officials, all standing around stunned. Michael jumped in the ditch, looked under the mangled car. No Barry. He looked in the back of the ambulance. No Barry there either. "Where's my brother?! Where is he?!"

An officer put his hand on Michael's shoulder and took him aside. "Son, we can't find him. There's no blood, no body, no trace of anyone. We're doing all that we can. There are men searching all over this place with K-9s. If he's out there, we'll find him. But first, can you confirm that this is Barry Gable's vehicle?"

"Yeah...yeah that's his. I don't understand, why can't you find him?"

"We don't understand that either. There is reason to believe, that he just...vanished."

...

Barry was never found, nor was there even a trace that an animal had dragged him off. Michael had stayed at the site for days, and then when the search was called off, he got his driver's license in spite of it all, just so he could drive back here every weekend, hoping that Barry would just show up randomly and everything be okay. With everything else, Michael just lost all care. Nothing mattered to him anymore.

A small memorial was held in Barry's name at the Gable home with just a few friends and family. Michael couldn't take it anymore, he was drunk again and ran out of the house leaving everyone in wonder about what he was up to. He jumped in his car and was about to drive off.

Chris ran out after him, called for him to stop, but nothing would get to Michael. Michael was now at his breaking point. The passenger door was locked, but Chris didn't stop from trying to get in. Michael sat staring ahead with the engine running.

"Mikey! Mikey, open the door. Come on man, I'm here for you."

"Go back inside Chris, you don't need this."

"No. Let me in." Michael put the car into gear, unlocked the door and let Chris in as they drove off together.

For what seemed like hours, they drove in silence. A blank stare never left Michael's face. "You didn't have to come."

"I'm not leaving your side man. Friends stick with each

other through anything."

"Well I warn you, this isn't going to be pretty." Michael took a turn on a back road, the same road where Barry crashed.

"Umm Mikey, what are you doing? Slow it down man."

"Don't call me Mikey! Barry called me Mikey, and I only want him calling me that."

"Michael! Come on man, don't do this." Michael drove faster, skidded around curves. Cars honked their horns as they pass by. Chris squeezed his seat belt, while his knuckles turned white from gripping the door handle. "Look, know it doesn't matter, but we've just got one week of school left. It's tough I know, but do you think Barry would want you to do this? He wants the best for you; for you to live it up while you still can. You have the rest of your life ahead of you. Don't end it now. Barry is here in your heart, and looking over you. He loves you. And I love you. Come on man, lets slow it down, finish school and get out of this town- see the world. What do you say? Just you and me."

Michael stepped down harder on the gas pedal, breathing heavy. He punched the steering wheel making the horn honk with each hit. The car slowed down as he let his foot off the gas. He slammed on the breaks as they came up where the crash happened. Tears rolled down his face. Chris stayed still as Michael turned off the ignition and walked under the yellow caution tape that swayed in the wind.

"I'm sorry Barry, I really am. I don't want to let you go. It's not right at all. I love you so much. You have been there for me any time I needed you, but I hate that I can't be there for you right now. I believe wherever you are, you are happy and that's all that matters. Please forgive me for being so selfish. I guess all I can really do is say good-bye."

...

Michael walked into the school the following Monday, ready to get this over with. But it turned out, he didn't have enough credits to graduate anyways. He had gone through so much school as it was that he didn't want to go through all of it all over again. Plus, he lost all respect for the school system after losing his brother at the time of the incident and they only shrugged it off and cared more about the grades. In the end, he made the best decision just to drop out. That night he packed his bags and left town, not even saying good bye to anyone except his folks and left his past behind.

Chris was the last to receive his diploma. He walked off stage a high school graduate-now on to the real world, free to do as he pleased. As he turned in his cap and gown, his phone vibrated from his pocket. Though he didn't know the number, he still answered anyways. "Hello?"

"Hey man, I'm glad you picked up. What's up?"

"Michael?"

"Yup, it is I." He laughed from the other end. It was

good for Chris to hear Michael actually laughing.

"Where you been man? I'm leaving graduation as we speak. I'm sorry you couldn't be here."

"Oh no man, no worries. I'm happy where I'm at. It's all okay."

"You do sound happy."

"Believe me, I am. Look the reason I'm calling is I've got a proposition for you. You know how you said it's going to be you and I? Well how would you like to get out of Knoxville and move in with me?"

"Move in with you? You have a place already for yourself?"

"Of course. Man, I'm living the dream. My boss pulled some strings and got me this house real cheap. I have an extra bedroom and waited to know if you'd like to have it."

"Whoa, dude that's awesome! I'm glad to hear you are doing well for yourself and just only a week. Yeah man, I'll definitely take you up on that offer. Where are you?"

"I'm living in Christy, Tennessee. I'll text you the address, so take your time getting here. No rush. Just thought I'd ask you before you made plans for the rest of your life, which I know how you are."

"Yeah I do rush things huh?" They both laughed like old times.

"And Chris?"

"Yeah man?"

"Thanks...for everything, you know? I love you."

"I love you too."

...

At first Chris' parents weren't too keen on him moving out so early, but they knew he was a man now and had to let him go. He packed the last box into his new car, and had a big dinner with them before leaving. Christy, Tennessee was only an hour from home, and gave him a good time to roll down the windows and let the fresh country air roll in. Which he definitely did.

He stopped at Benny's Gas and Auto Repair, just outside of the Christy town line. While filling up, he looked around the open fields that surround him. Crickets chirped in the peaceful night air. The latch clicks on the gas pump, completely full. He set the nozzle back and put the gas cap back on. His ears suddenly began to ring and pop as if he was driving up a steep mountain.

Chris turned around to a floating green light, humming above him. It vanished toward the sky before he could even get a glimpse of what it was. The ringing in his ears have stopped. He looked around, everything seemed fine. Now back in his car, Christy County here he comes.

<u>Chapter Twenty-Five</u>

The last picture Chris looked at on the wall after the graduation picture, was a newspaper article of Charlie Dunzy shaking hands with Michael after signing him on as a co-owner of Dunzy's Coffee Shop. Underneath that was an article from the sales paper of Chris' 1st book sale. This of course was seven years ago.

Chris and Michael lived together for the 1st seven years after Chris had moved to town. They worked together at Dunzy's Coffee Shop until Chris had become a published writer. Now they lived next door to each other and living the dream as Michael liked to put it. Though things were peaceful, they were about to change.

After locking the door behind him, Chris walked down to his mailbox, taking in the fresh fall air. Halloween was right around the corner as his neighbors began to decorate their houses. They all waved hello as they notice one another. Christy is a town like your typical Mayberry town. Everyone knew each other and were kind to one another.

He opened his mailbox, reached in and pulled out a single postcard from Roswell, New Mexico.

Chris, I'll be seeing you soon. Things are about to get real. Be careful- David.

<u>Chapter Twenty-Six</u>

Chris lived across the street from the Christy County church. From the sidewalk, he waved at Reverend Brown who raked leaves on the front lawn. He turned left on to Old Christy Highway, and began his walk into town.

Along the way, he passed a used cd, book, and movie store on his right called The Max. A Halloween theme of horror movies and books filled the display window. Then, beside there was the grocery store, which of where the windows had ghosts painted on them. The barber shop to the right of that had stringed orange pumpkin lights around the door frame. Next door to that, the hotel had a carved pumpkin on either side of the entrance. Then, on the other side of the street, Dunzy's Coffee Shop and the combined Christy County Hospital and Christy Fire Department have yet to decorate for the holiday.

On down at the other end of the road, Sheriff Boston's Police Station and to the right of that- the town library both were also undecorated. The county park between the library and hardware store was empty of kids, while the swings swayed in the breeze. The hardware store had cardboard cut outs of horror movie characters whom used power tools as their choice of weapons. Reels 8 Cinema was set up for a month-long horror film festival. And lastly, Dusk's Fashion and Design clothing store had dressed the mannequins in an array of costumes on display. He could only imagine what the schools and Camp Full Moon on Craven's Lane, and the other town homes on Old Jack Belvadeer's Lane had come up with for their decorations.

...

"Hey man, how's it going?" Michael asked as he wiped down the counter top. The warm aroma of fresh brewed coffee instantly relaxed Chris the second he walked into Dunzy's Coffee Shop: his home away from home. Dunzy's is where Chris did most of his writing.

"Oh, you know, same ole' same ole'. Here, check this out." Chris took off his jacket and set it down at the counter and then handed Michael the postcard from David.

"It's a postcard, so what?"

"Yeah, but look who it's from."

"David? Who's David?"

"My old neighbor, the one Detective Acuff and Marshall were after."

"I wouldn't worry about it, it's probably nothing. What, you're not scared are you?" He smiled.

"Well...no, not really. Just odd- haven't heard from him since the night Old Spooks' place burned down. That was what, 12 years ago? Sure, we were just kids, but think about it, didn't the detectives say something about not being able to find any record of David's existence? It's spooky."

"Wow, yeah you better sleep with your lightsaber toy by your bed from now on."

"Oh yeah, like that's going to do any good."

"Look at you man, you *are* creeped out. Okay, you're the writer here, do you honestly think if David was going to do anything, he'd send you a postcard first?"

"It's happened before, well in a letter. You ever hear of the Zodiac?"

"Yeah, but they never caught the guy did they? I mean the letters stopped after a while."

"Well they never caught David either. They did, but he escaped. This isn't helping me!"

"Here." Michael poured a cup of coffee. "Have yourself a cup and relax. Don't worry, I got your back, son."

"Oh that's reassuring."

"My specialty."

"Right, well I'm going to my corner and get some writing done."

"That's right, you get in your corner and think about what you've done."

"What? Hey, do me a favor and try some decaf every once and awhile."

Chris walked away laughing.

Michael said aloud, "Hey, got you laughing, now didn't I?"

Chapter Twenty-Seven

Chris yawned as he put his leather satchel across his shoulder and made his way to the counter. "Shew, it's been a long day."

"How far did you get?" Michael asked as he was cleaning up.

"A couple of chapters, not much."

"Hey it's progress, can't complain. You heading home?"

"Yeah. Yeah, I think I am. You want me to stick around?"

"No man, you're good. I'm just about to close up anyways."

"Okay. I'll see you later then."

"Take it easy."

...

Michael rechecked the shop and made sure the machines were off as well as the lights in the back room were off. He checked to make sure that the floor and counter tops were spotless, mugs and to-go cups were stacked neat and tidy. All set. He stepped out into the chilly air, turned off the main lights, turned the Open sign to Close, and then locked the doors behind him. Another long day down.

It wasn't a quarter after 10 p.m., the town was quiet and dark as a ghost town- not including the marquee of late-night movies at the cinema. He looked up to a blinking street lamp that buzzed on and off. Pretending he was smoking a cigarette, he blew puffs of air into the night. Two cats were fighting rough nearby and knocked over a trash can. Michael jumped and turned toward the sound of the can as they smashed against the concrete sidewalk.

"*Wow, look at that.*" Michael thought to himself. He looked up at the sky. A green aurora borealis glimmered over Sheriff Boston's Police Station. He ran down the sidewalk to get a better view as he reached in his pocket for his cell phone to snap a photo of this event. Oddly enough, the battery had died which it was full only a few minutes ago. One by one the street lights and the theater marquee as well all went black. Michael stood in nothing but a green glow.

Something didn't *feel* right; the hairs on the back of his neck stood up. An eerie feeling that he was being watched came over him. He looked around, but could only see darkness.

"Is someone the-. Never mind, I'm not going to ask that. I've seen way too many movies to know that if I was to ask 'is someone there?' someone would surely pop up and get me. But on the other hand, here I am talking to myself in the middle of the street. Sooo, yeah, I don't know."

A small part of Michael didn't believe anyone else was lurking in the darkness, but another part of him was straight up frightened- frightened not because talking to himself was easing the fear, but because the hair on the back of his neck would NOT go down.

"Oh Mikey, it's probably just the air that's getting to you. Let's go home, what do you say? I say we shall. We shall." He headed down the sidewalk toward home. Hardly anyone drove in the town of Christy, everyone lived so close that it was pointless.

"Mikey." A small quiet voice whispered out his name behind him.

"Chris, if I turn around and that's you, I'm going to be really upset with you."

"Mikey."

"Great." He said under his breath and turned to see a teenage girl glowing in white. "Angela?"

She floated down the sidewalk backwards, made a turn around the corner of the hospital and disappeared on to Craven's Lane.

"Angela wait!" He chased after her, but she was gone.

Chapter Twenty-Eight

Chris woke to his alarm clock flashing twelve a.m. The power must have gone off last night, no telling how long he had slept in. He wasn't used to sleeping that long, but he did appreciate the much-needed rest.

He checked his cell and it was 2 p.m. His parents would be there for dinner five hours from now.

...

After he took a shower and trimmed up his goatee, Chris dressed himself in baggy blue jeans, black t-shirt, and orange Tennessee hooded sweatshirt. He slipped on his house shoes and then checked the mail. There was nothing except for a town reminder of Farmer Johnson's Halloween Party. He headed back inside and made a cup of coffee and sat by the fire while he studied the book of John.

...

He sat a bowl of salad on the table by a chicken casserole and a batch of rolls just as there was a knock from the front door. His folks were right on time.

"Hey come on in, make yourself at home." Chris greeted them with hugs, amazed at how much they had aged the last time he had seen them only a few months ago.

"Mmm something smells good." His mother implied.

"Thanks, I hope you like it. It's ready whenever you are." Chris helped them both to the table, holding each of their chairs until they sat down. "So who would like to say grace?"

"It's your house son. You go ahead." His father said.

"Alrighty." They bow their heads. "Lord, heavenly father, we thank you for this meal we are about to receive. Thank you for our lives each day we are alive, and the love we show for one another. Thank you for your many blessings upon us. Please bring peace to those who are sick, and bless those who don't believe in you. In heaven's name we pray, Amen."

"Amen." They dug into their food.

His dad looked up. "So what are you writing these days?"

"I'm working on this book about a couple with which the guy is religious and the girl is an atheist. It's about the life they share together."

"How does that work?"

"Easy, Jesus tells us to love our neighbor and love our enemies. The male character will love her through anything which will cause her to turn to Jesus and welcome Him into her heart."

"I like that."

"Thanks. How are you and mom doing?"

"We're hanging in there. Can't complain though- tired

a lot."

"Tired? You should be resting since you're both retired now."

"We do, after we help the church first. Church comes before anything we do. Besides pray and thank God every day, of course."

"That's really good. You know I have the room here if you and mom ever want to move in. You'll love the church in this town, wouldn't have to travel far. It's just right across the street."

"Honey, we don't want to leave our home. We'll be okay. If anything was to happen to us, you're only an hour away." His mother pointed out.

"Yeah, a lot could happen in that hour also."

"Don't worry, anything that happens is in God's will, can't ever forget that. You know He's in control." She added.

"I know He is. And I know He keeps you two safe. Sometimes it's hard to keep that faith, but that's His way of testing us. Which, speaking of tests, you'll never guess who I got a postcard from."

"Was it that David kid?" His father asked.

"Yeah! How did you know?"

"He called us. Wanted to see how we were doing."

"What did you do?"

"Nothing." His mother said. "We just said we were fine and hoped he was doing well. You see, this *is* like a test of faith like you said. I think that's what you were thinking of also. Just like your story, we can't judge him, but we can show him our Christian love. That's how God wants us to live."

"You sure weren't like this before- granted I was still a kid and you were protecting me all the time, but you all were still young and naïve yourselves. That's how I felt about showing Christian love. I was confused at the same time because we're supposed to walk away from the wicked people. You are right though, we can't just judge him, after all we never did see him do anything. Just the way the detectives described him. It was pretty creepy."

"Right, but that is going off of what someone else is saying. Not everyone tells the truth." His dad mentioned.

"Oh yeah, I know. So, what if I do the right thing if he shows up and I end up getting hurt?"

"You can't let yourself worry. Just have faith in God and do what He tells you in your heart."

Chapter Twenty-Nine

3:30 a.m., Melissa Stetson stepped outside from the diner for a smoke. This time of the morning business was slow- not many travelers drove through Christy. She watched her brother-in-law, Joe, as he dozed off behind the counter across the street at her husband's gas station: Benny's Gas and Auto Repair. How Joe could even keep his job was beyond her, but her husband Benny had a big heart and didn't leave his family behind.

Joe's head fell over and bounced on the counter top. Melissa coughed on her smoke and laughed at Joe. She didn't hear the footsteps behind her. As she wiped her teary eyes, she turned and looked up to a man that stood a foot away from her. She screamed and then after she caught her breath said, "Wow, I'm sorry...you startled me."

As he rubbed his head, Joe heard the scream and then jumped out of his seat and ran outside to Melissa's aid. He yelled from across the street, "Hey you okay?!"

"I'm fine Joe, go on back inside. Everything's okay."

"Alright then." Joe hesitated at first and then headed back in. The man didn't look safe to him. He had on crinkly faded brown clothes which were torn in many places. His hair and beard were long shaggy. And a duffle bag hung over his shoulder, along with sandals on his feet.

Melissa looked in the man's eyes who stared down at her with sadness. "Are you hungry? Could I get you something to eat?"

He looked in at the diner and grinned. Melissa smiled as he nodded his head and she replied, "Yes? Okay, come on in."

The gentleman took a seat at the counter and placed his bag on the floor beside him. He took a glance at his dirty hands and decided to go to the restroom to wash up first.

"There you are." Melissa said sweetly as he sat back down. "How would you like your coffee?"

"Bl...ack." He struggled to say.

"Will do." She poured him a cup and placed a menu in front of him. After a moment she asked, "Do you see anything you would like?"

He looked it over and pointed to the first picture of biscuits and gravy, bacon and hash browns. "This...please."

"Good choice. It'll be right up." She watched him sip on his coffee while she cooked his meal. Quiet, he looked out the window and silently hummed 'Amazing Grace' to himself. "That was really sweet."

"Sorry, I...didn't know I...was...doing it...out loud."

"No, no it's okay. Really."

"Okay, tha...nk you."

"It's no problem."

He drank some more of his coffee. "Mmm this is good coffee. Sorry I was stuttering, I haven't talked at all in a long time; besides to God of course."

"Really? Anyone?"

"Nope, it's okay though. People tend to judge me because I'm homeless."

"He shall judge thy people with righteousness, and thy poor with judgment."

"I'm sorry?"

"Psalms 72."

"That's exactly how it is. Sad really."

"I totally agree. Don't worry about them. When someone puts you down, God will bless you double."

"He's blessed me plenty. I know what He wants from me."

"Well, He isn't done with you yet. Here is you some food to fill your tummy." She set down his plate. "It's on the house, so take your time."

"Thank you ma'am. You are too kind."

...

"Good morning!" Chris announced as he walked into Dunzy's Coffee Shop.

"Morning man." Michael said from behind the counter. "You want the usual?"

"Of course." Chris headed to his favorite seat, but stopped to notice someone else sitting there. He instead sat by the counter, whispered to Michael, "Hey, who's that guy?"

"I don't know. He's been here all morning, just reading his Bible."

"That's perfectly okay with me."

Chris pulled out his laptop and let it load up. He glanced over at the gentleman who when he read his Bible just smiled and completely tuned out of the world around him, as if he didn't have a care or worry left. The man, from what Chris could see, was totally happy.

Noon, Chris ordered two vanilla cappuccinos with two bagels for lunch. He handed the gentleman one of each and went back to his writing. He didn't know who he was, but it just came over him, suddenly, to do a good deed. As the man finished his meal, he slowly closed his Bible and headed for the exit. Something dropped to the floor as the man exited. Chris barely heard it fall and he reached down and picked up a gold cross necklace, then followed the gentleman.

"Sir? Excuse me sir. You dropped something."

The man turned around and said, "Why thank you kindly. And I didn't thank you before, thank you for the meal. That was Godly of you."

"It was no trouble at all. Well you take care." Chris turned to walk back inside.

"Will you sit with me for a minute? I'd like to talk with you."

"I should be getting back to my work, but why not? I need a break."

They sat on the bench out front of the barber shop next door. "I won't take up much of your time. I know you young'uns like your work. I just wanted to say that God wants me to tell you that He has big plans for you. He wants you to be patient and keep your eyes open. A lot of changes are about to happen in His favor. So just be ready." He looked at the necklace. "Here, I want you to keep this. Use it as a reminder that Christ died on the cross for you. And that He's always here. Thank you for taking the time to listen. That's all I've got to say. God bless."

Before Chris had a chance to speak, the man walked directly into traffic and was run over by a truck that carried cows from Farmer Johnson's farm. The man died in an instant.

Chapter Thirty

As the sun rose over the mountains, Reverend Brown said a blessing over the food Farmer Johnson, Chris, and himself were about to eat. They ate in peace and drank coffee while they watched the sun rise from Farmer Johnson's back porch. A nice way to start the day.

After breakfast, they decorated the farm house and hung spider webs around the wrap around porch railings, and had ghouls and goblins stuck to the windows. Following that, they did maintenance work that needed tending to: raking gravel on the walk way down to the bonfire pit, cutting a trail through the cornfield for a haunted tractor ride, cleaned up the grill for the barbeque, set up mechanical zombies to jump out of haystacks in the barn, and for last, carved pumpkins that of which were placed on each side of the steps on the porch of the farm house.

Reverend Brown held a board as Chris hammered in the nails to replace old boards in the bleachers by the fire pit. Two cars pulled into the driveways of the two empty houses across the street besides Chris' house. Each driver got out of their cars. One girl was a blond in a sunflower sundress. And the other girl was a girl with black and purple hair, along with black and purple Tripp pants. They help each other take boxes to each house.

"Ow! Dagnabbit Chris!" Reverend Brown yelled out. "Watch it, that hurt!"

"Sorry Reverend." Luckily, the girls didn't see him smash the Reverend's thumb with the hammer.

"Son, pay attention. What's got a hold of that head of yours?"

"Who's that?" Chris pointed at the girls.

"Oh, that's our new neighbors. I don't really know much about them."

"New neighbors? That was fast, those houses just went on the market. Besides that, they are gorgeous."

"Chris, put away that lustful mind and get back to work."

"Right. Sorry." Secretly, he kept taking glances toward them any chance he got. He was in love at first sight with the girl in black.

Chapter Thirty-One

"Is this okay for our date?" a boy of 15 asked. He was nervous to look his date straight in the eye.

"Yes Evan, this is fine." she smiled and placed her hand on top of his. He jumped. "Relax, it's only me...Carrie."

They sat at Dunzy's Coffee Shop, which was the biggest place for dates in Christy, besides the movie theater.

"I'm trying, it's just...well, you're really beautiful tonight. Not that you aren't always beautiful. Just, you know. I-" she cut him off laughing. He blushed. "What? What's funny?"

"You're cute." she smiled at him, hoping he'd smile back.

"Thank you."

"You're welcome. And thank you for taking me on a date. I'd thought you'd never ask."

"Really?"

"Of course. Evan I like you. I just waited for you to make the first move."

His eyes light up. "I really didn't expect this to happen."

"How come?"

"I just figured you'd see me outside of school as shy as I am in school and not want anything to do with me."

"But I like that you are shy; you're a good person. So what if nobody else sees who you are. It only matters how God sees you, which He loves you."

"He *must* love me if I'm on a date with the most beautiful and popular girl of the school."

"Awe, thank you. If we truly believe and love Him, He'll guide us where we need to be. I think you and I were brought together by Him. I prayed for someone whom I could spend the rest of my life with and not be hurt. And then that's when you asked me out."

"Psalms 149: For the Lord, taketh pleasure in His people: He will beautify the meek with salvation."

"Exactly! So tell me Mr. Evan, where do you see yourself after graduation?"

"Well I-" he began to say. A green light zoomed by the window. "What in the world?"

Evan looked over at Michael, frozen behind the counter. He knew from his reaction that Michael saw the same thing.

"What was that?" Carrie asked.

"I don't know, but I want to find out." Evan said.

"No! Don't go out there!" Michael yelled out. He jumped over the counter and locked the doors. Michael thought of the nightmares he had when he was younger, and it didn't feel right. "It's not safe, trust me."

"What are you talking about? It's probably nothing." Evan said.

"Probably not, but I don't trust that..." Michael pointed up to the sky. Three triangular green lights circle around each other and hover over the park. Mothers and fathers grabbed their children from the playground and ran for shelter in nearby businesses. Lights and power go out around town, leaving only light from the setting sun through the windows.

"This is too weird. Should we be by the windows like this?" Carrie asked.

"I don't guess it matters, if whatever those things are wanted to get in, they could." Michael added.

"Well, this sure makes an interesting first date. Wouldn't you say?" Evan smiled.

"Ha-ha I knew there was some whit under that quiet voice of yours." Carrie sat back down in her seat. Evan scooted beside her, putting his arm around his shoulder.

"Michael, sit down man. Relax." Evan insisted.

Michael reached behind the counter and pulled out a kitchen knife. "No thanks, I need to be on guard. I don't know about all this."

"But a kitchen knife? Seriously?"

"Hey, at least it's something. I've got a spatula, would that make you feel any safer?"

"Well yeah if you want to *flip* the situation, get it?" Evan said, but Michael didn't show the least bit of amusement. "Okay then."

They all sat in silence while they watched the lights twirl around one another, not moving from the same spot. It was almost as if the lights taunted them. Or even worst...they could be watching and studying their every move.

"What time do you have?" Carrie asked. She dozed off in Evan's arms.

"I don't know, my phone died. Feels like it's been hours though."

"I'm getting tired and hungry."

"Same here." Evan then called out to Michael. "Hey man, do you have anything that we can eat? Or at least nibble on until the power comes back on?"

"Yeah, just breads and donuts. I think the coffee is still warm if you want some of that." Michael leaned against the counter twirling the knife.

"That'd be perfect actually." Carrie said.

"Okay, coming right up."

"Hey, I think they are leaving." Evan said. He stared up at the sky as the green lights race off one by one. Street lights turn on up and down the street followed by the power. "Yay! Food!"

Michael watched the kids leave. He was shaken the rest of the night.

Chapter Thirty-Two

October 31st, Halloween

5:30 a.m.

Opening up the coffee shop, Michael scanned through the morning paper. Not a word about the unexplained lights, nor the power outage in town. Odd.

...

Farmer Johnson didn't wait for the roosters to wake him at sunrise, he was always the type of person who got up earlier than that. This morning he felt somewhat uneasy as he pulled himself out of bed careful not to wake up his wife, even though she has been dead for years now. He still wasn't used to her being gone. He half expected her to be in the kitchen cooking homemade biscuits and gravy while she danced along to Jimmy Rogers or Roy Acuff's music. But he knew she wasn't there.

He turned on the record player and let the tears fall while he threw sausage in a frying pan. Oh how he missed her. And then, as he ate, he stared up at their wedding pictures on the wall; so young and so in-love.

He then washed the dishes and looked out his back window to see something run into his cornfield. "Dadgum racoons."

Ted grabbed his shotgun from the hall closet and limped off the back deck and stopped to listen. All was quiet, except for the cool morning breeze rustling through the leaves. He broke the silence with a whistle and then yelled, "Come on out here varmints! Stay away from my corn!"

With his gun raised to the night sky, he took a shot in the dark; something metal was hit. "What in the world?"

The ground underneath him began to vibrate. Through the corn, a green dim light grew brighter and brighter before balls of light shot up into the sky and disappeared behind the clouds. Ted pulled out a cigar from his overall front pocket and lit it. "You'll be back, and I'll be waiting."

...

Reverend Brown was woken up by the sound of Farmer Johnson's shotgun. Startled, he grabbed his Bible from his bedside table and threw on his robe before he ran downstairs.

"Lord give me the strength." He stepped outside, closed his robe tightly to keep out the air. It was then he saw the green lights shoot up to the sky. "Lord help us."

...

Smoking the rest of his cigar, Farmer Johnson leaned

against his porch railing. Headlights pulled up into his gravel driveway and shined on him.

"Morning Reverend. What brings you out so early?"

"Is everything okay? I heard shots so I figured it came from this way."

"Everything's just dandy. I think I hit one of them space men."

"Was that what I saw? I didn't know what to believe. I thought maybe we were under attack."

"No worries Reverend isn't nobody gonna be stepping foot in Christy. Nothing here they'd want anyways. And yes, we have the right to bear arms. Somebody steps on my property, they ain't leaving without a missing limb or a bullet hole in their body. You can guarantee that."

"Not me, I'll fight with the good word and put on my armor of Christ."

"My gun is my sword, I live by the sword- I will die by the sword."

"To each his own I guess. Are you sure you're okay?"

"I'm fine Reverend. You can go on home. I'm sure you scared Sister Wilma rushing out the door."

Reverend Brown's faced slumped serious in that second with his eyes wide. "You know what? I didn't even think about that. I was up and out the door in a matter of seconds."

It was then they both heard screams from down the street.

"Reverend, I hate to tell you, but I told you so."

...

Margarette Billings heard the shot and was awoken from a dream of her late husband. Her first thought was that it was her gas that woke her, but she ran to the restroom and didn't have a bowel movement. She slowly, but surely, made her way down to the kitchen for her morning breakfast. It was almost time to get up anyways.

Cooking, she listened to her own humming of church hymns; not noticing the little feet enter the room. "Grandma, who are those men outside?"

She jumped and dropped the frying pan onto the stove. "Lordy, you startled me...what men?"

"The ones in the back yard. Look..." He pointed out the back door window.

She looked. "I don't see anything, sweetie. You had a bad dream. Go on back to bed."

"No, no, I promise you, they were there- behind the bushes."

Curious, she looked again. "Sweetie I don-"

Something dashed by the window. Margarette grabbed her grandson and pulled him back against the wall and turned off the kitchen light in the process. She held him tight against her with her hand over his mouth. "Shhh, be quiet."

The door handle shook, trying to open. Whatever was outside was desperate to get in. A green light shined through the windows and cracks of the door. The house shook like an earthquake, causing the dishes to fall and brash to the floor. Doors inside the house opened and slammed shut over and over.

"I need you to run upstairs okay? Just run-" The chaos stopped in complete silence. The back door slowly opened with nothing but darkness on the other side. No more green light. *Something* stepped inside the door way. Margarette screamed as loud as she could. Though she couldn't see what it was, but she knew that something was there, she heard its footsteps.

...

"Sister Margarette! Sister Margarette! Open the door! Are you alright in there?" Reverend Brown banged on the front door.

"I can hear crying." Farmer Johnson said at the same time he cocked his gun. "I'm going around back."

"Be careful."

"Pray for me." He limped around the corner of the house, but didn't see anything. Moving closer to the back, the cries become louder. "Sister Margarette? Honey, is everything okay?"

"Ted? Ted! Don't come back here. Something's here with us." She replied from inside the house.

He leaned against the back of the house, listened. There was silence except for the morning birds. "Margarette, I don't hear anything. I'm coming in in one...two...three!"

Margarette and her grandson both knew he was

coming and yet they still screamed when Ted entered in with his shotgun raised.

From outside, Reverend Brown's frantic, but yet concerned yells could be heard. "Margarette! Margarette, answer me!"

"Hang on. Sit tight. I'll be right back." Ted said, he glanced around to make sure that there wasn't anyone else in the room. He crept through the house to the front door, not leaving his guard just in case. Though nothing, he opened the front door. "Yes? Can I help you?"

"Is everything okay?" Reverend Brown ran in past Ted.

"They're fine, though sitting in the kitchen floor a little shook up."

Reverend Brown didn't waste one more second and ran to them.

"Hey Reverend, thank you for coming." Margarette said. She looked to her grandson. "It's okay now, you can go back to sleep on the couch if you like. We will be just right here."

"What happened?" Reverend Brown asked.

"I'm not exactly sure. Bright green lights and someone tried to get in." She pulled herself off from the floor.

"Well whatever it was, it's gone now." Ted said from the doorway, keeping watch.

"I think we better call Sheriff Boston." Margarette said as she picked up the only phone she had, a landline.

"I don't think that's a really good idea. He'll just think we all fell off our rockers. What's done is done, and no danger that I can tell." Ted stepped in.

Shocked, Reverend Brown asked, "Do you think that's a good idea?"

"There's just nothing we can do. If we started talking about aliens and UFO's and what not, they'd surely take us away. I've seen it done."

"Well if anything happens, I'm telling the sheriff. I can't tell a lie."

...

10:03 a.m.

While mothers sit and gossip on the park benches over coffee and cookies, the children play. One child, a little four year old girl, swings on the swing set. Two boys around the age of six play David and Goliath while on top of the jungle gym. They pretended they were on Noah's ark as they fought against each other. Ah, what the imagination of children's minds can create.

The little girl watched the boys play, stops swinging and stared toward the woods behind her. Someone she has never seen before lingered beside a tree. She walked over to him, "Hi, what's your name?"

The man didn't speak, just stared down at her and tilted his head from side to side like a confused dog questioning what she was.

"Can you talk?" Still nothing. "You look funny and

have some really big eyes. Are you an aliem?"

She reached out her hand to grab a hold of his. "Ewww, you feel like a slug. Come on, I want you to meet my friends."

"Hey guys!" she turned to her friends and let go of his hand. "Come here!"

The man faded into the woods before she turned back around.

The boys don't notice her. From top of the jungle gym, they stop playing and point to the sky over the woods. "Oooh look! Look! Pretty colors!"

The little girl ran over to the boys, but it was gone before she nor the mommies could even see it.

"Aww I missed it!" the little girl whined. "What was it?"

"Spaceship."

...

4:10 p.m.

About to head out of the door, Doctor Greg Stalls sighed as his work phone rang in his pocket. He was exhausted from a 15-hour shift. "Hello, Dr. Stalls here."

"Doc...help! Mental...Wind...(chatter)...Patient..." The call ended. From what little he could hear over the chaos of screaming voices, he dialed the Christy County Hospital Mental Wing. Getting no answer, he headed toward the elevator.

The ride up was quiet, he closed his eyes only for a second, soft music played softly. 13th floor, the doors open to the mental wing where the chaos runs through the halls: patients screamed and ran around. Nurses tried to calm each one of them down, some scratched the halls, some banged their heads on the windows, some rolled on the floor crying, and some who were strapped in wheelchairs shook from side to side. Everyone was in an uproar. Panic alarms went off in every room. Pillows, blankets and clothes were thrown all around.

A nurse ran out of room 330 and grabbed Doc Stalls by the arm. "We need you. Right. Now."

"What in the world happened here?"

"Mr. Dillingham went through one of his rages and escaped his room. He ran down the halls and let everyone out. We can get him or anyone in control."

"Okay, I'll see what I can do."

Doctor Stalls walked into patient Dillingham's room. He was backed against his window sweating profusely, holding off the staff who are circled around him with a knife. He swung it back and forth the closer someone came near him.

"Stay back! Stay back!" he yelled. He then noticed Doctor Stalls enter and got excited. "Doc! Doc! You've got to help me, man!"

"Mr. Dillingham, what are you doing?"

"They're coming!"

"Who's coming?"

"Them! The men from the sky!"

"Relax, there's no one coming."

"I promise you, they are here; and they are coming for us all!"

"Okay, okay just put down the knife and we'll talk about it."

"No sir, no, no, no. That I will not do. We'll talk, but the knife stays with me. That's my protection."

"I'll protect you. We'll all protect you, that's what we're here for. You've just got to trust us."

"I trust you all, but I don't trust *them*." He pointed to the sky.

"Why don't you trust them?"

"You don't get it, they want to kill us! Use our bodies as a vessel for their dying souls."

"Why do you think they will do that?"

"Because they've taken me before. They'll do it again."

"There is nobody going to take you, I promise. What would you like us to do? Strap you in bed? Lock you in the padded room? What?"

"I...I..." He fell to the floor, dropped the knife beside him. All he could do was cry in his hands. "I don't know, I just want to die."

A nurse kicked the knife away while the others calmly guide him to his bed. Doctor Stalls gave him a sedative that calmed him down almost immediately. They got the rest of the mental wing in order.

•••

6:42 p.m.

Sheriff Boston walked into the Sevier Family Store, west on Craven's Lane down the road from the Camp Full Moon entrance. The screen door slammed shut behind him. Behind the counter Granny Sevier dropped a box of napkins and yelled, "Lord Sheriff, can't you be any louder? You startled me half to death, and I ain't too far there as it is."

He sat down at the counter, looking around at how nothing has changed since they opened up since the 70's. "Sorry ma'am. I'll be quieter next time."

"You better. What brings you around these parts?" She poured him a cup of coffee.

"It's Halloween, you know I can't pass by on a chance of your pumpkin pie."

"Best pie in town I've heard."

"Well now I can agree with that. How are things going around here?"

"Couldn't be any better. Peaceful as always. Well besides the green men."

"I beg your pardon?"

"Oh yeah, trespassing on my property at night." She turned to the kitchen. "Hey Gus! Gus, come on out here and tell ole' Sheriff what ye been seeing with these green men."

Gus walked in dressed in a greasy apron and hair net. "Evening Sheriff."

"Evening." Sheriff Boston doesn't know what to think, just sat and listened.

"Go on, tell him." Granny insisted.

"Mom, it's really nothing. Probably just kids playing Halloween games." He looked at Sheriff Boston, nervous as could be. He was 6' 2" and towered over him at the age of twenty-one years old. "Sheriff, the other night I hear some noises outside when I was closing up. Figuring it was only 'coons or something, I still went out anyways and three people in green costumes ran into the woods when they saw me. It was nothing."

"Well I've heard around town stuff like this has been going on since early this morning. Nobody knows what it is. But between you and me, I believe it's aliens." Sheriff took a bite of his pie.

"Aliens?!" Granny yelled. "My, my, my what's this world coming to?"

"Nothing that the government hasn't already hid from us in the first place." Gus whispered under his breath.

"Hey!" Sheriff Boston laughed.

"Oh sorry Sheriff. You didn't hear me, that's the grill talking." Gus slid on back into the kitchen.

"What are we supposed to do?" Granny asked.

"Granny, the best I can tell you is if something like this *is* happening, then I honestly don't have a clue on what to do. It's not like they train us for alien invasions."

He stood and left her a ten-dollar bill on the counter, more than double the pay for the pie. "You have a happy Halloween, Ms. Sevier."

"You too, Sheriff."

"Would I be seeing you at Farmer Johnson's BBQ tonight?"

"Oh, maybe. You gonna have a dance waiting for me?"

"For you? Any day." He smiled and then yelled to the kitchen, "Happy Halloween, Gus!"

Gus replied back with a grunt.

Sheriff Boston closed the door of his cruiser and turned the ignition. No start. He tried again, yet still nothing. The doors automatically locked. He tried to manually unlock the doors, but the locks wouldn't budge. Static blared from the radios. His laptop went haywire with numbers all over the screen. A bright green light covered the cruiser, shining through the instrument panel. His sirens and lights went on and off while the car shook as if in a strong wind.

He tried to scream, but the horn of the sirens and the static of the radio blocked him out. Just as fast as the chaos began, it stopped in a bang of gun shots outside the vehicle.

Sheriff Boston turned to see Gus shoot up in the sky with a shotgun and then walked toward the passenger window. "It's alright Sheriff, they're gone now."

"What in the world was that?!" Sheriff Boston asked as he rolled down the window.

"It's those green men I was telling you about. Dagnabbit, they flew away before I could shoot 'em down. Hey, do you think our friends in the government would pay me a pretty penny if I shot one down?"

"I'm….not…sure…Gus."

"Ok, okie dokie then. Carry on." Gus unloaded his gun and casually walked back into the store as if nothing had happened.

Sheriff Boston started the cruiser and sped out of Sevier Family Store's gravel driveway and back towards town.

…

7:02 p.m.

"I'm not lying! That's what just happened!" Sheriff Boston yelled at Mayor Davis.

"Calm down, calm down. I'm sure there is nothing to worry about. You've been working hard lately, relax and have a good time." Mayor Davis insisted.

Chris and Michael entered through Farmer Johnson's wooden gate to the commotion between the Mayor and Sheriff. Christy Halloween BBQ's in full effect.

"Mayor, there is something terribly wrong here in Christy!"

"What's going on?" Chris asked, concerned.

"This doesn't concern you Mr. Wilson." The Mayor interrupted.

"It concerns the entire town!" Sheriff Boston blurted out.

Farmer Johnson stomped over to the commotion. "What in the blazes? Men calm yourselves. I don't care if the world is at its end, right now we've got a whole town of people down there having fun. Do not ruin this for them with your bickering! Set aside whatever nonsensical problems you both may have and get over there and have a good time. It's a holiday men!"

"I couldn't agree with you more." Mayor Davis grinned.

"Oh no, don't you dare start in with me! Keep on doing what you're doing with your greetings. I've got stuff to do. Sheriff, men, come lets chat." Farmer Johnson angrily replied back, leaving Mayor Davis in a state of shock.

Chris, Michael, and Sheriff Boston followed Ted to the BBQ grill. Kids ran around in costumes laughing and playing. Screams rang out from the haunted tractor corn ride. Couples line danced to a local Tennessee country band as couples also relaxed and cuddled around a bonfire drinking wine. The town was together and the town was having fun while showing love to one another.

"What was that about?" Chris asked.

An angry look on Ted's face quickly turned into a mysterious grin. "Nothing, just getting under Mayor Davis' skin. I don't like politics and that man thinks he can rule us all. Like I told Reverend Brown this morning, all I need is my gun, my farm, and my faith." He looked toward Sheriff Boston. "And you Sheriff, here...have a beer. I overheard what you were saying. I agree *something* weird has been going on, but don't you worry. If anything was to happen, this town will get together and stop it and erase it faster than it'll reach the authority and media, who'll twist the truth so far-"

"Whoa Ted, easy. You're right, but easy does it now." Chris interrupted, he knew that once Ted started on a rant he would last for hours, possibly even through the entire party. "So, serve us some of your BBQ sandwiches and we'll be on our way."

"Boy, you get it yourself. I just do my part and cook it. And Sheriff, wipe that look off your face. I know you are scared, but show some guts for the town's folk."

"But the lights...the sounds...the green men...the-"

"Sheriff! Do you want me to call Doc Stalls and put you in the mental ward myself? I will if you don't man up. It's all over with."

...

"So what do you want to do first?" Chris asked Michael.

"Well I think I'm going to help Mr. Dunzy at the coffee booth."

"Seriously? Man, you worked all day and you want to work some more?"

"What can I say, I love what I do."

"Yeah, yeah, yeah leave me hanging. Get on then." Chris laughed. He scanned around the party, trying to decide on whom to mingle with first. Sitting by the fire on a haystack was the new neighbor gals, watching the town's folk. They both seemed to be nervous and discontent. One of the girls was dressed in a black hooded sweatshirt with a picture of a zombie named Shteeeve embedded on the front, along with black and orange Tripp pants. In the breeze, her black and purple hair blew freely. The girl wasn't a skinny girl, a bit on the plump side; though as with the other girl who sat beside her-skinny-with blond hair and a knee length sunflower sundress. A thin shawl was wrapped around her shoulders.

The girl in the black caught Chris' eye. Closer he got, nothing else seemed to matter around him. She noticed him coming; a big smile on her face as she whispered excitedly to the girl beside her. In his mind, he was to respectively welcome the girls to town, but as he stood in front of them- the fire glowing and reflecting off the girl's eyes- he melted.

"I umm…welcome…umm…hi. My name is Chris…uhm Chris Wilson."

The blond stood up and shook his hand with a bright cheerful smile. "Hi Chris, I'm Michelle Owens, and this is Emilee Campbell. I'll leave you two be." She saw the look in Chris' eyes when he saw Emilee, the same look that guys give her every day. "It was nice meeting you Chris. And thank you for welcoming us to town, it's a really nice place."

Michelle walked off toward the food and coffee stands. Chris motioned to the empty spot on the hay beside Emilee. "May I?"

"Yes you may." Emilee blushed, thankfully it wasn't noticeable from the fire. What was noticeable though, was her smile that she couldn't hide. It took all she could just to even look at him.

"What? Do I have something on my face?" he smiled. "Or is it just my face in general?"

"No, no it's just…you probably hear this a lot, but…oh wow, I can't believe I'm saying this- I'm your number one fan."

"Well thank you very much. Honestly, you're the first person to ever say that to me. I'm honored. Do you have a favorite book?"

"No, just every book took effect on me and held my heart in certain ways. I love the fact that you write Christian books, and yet have a sense of the horrors of this world mixed in."

"Thank you, that was actually easy to do. The way I see it is God puts us in horrible situations to test out faith, and in that brings us closer to Him because of our love for Him. He isn't here to harm us."

"I totally agree with you there!" she fidgeted where she sat. "Sorry, I just can't believe I'm *actually* sitting here with Chris Wilson."

"It's okay, I'm just another Christian in the world. No bigger of a person than you." Chris stopped. "Wait, I don't think that came out right"

"Ha-ha, I know what you were meaning. I didn't take it wrong. I know I'm not a skinny woman, definitely not like Michelle and I'm okay with that. Really."

"And that makes you beautiful." His eyes widened when he realized what he just said, but he kept going. "It was the first thing I noticed about you and not many people in this town dress in black and Tripp pants like you and I do. I can tell you this though, they won't judge you for it. This is the most loving town I've ever seen."

"Do you really think *I'm* beautiful?"

"Oh I do." he grinned. "I know that's not right to just come out and say that first off meeting someone. But yes I do."

"Coming from you I'm perfectly okay with it. And I'm guessing that was you who was helping the preacher and farmer guy the other day?"

"Yes that was me, and they were Farmer Ted Johnson and Reverend Brown. In this town, everybody knows everybody. It's a pretty small place, you'll get the hang of it."

"I hope so. And I thought it was you, but I wasn't for sure. It could've been my mind playing tricks on me. Blew me away, because I wouldn't have expected you to live here."

"Why do you say that? And I was born and raised in Knoxville, Tennessee but moved here after my high school graduation. This place has been my inspiration, though all of my books are based in Knoxville. Of course if you've been to Knoxville you'd understand why, those people are nuts. And I mean nuts- especially this community called Halls. I swear there's something in the water there, shew."

"That's so awesome though! I just thought you'd be off in Hollywood or somewhere like that, *big*, writing your books. Not this quiet town. And yeah, we drove through

Halls to get here; people can't drive...at all there. It was weird, we went all through town just fine, but the closer we got to Halls the more people would ride our tail. It was just crazy. And not to change the subject or anything, but do you see Michelle anywhere?"

"Ohh I'd say she's a bit occupied at the moment." Chris pointed up the hill to Michelle and Michael at the coffee booth.

Michael, who poured a cup of coffee glanced up to see a beautiful woman walking toward him in a yellow dress. Everything seemed to be in slow motion- her hair swayed back and forth, and his eyes locked onto hers.

"Michael!"

He heard the woman calling his name, but her lips stayed perfectly still.

"Michael!"

She said it again. He couldn't believe what he was hearing.

"Ow! Michael!!"

He broke free from his trance to Charlie Dunzy kicking his burnt foot. Michael had forgot about the coffee. "Oh, sorry about that Charlie."

"Watch what you are doing next time, son. I'll be back in a moment- put my foot on some ice."

"Okay sir." the girl walked up to the booth with the most cheerful smile Michael had ever seen.

Concerned, but still not losing her smile, Michelle asked, "Is everything okay?"

"Uh…oh yeah, how may I kiss you? Uh- help you?"

She laughed. "Well let's see, first off, you've got to tell me your name, and then take me on a date. But until then, let me just have a cup of coffee, Michael."

The confused look on his face was priceless. "H-how do you know my name?"

"Um your name tag."

"Huh?" he looked down. "Oh yeah! Right. One cup of coffee coming up."

His hand shook as he poured, but continued to ask. "So uh, what's your name?"

"Michelle Owens." she held out her hand.

Michael stopped pouring first this time, set the pot down and shook her hand. "I'm Michael Gable. Here you go ma'am, no charge."

"Thank you." she added a little cream to the coffee and looked around. "This seems to be a pretty nice town you live in."

"Yeah it is, we've got the best coffee around."

She took a sip. "Mmm yummy, it is. My friend Emilee and I moved in a couple of days ago. Couldn't beat the deals of these houses. Right over there actually. We saw everyone coming over here, so we decided to come out and see the town."

"Well I'm glad you did." Michael smiled and blushed.

"Thanks."

"You're welcome. I should be taking a break here in a few. Would you like to dance?" He didn't know where that came from, but he liked it.

"Sure, I'd like that."

...

9:18 p.m.

"I'm getting bored with these movies." Craig Leeper had said.

"What are you talking about?" Marty Simmons replied back. "These movies are classics."

"They may be classics, but they *are* pretty boring." Calvin Cole had cut in.

"You guys stink." Marty stopped the movie. "It was your idea anyways to have a horror movie marathon."

"Yeah, but we let *you* pick the movies. That was our mistake." Craig grabbed the last beer from the refrigerator. "We're out of beers anyways."

"Okay, so what do we do now?"

"All of the girls are at the Halloween barbeque." Calvin said.

"Hey that's a great idea! We can go through the haunted forest!" Marty burst out.

"Marty, how old are you?" Craig asked.

"Umm, 15?"

"Yeah, then no. You're too old for that crap. We all need to get out and do something fun for a change, that doesn't have to do with the ignorant people in this boring town."

"What about breaking in to Camp Full Moon? You

know that place is shut down until the summer." Calvin added.

"Calvin, Calvin...hey Calvin, you're a genius man."

"My pleasure."

"No. No guys. I don't think this is such a good idea." Marty put the DVD back in its case.

"Oh come on Marty, don't wimp out on us now. We need you: Three's Company, Three Musketeers, Three Times a Day. You know?" Calvin asked.

"Three Times a Day?"

"Oh they were this old local band I once knew. But anyways, Martin no questions, you're going. End of story."

The boys had lived on Old Jack Belvedere Lane. At this time of night, it was deserted from the rest of the town attending Ted Johnson's barbeque. There was complete and total darkness besides jack-o-lanterns on neighbor's porches. They pass by Sheriff Boston's, and the Mayor's residence on Craven's Lane, as well as the Christy County High School on the left. And across the street on their right was the elementary and middle schools combined- home of the Christy County Deers.

Five miles down the road they end up at the Christy Highway and Craven's Lane intersection. Heading right of course would lead to town, while left would lead them toward Knoxville, Tennessee. The boys though were heading straight ahead another five miles to where they'd pass the Sevier Family Store and then Camp Full Moon before the dead end of the road.

With a bike each they slid to a stop on the gravel drive of Camp Full Moon, though they had spent more time than planned due to pitch black roads, they still made it with much time to spare. A single chain stretched across the entrance with a wooden plank hanging in the center that said, 'Closed for the season'. This wasn't stopping them for they stepped over the chain and walked up the pathway with only flashlights to point the way. It was so quiet, that the only sounds that could be heard around them was their feet crunching on the gravel beneath and the obvious creatures of the night.

"I don't like this." Marty had said. The closer they made it to the camp they could hear the wind slamming window shutters on deserted cabins. His friends didn't care and didn't even say a word. "Okay, so, what now?"

Marty sat down on the top step of the Welcoming Center. To the right, the five-foot tall owl statue stared down at them. It was one of those statues that no matter where you moved, the eyes would follow your every move. Creepy. Keeping his eyes off the statue, Marty stared up at the moon that reflected off of the lake down the way.

"We could go smoke at the fire pit." Calvin replied.

"Pssh, too easy. We've got to do something more than that. *Something* outrageous." Craig said, he leaned toward the statue, but yet fell into the bushes surrounding it. "Humph."

"Good job you klutz! Or should I say, Michael?

Remember when he did that one year…crazy." Marty had said while he laughed.

"What a rush." Craig pulled himself up. "Michael, you mean that weird guy at the coffee shop?"

"Noooo, our old camp counselor."

"Ohhh, no I don't remember him. Anyways. Come on guys think!"

"Smoke at the fire pit?" Calvin asked once again.

"Ugh, fine." Craig sighed.

"Guys, guys, we don't have much time, the party won't last much longer, and we won't get home in time." Marty implied.

"So what? If you are so scared, why don't you just leave then?" Craig asked.

"Umm I'm not going alone."

"Okay then, well we ain't leaving, soooo you are either going to have to go alone or stay with us."

"I….fine. I'll stay."

"Hey fellas…is it me, or is something flying over the water?" Calvin asked.

"Probably a bird." Craig suggested.

"That's no bird." They all squint trying to look at a large object hovering over the lake, too dark to be seen. Marty shined his flashlight toward it, but it was too far to be seen.

"What are you nuts? Turn off your light!" Craig whispered. Marty does, but a light shined over them. "Marty!"

"What? I did. It's not me!"

Craig turned from Marty to see a light that shined on them from the object that turned from white to green. They stared looking like three deer caught in headlights "On the count of three, we run."

"Craig I-" Marty began.

"One."

"This doesn't seem safe."

"Two."

"No!"

"Three!" Craig and Calvin both ran toward the exit leaving Marty alone to himself. The object chased after them. In only seconds it hovered straight over the boys. There was nothing Marty could do, but watch as the green light flashed a single flash like lightening and then the object was gone. Disappeared into thin air.

Not only was the object gone, but so was Craig and Calvin.

"Gu-guys? Guys?" Marty whispered. No answer. He shined his flashlight towards where they last stood. Though he shook, his light skimmed over two smoky circles that stained the gravel. Fear and adrenaline over takes him as he breaks into a run. Over the chain he jumped onto his bike, taking off toward town.

···

Chris and Emilee both had a blast as they walked from the haunted cornfield, and then stopped to watch a child speeding down Farmer Johnson's gravel walkway on a bike as he screamed "Somebody help! Help me! They took 'em!"

Michael and Michelle stop from their dance that kept on going long after the band had stopped playing from the shouts. At the same time, Charlie Dunzy was startled and dropped yet another pot of coffee on his foot.

"Son, what's wrong?" Sheriff Boston asked as he stopped the frantic boy. The town's folk walk toward the two huddled together.

In tears, Marty tried to calm himself down. "I...I...I don't know...bright lights...flying saucer...they...they took 'em."

"What in the blazes is going on here?! What's all this commotion about?" Mayor Davis hollered through the crowd.

"We're trying to find that out Mayor." Sheriff Boston said. He turned to Marty, his hand still held onto his shoulders. "Okay son, slowly explain what happened."

Marty told the story and confessed to breaking and entering to Camp Full Moon to the disappearance of Craig and Calvin, all at the same time with the gasps of towns folks. He broke down crying and held onto Sheriff Boston.

A hush had fallen over the crowd except for **CLICK** from Ted Johnson's shotgun. "Okay, let's go."

"Now hold on a minute there Ted." the Mayor had cut in. He turned to Marty. "Now son, I smell alcohol. Have you been drinking?"

"They were...well yeah, I had a little." Marty admitted.

"So you admit you were drinking?"

"Yes, sir."

"Okay then, it's settled. He's obviously belligerent and thought he has seen something that didn't happen. And imagined the whole thing. Those boys are probably off passed out in the woods somewhere. Sheriff, he's confessed to two crimes already, book him for those and then go out to the camp and find the other boys and arrest them also. Enough said."

"I didn't imagine it, I promise! The ground was smoking!"

"I believe you Marty." Sheriff Boston said. "Look, Mayor, we can't jump to conclusions. I'm going to take him back out there and we'll see what's going on. You just stay here with the town's folk. Everyone else, stay calm and be as you were. I'll inform you if anything comes up."

"Mom! Dad!" Marty yelled out as he ran to his parents whom made their way to their son. His mother was in tears.

"I'm coming too Sheriff." Marty's father sternly insisted.

"Okay."

Sheriff Boston pulled up to the entrance of the camp before he ran over Craig and Calvin's abandoned bikes. Marty's father stepped out from the passenger seat as Boston let Marty out from the back. "Okay, show us where it happened."

They all follow along the path- Sheriff Boston, Marty, and his father- until Marty stopped at nothing but gravel.

"Right there, it was right there, but...but it's not black anymore. I promise there was two black spots. They *were* smoking."

Boston leaned down and placed his hands on the gravel. "Cold. Are you sure this is...?"

"Positive."

"Okay. Let's walk a little further then."

"What are you thinking Sheriff?" Marty's father asked as they ended up at the Welcoming Center where it all began.

He stared out at the lake thinking for a moment. "Well, I don't see anything that explains the situation. I'm not saying I don't believe Marty, there's just no proof. We can't really rule them out as missing until three days, but we can walk around the camp some more. Maybe they have wandered off into the woods or are at home right now. We don't really know for sure. If they don't show up in the next few days, then well...we'll go from there."

<u>Chapter Thirty-Three</u>

"Well look who it is." Michael said with a smile at Michelle whom had walked into the coffee shop. "Miss me already?"

"Don't flatter yourself Gable." Charlie grinned as he entered in from the back with a crate of mugs.

"I miss you so much that I'm starting work here today." Michelle made her way around the counter. Charlie threw her an apron. "Surprise! Ha-ha."

"Wait, when did this happen? Not that I'm complaining, just lost."

"Last night, at the barbeque when I had you take down the booth. Miss Owens had asked for a job so I hired her. You got a problem with that?" Charlie asked as he stapled a stack of papers.

"Yes I very do have a problem with that! I have a problem with you over stepping my authority. I own part of this shop also you know! Forget this, I quit! Michael threw a dish towel at Charlie's face.

"For your information smart guy, this shop is owned three ways: you, my brother Brad, and myself. So go ahead and quit, it just leaves more money for us. And by the way! Are you going to check the toilet paper in the restrooms?" Charlie was calm as could be.

"I'm heading there now woman!" He walked off, opened the restroom doors with force. Though as he entered in, he closed the doors as softly as could be.

"Don't worry about that, we have fun all of the time. He's not really mad." Charlie mentioned to Michelle. "Come on, lets fill out some paperwork then we'll get started."

Later on in the evening, Charlie clocked out. "I'm heading out. You've don't a great job today Miss Owens. Glad to have you aboard. And Mikey?"

Michael rested his head on the counter, sat up real fast. "What's up?"

"Stay out of trouble."

"Ohh you know me. No worries."

"I do know you. Don't make me put Miss Owens in charge of you."

"Grrrrr."

"I'll keep an eye on him. Thank you sir, have a good evening." Michelle insisted.

"You too." He headed out the door.

"Okay, nap time." Michael poured himself a cup of hot chocolate and sat down by the fireplace.

"Are you serious?"

"Yeah, come on take a load off."

She sat in the matching leather chair across from him. "So how long have you been working here?"

"I think 12 years. We were fresh out of high school when we came here."

"We?"

"Oh, my friend, Chris and I."

"Oh I know Chris very well."

"How so hmm?" Michael smiled.

"My friend Emilee just adores him. Anytime he had a new book coming out, she was there at midnight to get it. She about died when she saw him at the party. I told her he's just like her and I. Just any other person."

"Ohhh I see you moved here to talk him right? Ha-ha. And that's true, he doesn't like fame. He tells anyone that wants an autograph to thank Jesus as he gives it. He's got a big heart."

"I wouldn't doubt it. And no we didn't move here because of that. We both thought this would be a peaceful town to live. Knoxville was just too crazy for us."

"You've got that right. That's where we came from. We just had to get away. After my brother and I got sober, he unfortunately passed away. Our senior year in Knox was terrible and such a mess."

"Awe I'm really sorry about your brother. I'm sure God got you through it in time though."

"I don't know. I don't believe in God anymore because of that. Barry was a great guy; he was there for me and was strong to get us clean. I just look at it that out of all the trouble we went through to get clean, he died a few months later. What kind of God could do that to someone?"

Michelle sat staring at the fire for a moment, thinking. "I suppose God did it because it was his time to go. He helped you clean up and helped you through all you needed to know. And now he's up in heaven looking down on you. God has a purpose for everything,"

"Hmm, I guess. Never really thought of it that way before." Michael looked at his empty mug. "I'm going to get more cocoa, would you like a cup? Or anything to drink?"

"Sure, why not? And I'll live a little, throw some whip cream on there."

"Ha-ha, you've got it."

He handed her the drink with extra chocolate shavings on top. "Sweets for the sweet."

"Thank you Michael, that was sweet of you."

He sat back down, getting comfy. "You're welcome. So how old are you anyways? You don't look a day over 20."

"Ha, well thank you. Guess."

"Oh no, no I'm not getting into that mess."

"Hey, you started it, so might as well ask."

"Ohh okay. I'd say 23, 24?"

"28."

"2- You're kidding?"

"Nope, I'm 28."

"Wow, you're really beautiful. Don't hurt me. Ha-ha."

"Awe thanks. Are you drinking more than just hot chocolate over there?"

"No, just straight up chocolaty goodness."

"Okay, okay, I believe you." She took a sip of her drink. "So how are the churches around here? Or should I say, church?"

"I couldn't tell you if the church is good to be honest, I've never been. But I can tell you that Reverend Brown is a great guy. I have never seen him judge anybody for their actions as long as they were in church on Sunday."

"So he doesn't say anything to you for not going?"

"No, I let him pray for me every time he comes in for his coffee and that seems to make him happy."

"How does that make you feel though?"

"Kind of awkward. It gives me chills."

"Hmm, so what would it take for me to get you to go to church with me in the morning?"

"What?"

"You heard me." She smiled, drinking more cocoa.

"Is it a date, or just me going? It'll take allot to get me to go to church."

"Then yes, it is a date."

"Really? Okay, no need to convince me then, I'm there."

"Going to church for all the wrong reasons, but it's a start. God does have a sense of humor."

Chapter Thirty-Four

10:30 a.m., the church bell echoed over the town of Christy, Tennessee to announce the singing service has begun. Town's folk greet Reverend Brown at the door up on entering with a handshake. Most of them would come early only for the good seats up front. Old fashioned in its ways, they sing straight from the hymnals with not a single microphone, piano or even an instrument of any kind.

"Morning' Reverend." Michael said as he walked up with his arm around Michelle's arm.

"Mor-" Reverend Brown stopped. "I'm sorry you just gave me a shocker. Gable, it's really good to see you at church. Good morning. And good morning to you too miss. How much did you pay him to come?"

"Ha-ha, nothing, just asked him to come and he did."

"Bless you ma'am. Go on and find yun's a seat."

They find a space in the middle row beside Chris and Emilee. Chris looked up at Michael and gave him the same look that Reverend Brown had given him. He patted Michael on the back as he sat down.

"We haven't formally met, I'm Michael Gable. You must be Emilee right?" Michael leaned over and whispered in her ear.

"Yes I am, it's good to finally meet you. And a fine place to meet someone also."

11:00 a.m., Reverend Brown opened the service with a prayer. "Dear Lord, we thank you for this lovely morning, and blessed day ahead of us. We thank you for the new faces in our little old church this morning. And we ask that you be with those who are sick and have fallen short from your glory. Bless them heavenly father. Amen.

It's been on my mind lately about love. Love is so simple, yet love is the most wonderful feeling anyone could have, or give to another in kind ways. As it says in 1 John chapter four that 'He does not loveth who does not knoweth God: for God is love.'

God loves us so much that he sent his only son to die on the cross for our sins. Because of this, it says in 1 John chapter three that 'Hereby perceive we the love of God, because he laid down his life us; and we ought to lay down our lives for our brethren.' The more we set aside our own selfish ways, and set aside our own greed to take time to love our neighbors and help them in their time of needs, or even doing something kind for them without asking, that God will bless us more.

Love is the first commandment, which Jesus had said, 'Thou shalt love the Lord God with all thy heart, and with all thy soul, and with all thy mind.' And in the second commandment Jesus then said, 'Thou shalt love thy neighbor as thy self.'"

Reverend Brown kept going with his sermon as Michael faded out thinking about Barry, and how Barry was always there for him. He never once gave up on

Michael, loving him through every little thing and never judged him for his mistakes. Michael looked over at Chris, who also never gave up on him, even when he didn't want anything to do with him. And now, here is Michelle-someone who didn't even know him, nor even his past, but still wanted to bring him to church.

All this time since Barry's death, he ran from love and was scared that if he even got close to love that it'll be taken away from him. Now he realized that love has been there all along: everything from Angela Stutts, Barry's death, and to Charlie Dunzy offering him a job at the coffee shop, to Chris stopping him from committing suicide, to now in a church pew with a beautiful woman by his side.

His heart pounded, breathing heavily. Tears tried to break free from his eyes. Though he didn't even think about it, he grabbed a hold of Michelle's hand. She looked at him in wonder with a funny smile that was on his face as he stared straight ahead at Reverend Brown.

"Is he okay?" Michelle whispered over to Chris.

Not even Chris could figure out what was the matter. "I have no clue. I've never seen him this way. Poke him, see if he's still alive."

"Oh he is, look at his breathing."

Michael let go of Michelle's hand as he stood and walked down the aisle towards the alter. Reverend Brown hushed along with the congregation. All were amazed at the look on Michael's face.

He dropped to his knees, the tears now flowed freely

from his eyes. "Lord! You've got me. I've ran from you for so long. I've pushed you away when I needed you the most. I never believed in you, but my God my God you have loved me through all of my mistakes and wicked ways. Thank you for never giving up on me and bringing me here today. I'm so sorry for everything. Please Lord forgive me. I give my life to you."

"God bless you son." Reverend Brown said to him. He kneeled beside Michael, his hand on his back while the church chimed in a singing of 'What a friend we have in Jesus'.

Chapter Thirty-Five

At work Monday, Michelle barely even spoke to Michael. Let alone even gave a glance his way. Evening came around where the times were slower and less customers. Dark clouds roll in throughout the day, covering the setting sun. Rain poured as thunder rolled through the Christy Mountains.

"It's really coming down huh?" Michael asked. He turned from the window and toward Michelle who sat over by the fireplace.

"Yeah." She whispered.

He sat down across from her. "Okay what is it? You've been distant with me all day. Did I do something wrong?"

"No...well...no."

"What is it?"

"I'm just...scared."

"Scared? What for?"

"*You* to be honest."

This caught him by surprise. "*Me*? Why me?"

"I don't know why I'm so scared. I guess it's because I barely even know you and...I like you. Then you grabbed my hand at church, I don't know. I just seem to get hurt allot. I'm not like most girls."

The look on his face was astounded. Michelle panicked, "Look I'm sorry. I...I shouldn't have said anything."

"No, I'm glad you did. Thing is, I like you too. I know you are different from most girls, and that's part of what I like. I didn't think such a beautiful girl like you would ever be into me. I haven't lived the best kind of life."

"Is that why you grabbed my hand? Because you like me? And it doesn't matter what a person's past is, only who they are now. It's not my place to judge anyone."

"Yeah that's why I grabbed it, I like you and I was feeling God for the first time and it just came natural to me."

"The Lord does touch our hearts in many different ways. I'm glad you did it because you like me and not looking for it to lead to a hook-up."

"Yeah He does. And how could that lead to a hook-up?"

"It's just possible; you don't know the guys I've ended up dating. I'm a virgin and I'd like to keep it that way until I'm married."

"Well I'm not that type of guy, you wait and see."

"I hope not because I'd like to get to know you more."

"And I would like to get to know you more also." He walked to the counter and poured himself a cup of coffee. "This is going to sound crazy, but what caused me to grab your hand was a feeling of love towards you. I was thinking of my brother and then I looked at you, Chris, and Emilee and it was like WHAM this is where you are supposed to be. I've never felt anything like that before."

"That's how Jesus makes us feel each and every day with His love once you accept Him. He knew that you coming to church was a next step in taking towards Him. So He came a knocking and you let Him in."

"I believe that, but I mean I feel that you and I were meant to meet."

...

Chris sat down at his desk in his den with a cup of coffee. He had already written a few pages already today with evening still around the corner. A storm just arrived as rain pelted against the window. He looked out the window to see a pumpkin rolling down the road in the wind. Out of the corner of his eye he noticed someone at his front door.

He saved his work and stepped out into the hallway-opened the door to Emilee who stood wet with a pizza and a stack of movies. "Hey there."

"Well hello to you too. I didn't expect to see you. I'm glad I did though, come on in." He said, letting Emilee by.

"Yeah, I figured you'd like some company in this storm. Brought the ultimate party supplies: pizza and horror movies. I'm not interrupting anything am I?"

"No not at all. I was just taking a break from writing."

"Oooh what are you writing?"

"A book about patterns."

"Ha-ha, oh right."

"Come on, let me give you a tour of my crib yo." He showed her the den to the left of the front door, the open living room to the right, restroom, guest and bedroom down the hall, the dining room and kitchen through a door from the living room, and also the laundry room out from the kitchen, and the back deck facing a field and woods.

He poured some drinks from the fridge and grabbed a couple of plates from the cabinet. "So what would you like to watch first?"

"It's your house, you can choose. Lovely home by the way. Ours isn't quite as nice." Emilee took a seat in the middle of the couch.

"You know you can take your coat off right? Relax, make yourself at home. And thank you, keep it up well. Yeah, umm...your house has a bit of a history." He placed the DVDs on top of the entertainment center and placed a few logs on to the fire in the fireplace.

"What kind of history?" She asked taking her shoes off at the door.

"Just that no one stays there long. Nobody really knows why either. Your modern day *Amityville Horror* story."

"That's okay, I've dealt with ghosts before. It's demons I'm worried about. But at the same time I'm not frightened by 'em, because I've got the Lord Almighty by my side."

"Yes ma'am, I agree with you there. Nothing stronger than the Lord's strength." Chris put in a movie into the player and sat down by Emilee on the couch. "*House on Haunted Hill* a good choice?"

"Yes it is and ironic 'cause of what we are talking about."

"Good. You know what's funny? I have all of the movies you brought over. Feel free to look at 'em if you like." He motioned her over to the three book shelves full of movies.

"I noticed that. I love your taste in movies. I should come over more often."

"I'd love that."

...

"You think we are meant to be? Or meant to meet really?" Michelle asked, setting her mug down not to spill it.

"Please don't think I'm crazy for that, but yeah I honestly do. I've not had the best of life, and then here you came along and kindly get me to church and see the good in me. Nobody has ever done that for me before. Sorry." Michael left his mug on the table beside him and scurried off to the back.

...

As he finished up his second slice of pizza, Chris set his plate down on the coffee table in front of him.

"I'll eat more later on, don't want to get full too fast. So, Emilee, what are you wanting out of life?"

"To be honest, *this,* watching movies with my husband, quiet times at home. Our kids playing in the floor or cuddled up with us. I don't really want a fancy life, just simple and relaxing."

"Really? That's what I want also. That's part of why I like to write books for a living. I could be able to be home with my family and keep the roof over my head at the same time. When that happens of course."

"Yeah, that's why I don't go out partying, I stay right with God and spend my nights at home with a cup of coffee and reading your books."

"I appreciate that. Quiet nights like those are the best. That's how I was when I was a kid, even though Michael and I would stay up most of the night playing video games. Those were the days."

"That's really neat. Michelle and I sort of did the same thing. We'd play board games with her family, or watch black and white classics with my family."

"Oh really? Do you like those classics?"

"Yes I do, I grew up on 'em. Don Knotts' were my favorite, especially *The Ghost and Mr. Chicken* and *The Shakiest Gun in the West*."

"Now see, I can agree to that. And I might add *Laurel and Hardy* or *Abbott and Costello*. I really enjoy those, and can't forget *the Three Stooges* or *Red Skelton*."

"That's amazing, I've never seen that in anyone. Comedy sure isn't the same."

"Oh no it's not. There have been plenty of movies that the younger generation calls 'funny' that I just couldn't even finish because they were so bad."

"Same here. I've had to stick to Christian films here lately, 'cause of how bad theatrical films have gotten.

Which by the way, are there any Christian stores around here?"

"Sadly, not in this town, which I have never figured out why. But the Max does sell any kind of cd, movie, and book known to men. So that would be your best bet."

"I'll have to check that out. But book I'm not worried about. I've got a job at the library so books, oh yes."

"Interesting. I didn't even know the library was hiring."

"Oh they weren't. The librarian is my aunt, so it all worked out."

"Oh so that's how you knew I lived here, I see how it is. Ha-ha."

"No, no she didn't even know who you were until I mentioned you- that I met you at the barbeque."

"Yeah, Mrs. Whiting's never really mingles with the town much. She stays in the library pretty much 24/7."

"Oh I know. She's even like that with the rest of the family also. She only likes me because she knows I'm a good person and all I've ever liked were books."

"That's a good thing though."

"Yes, sir. I guess ha-ha."

Chris looked at his almost empty glass. "Would you like more to drink?"

"Yes please."

"Excuse me." He said as he took their empty glasses to the kitchen. Emilee walked over to his movies, not hearing Chris walk back in the room. "See anything you like?"

...

Michelle walked into the back where Michael furiously washed dishes in a sink full of soap. "Are you okay?"

"Yeah, just made a fool of myself. Nothing new."

"You really didn't, I promise."

"Okay. You're going to quit now huh?"

"Nope. I like working here. And I like you too."

He dropped the dish rag on the floor and turned to Michelle. "Do you really?"

"Yes I do. I believed what you said and I'm just afraid of being hurt. That's all."

"If it was me, I couldn't hurt you."

"That's really sweet of you Michael."

...

"You scared me, I didn't hear you come back."

"I'm a quiet person. It happens." Chris said and handed Emilee her drink. "Hey, come here, I'd like to show you something."

"Yeah, that never ends up well, but okay."

...

"I just feel like a totally different person around you." Michael said. "I don't know what it is."

"Is that a good or bad thing? I'm guessing good."

"It's a really good thing. I'm happy, and I haven't felt

this happy in years."

Michelle began to blush. "...oh Michael."

"I'm sorry, I just...when I like something I say things too far. But, anyways, since you asked me on a date to church, would it be okay if I took you out on a traditional date? Maybe get some coffee?"

"Michael."

"Yeah?"

"Where are we right now?"

"Umm backroom?"

"Of where?"

"Ohhh, coffee shop duh."

"That's right, yes you can take me out on a date. How about now?"

"Working and on a date at the same time? Fine by me."

...

He sat behind his desk, and handed Emilee a folder. She sat across from him in a leather chair. "What's this?"

"Take a look." There was a mischievous grin on Chris' face.

She opened the folder and almost fell out of her seat with excitement. "Chris? Is this? No way..."

"Yes way, my new book."

"But...why are you letting me read it early?"

"All I can think of is, 'why not?'"

"You're amazing!"

"Na, but have fun."

Chapter Thirty-Six

Under three brightly lit chandeliers hanging in the Christy County Library, Emilee propped her feet up behind a large dark oak desk, reading Chris' new book. Noon, the lunch hour went by slow with children in school and everyone else at work. She had all the time she needed to read, along with a cup of coffee by her side and a throw blanket over her legs.

Really deep into the book she almost jumped out of her seat as the phone rang from the office behind her. Not even bothering to pick up the book she had thrown across the room, she answered the phone with the door open to hear if anyone entered the library.

Minutes later, she came back to find the book sitting on the desk- closed, with a book mark where she left off. Taken off guard, she was for certain she did not close her book beforehand. Something surely did not feel right. Maybe it was her instincts and horror movie fanatics getting the best of her, but it was still a feeling of unease. Not taking any chances, she grabbed the first thing she could see- a stapler. All though it wasn't a knife, nor even powerful weapon as say a gun, but with a frightened woman a stapler could be very harmful.

She listened with caution each step she took. Her breathing and tennis shoes against the carpet was all she could hear- except for the hum of the overhead florescent

225

lights that hover over each aisle. One by one, nothing was amiss. Every door, excluding the entrance and restrooms, were locked.

Giving in to the possibility that this was all just her imagination, she let her guard down and relaxed. Well, tried to relax at least. There was still a small feeling that someone was watching her. *Somewhere* she could feel eyes-piercing eyes-that which would follow her every move.

Finally, she sat back down at the desk, after rechecking every door and aisle on the way back. Suspicious? Maybe. Discreet? Without a doubt. Her love for horror movies has given her a quick witted mind belonging to incredulous situations as this.

She checked her watch, 3:45. An hour and fifteen minutes left of work. The time began to slow down even more now. Once again, she opened her book and didn't hear the entrance door open and close. Her mind was in a totally different place at the moment.

"Excuse me ma'am." a man in front of the desk had said.

"Lord almighty!" Emilee screamed and threw the pencil in the air that she was twirling between her fingers.

"Praise Jesus!" The man grinned.

"Sorry about that, I-" They both look up at the pencil stuck in a ceiling tile. "I didn't hear you come in. What can I help you with?"

He loosened his tie. Emilee took notice how well he

was dressed: black suit and tie, dark purple button up shirt under the jacket. Not to mention shaggy hair and a scruffy beard.

"No worries, miss. Always a good day to praise our Lord. And I believe you can help me; would you all happen to have an archives section? Possibly with *this* town's histories?"

"Yes we do, though I'll tell you now, we don't allow anything from the archive room to be checked out. Anything you look at you must sign and date your name to a list. Record purposes, you understand?"

"I can handle that. Not a problem."

"Okay then, let me take you back there. We'll be closing shortly, take your time though. No rush."

"I won't be long."

Chapter Thirty-Seven

Emilee checked her watch for the umpteenth time in the past hour. The last hour of work always seemed to creep by. Ten minutes left before she could lock up and leave for home, she bookmarked her book with a little less than half way to go.

Before she logged off from her computer, there was one thing left to do. She hadn't heard from the man since she last left him in the archive room, and though still being new in town herself, he wasn't someone she recognized. Not someone she'd fully put her trust in right away.

With courtesy, she knocked before entering. "Excuse me sir, I'm sorry but we're clo-"

The archive room was empty. The man was nowhere in sight. Quickly, she glanced around the room, nothing seemed to be out of place as far as she could tell- not even a chair out of alignment with the rest of the chairs. Interesting. She knew she wasn't crazy, his name was signed on the sign in sheet along with a list of newspapers he looked at, that of which were still in their appropriate places. And she did *see* him come in the archives, but of course didn't see him leave.

It must have just been a long day. Being on the safe side, she made yet another building check. All safe and sound, though it didn't take away the cold chills from her arms.

"Hey, where are you at? You busy?" Emilee asked Chris on the phone.

"No I'm not busy. I'm sitting outside your work actually. Wait that sounded wro-"

"Okay good, I'll be out in just a second. I'm really glad you are here."

"Everything okay? You sound as if you just seen a ghost or something."

"Well not a ghost...I don't think. You wouldn't care to take me to my car would you?"

"No not at all. Are you hungry?"

"Starving actually."

"Would you like to go out to eat?"

"Sure, that would be great." She smiled and hung up the phone. Chris made her day just from hearing his voice. She had forgotten everything that had happened in that very instant.

Her feet propped up on the dash, Emilee relaxed during the lengthy drive out of town. She had her nose in his book, reading as much as she could. It didn't bother Chris one bit; that's what his books were for-to be read. He had other plans in mind for the evening, though they were a surprise to Emilee. She had no idea what they could be, only that she did know they were on a back-road surrounded by woods.

"Okay, here we are." Chris said as he turned off onto gravel.

"Oh wow!" Emilee almost dropped her book from

amazement of the restaurant Chris had brought her to.

Being on the lake, the restaurant had a wraparound porch with a dock on the back. Live bands played on the dock by tables and a dance floor. Clear icicle lights were hung around the banisters above the dock.

"I thought you'd like it. Shall we?"

"We shall, Chris Wilson."-

Seated in a booth on the inside by a window, Emilee gazed around the room at the pictures of boats on the walls along with decorations that gave off the feel of a fisherman's wharf. Sunset reflected off the lake. Candles were lit on each and every table. The perfect setting.

"What are you thinking about?" Chris took a sip of sweet tea.

"Two things actually: one, that this place is really amazing. And that I'm not special enough of a person to be treated this way."

"And the second?"

"That this is the exact setting in one of the stories in your short story collection."

"Ha-ha, you caught me. I wrote that story while I was here actually. Just one of those moments where I was inspired the second I walked into a place."

"Uh huh, you know you bring all your other girlfriends here on a date."

The waiter placed their food on the table along with a complementary bottle of champagne.

"Thank you sir," Chris said. "And nope, just you, my dear. And for the record, you really are special to me. I don't expect nothing from tonight, I'm only doing this for you and to see that beautiful smile of yours."

"Ohh Mr. Wilson, you are such a charmer." Emilee laughed.

"We writers have to be good for something you know? Ha-ha."

"Whit, charm, and a sense of humor. I like that."

"Good, because you know I like you."

"You're just being modest." The smile on Emilee's face faded with cold chills down her spine as her eyes followed a man whom walked passed the table in a suit and tie with a purple shirt. She thought it was the man from the library.

"Hey you okay? What, was that a guy you didn't want to run into or something? Maybe an ex-boyfriend? I'll put a lobster down his drawers if you like."

"Ha-ha, no I'm okay. And yeah, that wasn't who I thought it was, but not someone I'd want to see tonight. Or ever again for that matter. It wasn't an ex either, mister; just a creepy guy from work today."

"What guy?"

"All afternoon I had the strangest feeling that someone was watching me. There was a certain eerie silence to the place. So I checked every door, walked down every aisle. And nothing. Well I thought it was nothing, but then this guy shows up out of nowhere. I didn't even hear him come in, which he seemed like a harmless guy, but his hair and beard didn't mix with his fancy suit. That was a little off to me. And all he really wanted to do was look for something in the archives, which was fine. What made it even more weird, was when I went to tell him we were closing, he wasn't there. It was like he just vanished out of thin air.

I checked all over the place for him, and still found nothing. Unless he went out when I was up doing that, I don't know. That's why when you called I was a little disoriented. Too many *Goosebumps* books I guess."

"That really creepy. Did you get a name? I know that anyone who even goes into the archives has to sign in, but-"

"Only thing he put was D.L. Do you know any D.L.?"

"No I don't." Only person he knew was David, but that possibly couldn't be him. Could it? And Chris didn't dare tell Emilee about him just yet.

"Then I don't know."

"Yeah, that's creepy. But it was probably nothing, I agree. And even if so, it was just the archives which is only town records right? Nothing big like the Declaration of Independence or anything like that. But if you want, I could do my writing there for a while, keep an eye on things."

"Thank you, I'd like that. I'm sorry I brought that up, don't want to down our night any."

"Oh no, not a chance. You are really fine. I always enjoy a good story. What if you say after we eat we go out on the dock and have a few dances?"

"Yes, please." The smile on her face returned in that very instant.

"Chris?" Emilee asked as she swayed back and forth in his arms. Moonlight and stars shinned overhead along with the crickets and frogs along the shore of the lake.

"Hmm?"

"You're really amazing. Why aren't you married by now?"

"In a way it's trust issues, but in another, I've never met the 'right' girl. I guess that consists of trust to a point. I've met some *interesting* girls to say the least. And I'm really not that amazing of a guy, I'm no silver screen buff, but I'm okay with that."

"Please don't get me started on *interesting* people. I've had my share of interesting guys for the evening. And trust me, you are far from them, which that's what makes you amazing. You aren't the screen buff type, but are the ideal family man. If no girl could see that about you, then quite obviously they were the type of party girl whom you definitely could not trust. Trust, yes, is a big issue- it is for myself also. And the girl lucky enough to win your trust has in their time found a lot of four leafed clovers because they'd be darn lucky to have you."

"Wow that's a first anyone has ever said to me. I'm not a kid anymore, that's for sure, but what you just said really brought back a certain giddy teenage crush feeling in my stomach. I've always had a belief that if anyone could make you feel that happy again no matter what age, then she is definitely a person's true love and dare I say, soul mate."

"I couldn't agree with you more about that. True love

isn't fairy tale as what most people believe. True love is a love from God, and that of which God has made for a certain someone."

"My point- soul mates." Chris smiled as he stared into Emilee's eyes from which the lights from the dock reflected off.

They danced through three more songs before Chris paid the bill. For the rest of the night, they walk along the water's edge, talked of both good and bad times. Really opened up to one another. And connected in ways only the two of them could understand.

"I have to be honest, tonight was really amazing." Emilee said as Chris parked in his driveway and walked her to her door. They crossed through the yard, careful not to disturb Michelle's sleep.

Emilee continued, "I really needed it from what happened at work earlier. Thank you."

"Really, no need to thank me. I felt it earlier that you needed a good night. It was my pleasure. I know it's late and you have work in the morning, so I don't want to keep you up all night. Heck, I'll be honest too, I loved tonight. It really was amazing, and I wouldn't want it to end if it was my choice. That's the teenage feeling talking again, even though I know we are adults that have responsibilities."

"Oh, I see, you are only just saying that because you are wanting to end this night so quickly. No, no I see your games. Ha-ha, I'm only kidding. You're right though, we do have responsibilities, I also wouldn't want this night to end. But I don't know how to end this night either."

"Hmm, maybe a hug goodnight and walk away before we get to talking some more."

"That could work I guess, ha-ha."

"Okay, goodnight."

"Goodnight." Emilee couldn't stop her smile. They embraced in a hug even more close than from when they danced.

Chris got as far as the bottom of the stairs, listened as Emilee's keys were in her lock. "You know what?"

"Wha-" Emilee tried to say, not the least expecting Chris' passionate kiss.

"I needed that, and wow. Goodnight." Chris left with the biggest smile.

"Oh my…" Emilee watched him leave before heading inside herself.

Chapter Thirty-Eight

Chris walked into his front door, took off his shoes and hung his jacket on a hook. It was still late, and yes he very well knew that- he was too excited for bed. To wind down, he sat in his office and wrote awhile.

Later on after he finally did decide to try and get some shut-eye, he tossed and turned. *Something* kept him from having a good night's sleep. For reasons unbeknownst to him, every time he had even dozed off he'd get an image of Angela and then of Becky in his head. It was though a sudden discomfort.

He then though gave into the realization that tonight wouldn't be a night he'd be able to sleep. Pulling himself up, he walked onto his back porch, wrapped up in a blanket. As he held onto a big mug of coffee, he sat in a rocking chair and looked towards Emilee's house and wondered what she could be doing at this hour. More than likely she was probably sound asleep.

How wonderful she would be sleeping, cuddled up with her head on my chest. Chris had thought to himself. *Oh yeah, that's not creepy. Good job Christopher, good job.*

But there was only one person who'd know how he really felt, or merely what was on his heart- "Lord, Heavenly Father, I haven't really spoken to you in a while. I don't really have an excuse for that, but I'm sorry. You've really been a blessing to me here lately, regardless of my being quiet. You really have blessed me with the most beautiful and amazing woman that has ever come into my life. Thank you for that, for making our paths cross.

I've felt this way before toward two women, Angela and Becky, which is why I'm talking to you tonight. It scares me having these same feelings, just because of everything that has gone on. I don't want to fall for her even more than I already have, just to turn around and lose her like I did them. I'm sorry for dwelling on closed doors, when I know YOU have a brighter future for me that all I need to do is let go of the past. Through YOU all things are possible. And so possible that I want to marry Emilee. I've never felt that way for anyone, even though I don't even fully know her yet.

I just have to keep the faith knowing you are guiding our very steps. Thank you Father and thank you for taking the time to listen to me. Amen."

Chris felt really good to get that off of his chest. Now that he was relaxed, he knew it wouldn't be long now before he was out for the night.

Chapter Thirty-Nine

Reverend Brown was up before the first rooster crow of the morning. Even though Sunday was a day of rest, he was the first in the church and last to leave. He laid the foundation for his sheep by cleaning up, making things right for the congregation before the service.

With a welcoming fresh pot of coffee brewing on a table by the entrance, Reverend Brown walked down each aisle one by one and neatly arranged the hymnals. He looked up as someone creeps in through the front door, catching him off guard. No one was usually at the church this early, besides him of course.

"Good morning Reverend. Sorry if I'm a little early."

"Well good morning Michael. How are you today? No worries at all about being early, I'm glad to see you came again."

"I'm doing okay, couldn't sleep so I went for a walk. Saw that you were up and took it as a sign, so I dropped by. And I'm glad to be back also, never thought I'd ever hear that come out of my mouth to be honest, but I am."

"Is everything okay? You know you can come talk at any time if you need to. God does guide His children's steps when we don't even realize it. When He closes one door, He opens another."

"Yeah I guess that's true. And I don't know if I'm okay or not, I have a lot on my mind. But, do you need any help with those?" Michael pointed to the hymnals.

"Sure, sure, be my guest. Would you like to talk about what's bothering you son?"

"Do I have to go into a confessional or anything like that? This is all new to me."

"No- sure confessing your sins to the Lord will set you free, but you can do that in prayer."

"How do you pray?"

Reverend Brown looked at Michael and smiled.

"What?" Michael continued. "Hey, if the church paid you on commission you'd be making your money's worth with me."

"I don't do it for the money- never have, never will. I've always done it for this very reason, and to see people smile and know they are happy with God."

"That makes sense. A very noble way to go."

"All for our Lord Jesus Christ. That's for certain. Everything we do in life, how we live and breathe, must be by Jesus Christ and for Jesus Christ. I'm not saying to go out and murder someone or steal from our neighbors and say that we've done it for Christ; we still do have our commandments. God knows we aren't perfect and that we all *do* sin and fall short of his righteousness. It's coming back to Him and asking for forgiveness and believing in your heart that Christ died for us that is the key to everything."

"Which that's what has been on my mind. I'm scared- scared that I'm not good enough for God. I don't feel as if I deserve all of this. That I've pushed Him away too much, and have done so many bad things that He doesn't want anything to do with me."

They were down to the last row, closest to the alter. Reverend Brown sat down. "Michael, take a seat. We ALL don't deserve Jesus, but He died for us because He loves us. It's okay to be fearful; God would rather us fear Him than forget Him. Let me ask you this, did God ever give up on you? Do you still feel His hand on your heart saying 'I'm still here'?"

"Yeah I do, well now that I've given into the knocking, knowing what it was all along, yeah."

"Then that's a no, He didn't give up on you. Just like with Peter- Jesus told Peter that he will deny Him three times before the rooster crows, and Peter did just that. But guess what? Jesus still forgave him. He forgave everyone who beat Him, stuck the arrows in His ribs and those who hammered the nails into His wrists. He forgave EVERYONE, which was the basis of Him on the cross, so we could live a free life."

Farmer Johnson's rooster crowed in the morning air.

"You see, He's listening." Reverend Brown had continued.

"I believe, but I'm just not understanding all of this just yet."

"Which is fine. Take your time with it and study at least 15 minutes a night in the Bible. And God will show His ways of revealing something when He wants us to see it. I know this all seems like a lot to learn, but it's why I say take your time and definitely stay faithful in your ways and to God."

"It is a lot and doesn't help that I'm a slow learner. I will admit, you have helped me with talking to me even now. I really needed it, thank you Reverend."

"Hey, hey, no need to thank me. Just doing my job. But give all the praise to Jesus- He deserves it more. There's nobody amazing as He is."

Chapter Forty

"...I now baptize you in the name of the Father, the Son, and the Holy spirit." Reverend Brown said as he dipped Michael into the pond on Ted Johnson's farm, washing all of his sins away.

Michael came up joyful and radiant with the biggest smile he has had in years. For once, he was at peace with himself, with the world, and most importantly- with God. Free.

"Michael, that's really awesome you did this. I'm really happy for you that you found your way to God." Chris said, who stood in between Emilee and Michelle.

"He's been here all along, I just needed to let Him in." Michael said. "And I know you, after every big event you want to go celebrate. So I think I just want to go to Knoxville for a bit and be with my family. Well, visit Barry some. Is that cool man?"

"Well yeah man, it's your day. Whatever you want. That's all I was going to suggest is we do that."

"Yeah, this is what I want. Hey, maybe you three could go do something together for a change." Michael suggested.

"Sure, yeah we could do that. It'll give me some time to get to know your friend that's the love of my friend's life...oops did I say that out-loud?" Michelle giggled.

"Real cute." Emilee blushed.

No better way to spend a Sunday afternoon than a drive up through the mountains. Chris was at the wheel while Emilee had her feet propped up on the dash. Michelle sat in the back seat of the truck while reading her e-reader at the same time. With the windows rolled down, cool fresh air was let in. Though it was November, Tennessee weather could be cool in the fall one day and then hot the next. Of course it was the same way in the winter and summer also- allergies could never make up their minds.

They pull off to the side of the road. Chris grabbed a cooler full of ice, food, and drinks and maneuvered around Emilee and Michelle. The girls grabbed the fishing rods and a tackle box.

"Do we want to eat or fish first?" Emilee asked as she pretended to cast in her line.

"You can fish if you like, Chris and I will get the food ready." Michelle insisted.

"But what if I want to fish?" Chris asked.

"You can fish later, I want to talk with you for a minute."

"Uh oh, I'm in trouble." Chris looked toward Emilee who shrugged her shoulders. Not even she knew what was going on.

...

Back in his home town, Michael didn't know how to

react. Everything was different- smaller somehow. It's been awhile since he even visited. Most, if not all, of the family owned stores and restaurants have all been replaced by conglomerate chain stores. Saddened from places that of which he spent his childhood memories are now gone and faded away.

...

"I didn't do it...whatever it is." Chris said, helping unfold a table cloth.

"Ohh yes you did, you stole my friend Emilee's heart."

"Oh that? She stole mine first though. So, pssh."

"I'm being serious Chris. You and I haven't really talked or got to know one another, but she's hopelessly in-love with you. And no, you stole her heart years ago with your first book. Once she read that she was hooked and wasn't the same ever again."

"I knew she was a fan, but I've never heard from anyone that actually changed from them. With constant books sales I just put two and two together and assumed either that was happening or I was just a 'good' writer."

"Oh trust me, you have no idea how much you changed her when she hasn't really had a good life, but God really worked through you to her."

Chris watched Emilee- how much fun she was having. She really was truly happy.

"What is it? Did I say something wrong?" Michelle continued.

"Not at all, it's just yeah I'm crazy about her also. She's really an amazing woman."

"I know you are, I can tell in your eyes, but my whole point of all this is please don't hurt her. She doesn't need another disappointment in her life."

"I could never hurt her. I promise you that. Hey, between us, I love that woman soooo much that given the chance I'd marry her."

"That would really make her world if you did. Chris, I mean that."

...

"Hey Bro," Michael began. He sits down in front of Barry's grave. "It's been awhile since I've been by. I really miss you. You'd be so proud of me. Things are really great now, but I'm sure you know that watching over me.

I'm really happy, and I mean really happy. I've got a great job, a home, and I'm dating the most wonderful woman in the world. Barry she's so amazing and she loves me for me. No matter how rough my past was, or what I've been through and the mistakes I've made, she still loves me and stays by my side. She really believes in me, and brings out the best in me. And she brought me to Christ. Can you believe it?

I was baptized today and it's one of the most amazing feelings ever. You know, up until now I never believed in God, but because of Michelle I know He's there. Maybe she's an angel sent to me by God for that very reason.

Either way, it's just so amazing. I wish you were here to share it with me, be like old times with it being you and me against the world. Michelle makes me feel that complete. It's crazy.

Speaking of crazy, I better get back home. Who'd have thought this would come out of my mouth, but I've got to get some rest for work in the morning. I really miss you Barry and I will always love you. Something my preacher told me, that with God all things are possible, so maybe you could visit me in my dreams some time. I'd love that.

I'll see you Bro."

<u>Chapter Forty-One</u>

She had just finished rinsing off the last dish from the sink when she heard the front door open and close. Watching the kids playing in the backyard, she waited patiently for his touch.

As if she was in heaven, his hands wrap around her waist and kissed the back of her neck. Cold chills ran up and down her spine. "Hey beautiful, how was your day?"

"It was amazing. The kids helped me with the house and then we baked cookies. Shhh, I know it was before dinner, but don't tell, ha-ha." Emilee turned around and faced Chris. "How was your day, did the meetings go okay?"

"It was excellent, they bought the book. They think it's going to be yet another hit."

"Honey, that's awesome! I'm really happy for you!"

"What can I say, you're my inspiration. And mmmmm what smells so good?"

"Awe, you're so sweet. And homemade pizza- trying something different."

"Well I love it. And again, it smells so good." He gave her a kiss. "Be right back, I'm going to say hi to the kids."

Her heart fluttered. She watched the love of her life step outside. Their kids ran full blast to their daddy. He kneeled down on one leg to embrace his little boy and little girl in a warm welcoming hug and kiss. She really loved her family. Even though nothing is perfect, she really had in her eyes a perfect life: a home, sweet and loving husband, and wonderful children with clothes on their backs and food in their tummies. A happy family.

As happy as things were, it would never last. Emilee woke up in tears that were both happy and sad. Happy because she knew she wanted to spend the rest of her life with Chris, but her dream really made her want it more. And that of course made her sad because she and Chris haven't really been dating that long now. She wasn't for sure what he wanted out of the relationship, or how serious he was with her.

All she knew to do was roll over and pray.

Chapter Forty-Two

"Michael?" Michelle asked, standing over him holding a broom. He was slumped down in one of the leather chairs beside the fire in Dunzy's Coffee Shop asleep.

"Hmm?"

"You're sleeping. Go on home, I've got this."

"No I ain't." He mumbled.

"Yes you are, honey. Come on before I whack you with this broom."

"No thank you Mommy, I don't want a balloon."

"Michael!" She whacked his feet with the broom.

He jumped up real fast. "What? What happened?"

"Go on home." She laughed. "And I'll be nice and buy you a balloon."

"What are you talking about? And I can't we're closing up."

"Ha-ha, no *I'm* cleaning up, you were sawing logs. Now, I'll tell you again for the fiftieth time, go on home and get some sleep."

"Are you sure? I can wait around and take you home."

"Yes I'm sure. Now go on. Scoot, scoot, skedaddle."

"Fine, fine." He kissed her. "Call me when you get home and let me know you're okay?"

"Of course."

"Okay good. I love you."

"I love you too." She kissed him again, and closed the

door behind her. Her eyes followed a man walk down the sidewalk in baggy pants and a sweatshirt. Something about him gave her the creeps. For a split second she almost called Michael back to wait with her, but instead she locked the door and let the blinds fall closed.

Michelle finished up closing: made sure everything was straightened up, all appliances were turned off, and the fire was out. She turned off all the lights and peeked through the blinds before she even stepped one foot outside.

The man from before paced back and forth behind a bench across the street. As if he almost knew that he was being watched he stopped and turned towards Michelle. She jumped back and bent down to the floor. With her mouth covered she wondered what she should do- abundantly frightened no doubt.

Only thing she knew to do, she pulled out her cell phone from her purse and called Sheriff Boston.

What was taking him so long? Michelle never left her spot on the floor. She was away from being seen that was for sure, and she kept a close eye on the man from underneath the blinds. He now sat on the bench staring at the shop as if he himself was waiting for something also- probably waiting for Michelle to walk outside and grab her. She surely was not going to move and apparently not him either. He was like a statue, and even a part of her if only her imagination didn't believe he was even blinking.

That was fear though.

And out of nowhere the coffee shop started to shake furiously. Lights flashed on and off as well as the blinds opened and closed all by themselves. Chairs and tables levitated off of the floor. Coffee mugs, plates and bowls clink together.

Michelle screamed and crawled away from the windows and turned around just in time to see the man running from the bench toward the shop. He banged on the door as well as kicking and kicking frantically trying to get in. Flashing red and blue lights shine through the windows as Sheriff Boston screeches to a stop by the sidewalk. The man doesn't run, just falls to the ground with his hands behind his head. He gave up on the spot as Sheriff Boston cuffed him and threw him in the back of the cruiser.

Knowing that she was safe, Michelle unlocked the door and stepped outside. "Thank you, thank you, thank you."

"No problem Ms. Michelle. Are you doing okay?"

"Yes I'm fine now, still a little shook up. That was some earthquake huh?"

The look on Boston's face was pure confusion. "Ma'am, what earthquake?"

"The earthquake that just-" Michelle fainted.

<u>Chapter Forty-Three</u>

"So there's been something I've been thinking a lot about here lately. Not to scare you, but I've been thinking about marriage- like what my life will be like if I was married. You know what I mean?" Chris asked out of nowhere to Emilee.

Her head was rested against his chest while they sit in the dark by the fireplace drinking wine.

"Why would that scare me off? I think about it all of the time to be honest. I even had a dream about it the other night- about us."

"Really what about us?"

Emilee's phone rang from inside her purse. "Shew, hang on just one second."

Chris didn't mind, he knew that a phone call this late at night was never good.

"It's Christy County Hospital," Emilee said on the verge of shaking. "Hello? Yes this is her...I'll be right down."

...

Michael fell asleep waiting for Michelle's call that she was home safe from work. His cell phone laid on his chest and a bible covered his face. He was out cold, but it was the call that woke him- really startled him out of his sleep where he threw the bible across the room.

"Hello? Hello? Randolph's Pizza can I take your order?" Michael asked.

"Who's Randolph? Michael, are you drunk?" Chris asked from the other line. He wasn't playing the least bit.

"Hmm? What, no, sorry just waking up. What's going on man?" He squinted to see that it was nearly past midnight on the alarm clock by his bed.

"I need you to get down here to Christy Hospital, it's Michelle."

...

"Where is she?! What happened?" Michael rushed in through the hospital entrance in his neon green pajama shorts and hooded sweatshirt.

Sheriff Boston stood in the Emergency Room with Emilee and Chris and quickly moved to Michael, placing his hands on his shoulders. "Calm down, calm down. She's okay. It was just a nervous breakdown."

"A nervous breakdown? She was perfectly fine earlier. What's going on?"

"We're not totally for sure yet, she called about a maniac trying to break into the coffee shop after her and then she fainted when I got there. She's pretty out of it right now, mumbling about an earthquake that didn't happen."

"Oh no. No. No. No. I was just there- I mean I was with her before I left. I didn't see anyone though. That's just…just, I don't know right now. Can I see her?"

"Of course, of course. Come on, I'll take you to her."

...

She slept peacefully. The room was dark despite the single lonely light above the empty bed beside Michelle's. Michael entered the room and pulled a chair up beside her bed. He quickly took ahold of her hand and kissed it gently, his eyes not leaving her face.

"Let's go get some coffee," Chris whispered to Emilee. They stood in the doorway and closed the door as they left to give Michael some alone time.

Michael leaned in and kissed her on the forehead and sat back down. "I'm so sorry. So very sorry."

Minutes later when Chris and Emilee returned, they each had a small cup of coffee which Chris handed one to Michael.

"Thanks," Michael whispered.

"No problem man. Any change since we've been gone?"

He shook his head. "She's just sleeping."

"She'll pull through," Emilee cut in. "After what had happened she'll just want to sleep. It's all she needs really."

"I know." Michael turned back to face Michelle. "She doesn't deserve to be here. I should have stayed with her. It's my fault this happened."

"No Mikey, don't say that. You are not to blame for that. These things just happen, no coincidence. We can't control them." Chris said.

"It's just that still small grievance I carry around because of Barry that's going to stay with me forever. I know I couldn't have saved him, but I could save her. Protect her."

"You didn't know that was going to happen. Nobody did." Emilee blew on her coffee.

"Neither did I with my brother. I just really love her and don't want to lose her like I did Barry."

"You won't Mikey, I promise." Chris reassured him.

There was a knock at the door as they all turn to see Doctor Cravens step in. "How's she doing?"

"She seems fine, resting." Emilee replied.

"Good, good, good. Well, all her vitals and tests look normal. Everything seems to be doing okay, so she can go home at any time. Just, I suggest, let her get some rest for a couple of days until she's better. Alright?"

"Sounds great Doc. Chris and I were talking and we'd like to get her away to a cabin for a while. Would that be okay?"

"I think a getaway like that sounds perfect."

Chapter Forty-Four

Michelle slept the entire drive to the cabin with her head rested against Michael's shoulder. Though still weak, she made it to the bed. Michael covered her up and then laid down in a recliner beside her and went to sleep holding her hand.

...

Both Emilee and Chris were in a hooded sweatshirt and toboggan as they cast out their lines into the lake below the cabin. The sun was high above their heads, cold from the breeze coming off the water. And a thermos of coffee in between them.

"It's so peaceful out here." Emilee glanced around at the trees, taking in the nature. "Very beautiful."

"Yes you really are." Chris said thinking aloud.

"Do what?"

"I mean...yeah it really is."

She knew she heard him the first time, but even still she blushed at the moment. "Oh Chris, you're just being modest."

"Or just being honest." Which even if he just thought it, it was still true to him.

Emilee didn't have to say anything, but smile and stare out at the lake. That's all it took. Chris though, was curious what was going on in her head. "What? What is it?"

"Oh nothing- I was just thinking about that dream I had the other night."

"What was that dream about anyways? You never had the chance to tell me."

"We were married and you came home from a meeting and kissed me. I watched you and our kids playing in the backyard through the kitchen window. I really loved it. And I woke up wishing that was how it really was."

"Well it's funny that you say that."

...

Michelle slowly opened her eyes. It took a moment for her eyes to adjust. And though she looked around the room, she was unclear of where she was and still groggy from the IV. She followed down her arm to see Michael asleep in the chair beside her still holding her hand. His head was leaned back against the wall with his mouth wide open and drool running down the side of his cheek.

"Michael? Wha- what's going on?"

He snorted and woke himself up. When he saw Michelle awake he pulled himself up. "Hey, you're awake. How are you feeling?"

"I'm okay. A bit thirsty though." She didn't know anything, nor what to think.

"Oh sure, here you go." He fumbled to pick up a cup of water on the nightstand between them and helped her take a drink.

"Thank you. Umm Michael, where are we?"

"At a cabin in the Smokies. You've been asleep for some odd hours now."

"I have? All I remember is-"

"Shh, shh don't go back there. You had a nervous breakdown. So, Chris, Emilee, and I brought you here to get away for a while to get better."

"Oh." This took her by surprise. "Where are Chris and Emilee?"

"Down at the lake fishing."

"Oh." She stared down at her feet still trying to comprehend everything. "How come you aren't down there with them?"

" 'Cause I wanted to stay with you."

She smiled and laid her head on his arm and stared up at the ceiling. Though quiet for a moment, she asked, "Michael?"

"Yeah sweetheart?" He rubbed her hair.

"Have you been by my side the entire time?"

"Yeah I have. Even in the hospital."

"But why though?"

...

"It's funny you say that." Chris reeled in his line and set the pole down beside him. "Because here lately that's all I've been thinking about- is marriage, with you. Emilee I've fallen hopelessly in-love with you. I know that's really soon, but it's true. It's something I've never felt before, and definitely something I never want to lose. And I'll be completely 100% honest, I want to marry you. I love you that much."

"Chris, you really don't know how much that means to me. I love you so much, it's not even a joke. It doesn't bother me the least bit how soon it is, because I truly believe that you and I were meant to be together."

"I believe that also. It's just too much of a coincidence that you moved into a house beside mine- not even knowing I lived there. Of course that's not the only reason I believe that, it just feels 'right' with you."

"Ha-ha, yeah God does really work in mysterious ways, doesn't He? And it really does feel 'right' with us. Which I felt that when I read your books, like you were someone I wanted to end up with. That sounds crazy, but I feel God did that with your books."

"That doesn't sound crazy at all, because I know how mysterious He could be...or really how He *is*."

"Oh yes definitely. But what's all this meaning?"

...

"For a couple of reasons really." Michael said. "One being is that I feel terrible about what happened. If I hadn't left then this would not have happened. I should've been there with you. And for another, I've realized that I don't was to be away from your side at all for the rest of my life. My life didn't really truly begin until I found you. I mean that because with you, I found Christ. And I'm not that smart of a guy, but I do know that anyone who could make me feel that way, or love me enough for me to *want* to do that, I shouldn't let go. I don't want to let go. Ever.

Emilee I love you. I love you so much. And because of this, because of Barry, because of life in general and how short it really truly is, I want to marry you. You are the best thing to ever happen to me. Will you marry me?"

...

"It means what's right in front of our face is the inevitable. What should be happening is something we should have already asked ourselves. Should we get married? Or should we already have been married?"

"I think we should've already been married. But that's just me. When I'm with you it does feel like we already are, though yes unfortunately we haven't made it there yet. What are we waiting on anyways?"

"I haven't got a clue. It beats the far out of me. So, you wanna get married?"

Emilee smiled. "I thought you'd never ask. Yes, I want to marry you."

...

"Michael, I don't know. I'm not questioning it, it's just it caught me off guard. I really love you, I do. I-" Michelle wiped a tear from her eye. "Do you want this? I mean are you really ready for that kind of commitment?"

"More than anything. Michelle, I know that with everything going on if God was ever telling me anything it's this- not to let this moment pass."

Even though this all felt like a dream, Michelle knew that it wasn't a dream and that it was real. This wasn't the meds the hospital had given her- Michael really was proposing to her. And despite the past 24 hours, this made her truly happy. She knew that if someone could make her this happy no matter what was going on that she couldn't let them go- and Michael truly did make her happy. This is who God meant for her.

"Yes Michael, I'll marry me. I mean I'll marry you."

Michael didn't know how to react, except breakdown in tears of joy and kissing her on the forehead.

...

"Is that crying?" Chris asked as he and Emilee were entering in the cabin. They drop their fishing gear on the porch outside and rush upstairs to Michelle's bedroom. "What's wrong? Is everything okay?"

"Yes Chris, everything is fine. Perfect actually." Michelle smiled. She was certainly better now.

"Thank heavens. From the sound, well, we really didn't know what to expect." Chris looked down at Michael on his knees whom the crying was coming from. "Mikey, what are you crying for? Stub your toe? Break a nail? Maybe even bite your lip? Hmm?"

"No you jerk, I'm happy. Michelle and I are getting married."

"Mar-!! Wow, creepy, us too! How in the world did that happen?" Emilee asked.

"With Chris and I there's really no telling. You should've seen us when we were kids- crazy moments."

"I can only imagine with you too." Emilee turned to Michelle. "I can see you are feeling better."

"Much better, thanks girl. And thank you both for bringing me out here. Well, I guess God was guiding us the entire time."

"And that He is, because I take it, we all have wedding plans to attend to huh? Or is that all too fast because of-." Michael said.

"I'm fine, trust me. This is just all what I needed." Michelle insisted. "Let's all get to work."

Chapter Forty-Five

"Are you ready for this?" Chris asked Michael. He stood in front of the mirror beside Michael, both adjusting their ties- Chris's purple tie and Michael in a baby blue tie. Michael had combed his hair in the style of a 50's greaser, while Chris had his black hair straight and touched up on his mascara.

"You have no idea how ready I am for this."

A knock came from the door.

"It's open." Chris said. "Come on in."

"Unless you're the devil, we don't want you here. Not welcome. You are definitely not going to ruin my wedding day. If you've ever heard of a bridezilla then prepare to meet a groomzilla."

"Our wedding day." Chris corrected.

"That's right my friend, *our* wedding day."

"So very far from the devil here." Reverend Brown poked his head in. "You boys ready?"

"You bet your sweet patootie we are." Chris said.

"What?"

"Nothing, I'm hyper. But yes, sir, we're ready."

"Okay then, let's begin shall we?"

Followed behind Reverend Brown, Michael and Chris made their way down from the cabin to the dock. It was a peaceful sunny day from a somewhat stressful week arranging the wedding. Everything was put together- rings, licenses, tuxedos, dresses, cakes, everything- in only a matter of a few days. No time was wasted, and yet came together perfectly except for the one single stressful night planning by a warm fire.

Chris and Michael both hug their folks who stand in the grass by one side of the dog, and then hug their mother in-laws to be on the other side of the dock. Fred Johnson leaned against a tree close by and just waved at the boys.

When Emilee and Michelle were escorted down the path with their fathers holding up the back of their dresses from the ground, it was like watching angels walking down to the men. They couldn't keep their eyes off their brides. And then they shook their father in-laws hands as they gave their babies away. It was time.

"Dearly beloved," Reverend Brown began as he prayed over the ceremony. "Thank you for this glorious day in the unison of your fine children- bringing them together as one on their wedding day in the name of your son Jesus Christ. We ask that you bless their lives in faith and in love. In Jesus name we pray, amen."

Family and friends, we are gathered here today in holy matrimony, to join together Chris and Emilee, and Michael and Michelle in their joyous experience as they pledge their love and commitment to one another. We rejoice as it was God's intentions that led them to each other and got them to the place where they stand today. As it begins in the book of Genesis, 'As for a man shall leave his father and his mother, and fast to his wife and become one flesh. The Lord made woman from the rib of man for man. It is not good for the man to be alone. God made a suitable helper for him'.

The book of Corinthians describes a perfect love. 'Love is patient and kind; Love is not jealous or boastful; it is not arrogant or rude. Love does not insist on its own way; it is not irritable or resentful; it does not rejoice at wrong but rejoices in the right. Love bears all things, believes all things, hopes all things, endures all things. Love never ends."

Reverend Brown turned to Chris and Michael, "Men, your duty as husbands is to never take your wives love for granted. To always stand by her side for good, comfort, love, support and encouragement. For protection and understanding. Do you both take Emilee and take Michelle, joining your right hands in consent, to be your lawful wedded wife to have and to behold from this day forward, better or for worse, richer or poorer, sickness and health, as long as you both shall live?"

Both men say together in unison, "I do."

"Ladies, as your duty to your husbands, it is your job to help him through any burden in life, love, support and comfort him unconditionally. Do you Emilee and Michelle take Chris and Michael to be your lawful wedded husband, to have and to behold from this day forward, better or for worse, richer or poorer, sickness and health, as long as you both shall live?"

Both ladies, "I do."

"The wedding ring is a symbol for an unbroken unity without a beginning or an end. Today these children of God will exchange these rings to show a confirmation of their vows to join their lives together. May the Lord bless these rings which they give to one another as a symbol of their love and fidelity.

Christopher and Michael, please repeat after me as you take this ring and place it on your bride's finger: With this ring, I thee wed. I offer you my hand, and my heart as I know they will be safe with you. All that I am I give to you and all that I have I share with you.

And now Emilee, Michelle repeat after me as you take this ring and place it on your husband's finger: With this ring, I thee wed. I offer you my hand and my heart as I know they will be safe with you. All that I am I give to you and all that I have I share with you.

Christopher, Emilee and Michael, Michelle you have given and pledged your promises to each other, and have declared your everlasting love by exchanging the rings. Your vows have been spoken, and your promises will last until your last breath, as one family before God and this community of friends. I now pronounce them husbands and wives. Y'all may kiss your brides.

Ladies and Gentlemen, I present to you Mr. and Mrs. Wilson. And Ladies and Gentlemen, I present to you Mr. and Mrs. Gable.

Chapter Forty-Six

It was a joyous and romantic honeymoon shared at the cabin. Though it was shortly lasted, many memories were created. Then as they made their way home, Sheriff Boston's cruiser sat in Chris'- and now Emilee's- driveway with an unmarked cruiser behind him. Chris parked next door at Emilee's and Michelle's house.

Followed by two gentlemen in black suits, Sheriff Boston made his way through the grass across the front yard as Chris, Emilee, Michael, and Michelle stepped out of the car and met them halfway.

"What in the world are *they* doing here?" Michael asked with a tension in his voice.

"It's good to see you Mr. Gable, Mr. Wilson. How have you gentlemen been? Been a long time." Detective Acuff said.

"Not long enough." Michael whispered under his breath.

"What are y'all doing here anyways? We haven't done anything- never have, never will." Chris said.

Detective Marshall cut in. "We know Mr. Wilson, but this isn't about you this time. This concerns your wives. Which congratulations by the way. Sorry for interrupting your moments."

Michelle turned to Michael and whispered, "What's going on?"

"Ma'am," Detective Marshall continued. "Is this the

man who attempted to attack you?"

He handed her a photograph.

"That's...that's...him!" She couldn't breathe and dropped the photo.

Emilee who stood by her side, leaned down and picked up the photograph. "Hey, that's the guy that crept me out at the library that one night."

"You've seen him too?" Detective Acuff asked.

Chris leaned over her shoulder. "No way...it's David."

"Yes Mr. Wilson, that's David. Now please, tell us where he is." Detective Acuff insisted.

"I honestly do not know. I haven't spoken to him since I was 17 years old. Do you know how long ago that was?"

"He should be in jail, I saw you and Sheriff Boston arrest him. I saw it." Michelle said as she grabbed onto Michael trembling where she stood.

"That's the thing- he escaped. We don't know how exactly, but he did." Sheriff Boston cut in.

Michael asked, "So you think he's *here*?"

"It's certainly a possibility." Detective Acuff admitted.

"If he is, we don't know about it. We just got home from our honeymoon." Chris said. "Look detectives- we're completely innocent. It may not have seemed that way when we were just kids but look around you: we've got a life now. Why do you all intrude on our lives like this?"

"Because we know you are innocent, okay? But until we find this guy, there will be a possibility that he'll come straight to you. And when he does, we've got him." Detective Marshall said.

"You're using us as bait. Do you know that?" Emilee asked.

"Yes, considering your husbands were the last people he was around. But if you don't mind, could we do a quick search through your houses and make sure he's not in hiding?"

"No, please go on ahead. That…that…oh that man needs to be found." Michelle wept.

"Oh we're going to find him, don't you worry." Detective Marshall smiled, but it wasn't such an assuring smile.

Chapter Forty-Seven

Everybody was settled in, except for Chris. He couldn't sleep the least bit, even though his wife was lying next to him- their first night them sleeping together in their own home. Minutes seemed to roll by with every toss and turn. He's happy though, happy to be married and have his wonderful life. Life has treated him well. Though now with David making a surprise visit in to his life once again, his mind has been on a constant rollercoaster that will not stop.

Trying his hardest not to wake Emilee as he slid out of bed, he threw on a hooded sweatshirt before heading down the hall. Chris tiptoed past the living room not to disturb Michael's and Michelle's sleep who because of recent events decided to stay at the Wilson's house for a bit.

He closed the front door behind him with no sound and walked down to the detective's cruiser that was parked along the sidewalk. Detective Acuff was sound asleep with his head against the passenger window and his mouth wide open. But Detective Marshall was up reading a book and jumped when Chris tapped on the driver's side window.

Marshall rolled down the window. "Wilson! What's wrong? Everything alright?"

"Yeah, everything's fine. Can I talk to you for a moment?"

"Sure." He turned to Detective Acuff. "Hey! Watch post, be right back. I've got a 10/100."

Detective Marshall followed Chris to the back porch.

"What's a 10/100?" Chris asked.

"Restroom break. Make this quick- what did you have to talk about? I can't stay gone long or Acuff will fall back asleep- if not already. I've seen him do it."

"Look, I'm going to be straight to the point- what in the world is going on here? What is so important about David that you and Detective Fart Face keep watching us? We're not kids anymore. Sure we were pretty ignorant at 17, but now we're both married. Be straight with me."

"You're not going to like this answer...but it's confidential."

"Are you seriously pulling the 'confidentiality' act on me right now? We tell you over and over again that we don't have anything to do with David and yet you are still staking out our house? And trust me, you've got Michelle all tore up which she really does not need that right now considering her breakdown a few weeks ago."

"I'm really sorry about that and I'm sorry are angry with us, but it's honestly not about you all. We just know given the first chance David he can he will contact you- which we believe he will- and then he's ours. Then we'll be out of your all's hairs for the rest of your lives. You can be able to live your all's perfect little marriages in peace."

"Just answer this one question so I know everything is truly okay- what did David do exactly? All I remember is you all trying to get him on arsine for the Old Spook's place burning down, and something about him not having a record in the United States. Don't get me wrong, I understand him being an illegal immigrant is bad, but chasing him this many years is uncalled for."

"Chris, you have to trust me on this one. You all are not in any danger I promise. Yes, David is an alien to the United States, that's it and nothing more. Everything is perfectly fine."

Chris knew there was something else that Marshall was keeping from him, but he knew that at the moment he couldn't get it out of him. "Yeah okay. Tell that to any horror movie victim that has ever heard that before."

Chapter Forty-Eight

"Are you sure about this?" Emilee asked as she and Chris pull up to the curb in front of the library. She glanced up in the review mirror- the detectives followed close behind. Detective Acuff stepped out of his cruiser and walked toward Chris and Emilee.

"Positive sweetheart. Detective Acuff will be with you all day on guard. Yes, he's a pain to Michael and me, so I'm sure he'd be a little easier on you."

"Then how come they aren't keeping guard on you and Michael? Why stick with us when this David guy knows you two?"

"I'm guessing because we're men, and they think we can take care of ourselves. At least I *know* I can, I'm not sure about Mikey though."

"Oh that's sexist."

"Hey, I didn't say it. Give it time to get to know these guys- they're jerks. Acuff is, I know that for a fact."

"I hope this doesn't last long enough for me to get to know them that well. And you know me, since I know how they are I'm going to take it to my advantage."

"Ohhh yes I know, and I love that about you."

"And I love you too." Emilee kissed him on the lips then on the forehead. "I'll see you after work. Have a good day."

Detective Acuff escorted her out of the car and into

the library.

...

Chris glanced both ways down the street and saw that there wasn't any suspicious activity before he entered into his house.

He threw his keys down into a bowl that was on top of a hallway table- one of many new things that came along with Emilee moving in. It most certainly wasn't a problem for him with all of the changes. He knew it was all a part of being married and living together.

It was a cool sunny day so he took a seat down at his desk after opening the window blinds. Time to catch up on his writing. He opened his top desk drawer, surprised to see a thick yellow envelope inside.

...

Emily watched the clock. Even though the day had only just begun, she knew with Detective Acuff seated by the entrance doors that it was going to be a very long day.

"Hey detective?"

"Yes Mrs. Wilson?"

"Hi."

"Umm...hi?"

"Would you like some candy? It'll make you feel soooo good."

"Mrs. Wilson, I'm going to only ask you this one time,

are you on drugs?"

"Who me? Maybe...wouldn't you like to know? Huh? Huh? Huh?"

There was no emotion on Detective Acuff's face. He didn't grin, but only showed a harsh stare.

"Geez, lighten up," Emilee continued. "I'm only playing- trying to pass time. And no I'm not on drugs thank you. I tend to act strange when I'm bored."

"Humph."

"You must be one of those straight-forward, no holds-bared kind of cop huh? Straight down to the book and ridiculously merciless unless you caught your perp. Someone hard to get along with."

"For the most part, yes."

"Interesting." Emilee checked out a group of kids and turned back to Acuff, "So Mr. Policeman, what has my husband done that's so terrible?"

"Nothing."

"Nothing? Really? With nothing there wouldn't be this extra special protection y'all got going on."

"But ma'am, that's just it- protection. We don't know what we're going up against with this guy, but we know he's had ties with your husband and his pal. Not to mention came in contact with yourself and Mrs. Gable."

"Well...yeah you've got a point. But who's this guy you are talking about anyways? What's he done?"

"Has Christopher not told you about him?"

Emilee knew that the tables were turned. "No...well if he has I don't remember."

"Then no. Maybe you should ask him, see what he says."

...

He picked up the envelope which had somewhat of a weight to it. It felt as if inside was encased with a book. For some reason it frightened him to the point where he had to lock his office door, shut the blinds, and check to make sure nobody was watching from the closet. Other than not knowing whom the envelope was from, he didn't know what was frightening him. He felt as if he was a teenager again hiding a naughty magazine from his parents, or getting caught doing something he wasn't supposed to be doing.

Chris sat back in his chair. His adrenaline ran sky high and shook as he opened the envelope. A brown leather-bound journal fell out onto his lap.

...

"I have to go to the restroom." Emilee rose from her desk and walked over to the restroom with a mischievous grin on her face. Detective Acuff followed behind like a lost puppy. "Oh no, no, Mr. you are not coming in here with me. Sit boy sit."

Detective Acuff sat at a table across from the restroom. To make things worse, Emilee used this moment to her advantage by taking her precious time. When she came out, Detective Acuff stood up in that very instant.

"Shew, I feel better." Her eyes caught a cart of returned books. Normally books would be put on shelves before closing time, but Emilee took it as a given opportunity to mess with Acuff's head. "Well, it's pretty quiet right now, I think I'll put up these books."

Step...by...step she zigzagged through each aisle with Acuff two steps behind. There was no particular way that she put up the books. Any other day she'd already have them arranged alphabetically on the cart. Going around the corner she tripped over a wheel and both Emilee and the cart fell to the floor. At the same time a group of children entered into the library.

"Oops, my bad. I'm sorry about that." Emilee pulled herself up from underneath a pile of books. "Would you mind putting these books back on the cart for me would you? I've got to help these kids. Thank you."

She scurried off before Detective Acuff could give any form of answer.

"Hey kids," Emilee continued, not even affected by the fall. "Would you like to have some fun?"

...

Chris opened the journal to the first page. The outside was cracked, faded, and well used many times.

Entry #1
Dear Chris, all of this will come as a shocker to you, which I

know you will be able to handle it. Everything I am about to tell you is just about everything your creative mind could conjure up. Truths will be told and a lot to take in. If I know you as well as I think I do, about now you'll be getting your coffee ready and bracing yourself from what's yet to come.

He took a sip of his coffee and thought, "Lucky guess."

...

Emilee waited patiently behind the desk: watched and waited for Detective Acuff's return.

The kids had done exceedingly well in causing chaos to Acuff in an utmost legal and nondestructive way. When given the permission to be troublesome, the kids dutifully accepted with joy. It wasn't every day they were *asked* to be 'bad'. Books were thrown. Carts were knocked over...again. Toilet paper tossed over aisles. Doors slammed. Chairs knocked over. Complete and total havoc.

Detective Acuff would catch one kid, only to be bitten on the calf or the ankle by another kid. They were out the front door before justice could be served. Out of breath, he leaned against Emilee's desk.

"Problems?" It took everything for Emilee to hold in her laughter.

He gave her a wore out, aggravated glare. "You...did...this...didn't you?"

"Maybe I did, maybe I didn't. Who can tell?"

"I...hate...you."

"Now, Detective Acuff, hate is such a naughty word. Don't you know that? You DISLIKE me right now."

"Very much so…and kids. I have to…sit down and…catch…my…breath."

"Yes, sir." Emilee gave him a salute.

…

Entry #2

Instead of leaving you in the dark about everything that has gone on since we saw each other last, I'll begin from that moment. You have my word that what I'm about to say is true, regardless that of which the detectives have told you about me. Which I'm guessing very little, if nothing at all. Certainly not what is the truth.

That night at Old Spooks' land, I did not run because the detectives were after me. I ran to find answers of why my Dad's flight jacket was in that man's house. Up until then, I was still David Lowery- at least to me I was. And I didn't have the slightest clue that they were after me.

Of course mom knew it though. By the time I arrived home, our stuff was packed and ready to move. Without a word of reason or even a goodbye, we were gone. I thought maybe Becky could shed some light on the situation, but she nor my aunt were anywhere to be found.

When I walked through the door, mom was walking back and forth in the living room saying, "No, no, no, no I knew this was going to happen." But then she saw that I was wearing Dad's jacket and stopped dead in her tracks.

Her eyes were wide and the look on her face was like she saw a ghost. "Where did you get that?! WHERE?!"

"Out of that old man's house. Why was it there? Mom, what's going on?"

"I really, really didn't want you finding out this way." She was in tears again. "We have to talk."

But we didn't talk until we made it to my aunt's house. The whole ride she stared up at the sky out of the window, clutching the jacket close to her heart.

We let ourselves into the house and all the lights were off. Everything was in complete darkness and eerie quiet. Not a soul in sight, or even a piece of furniture. The floor was covered in dust and it didn't even seem like anyone had even ever lived in the house. As if the house was abandoned. But then there was that same triangular symbol burnt into the wall that we saw at Old Spooks' house. Mom saw it and started to fall.

"Mom!" I yelled and grabbed her before she hit the floor.

"David, I'm so sorry." Her eyes never left the symbol. "Have you seen that before? Yes, yes of course you have. It's our family emblem brought down from our home planet."

"What? Family emb-? I'm calling 911. You're having a mental breakdown."

"No David! Please just listen to me." Mom pleaded and gripped onto my wrists. "I'm perfectly fine. I'm just...nervous about Becky. She's taking over. I knew this day would come, but not so soon. Not so soon."

"Mom what are you talking about? You're not making any sense."

"Your great grandfather was our king and he wanted peace, but our planet wasn't following his orders anymore. He was once a great leader- the best we had ever seen in ages. Something happened though that corrupted the people, everyone turned against one another. We just couldn't do it anymore and our family fled to the nearest planet: Earth. Our hopes were to make peace with the humans like we were on our planet and create a nation joined together as one.

Until that day was to come, we had to observe and learn how to adapt to their society. In doing so, we invaded bodies to blend in, but the bodies mutated with ours and now we all looked alike. You couldn't tell the difference- which was fine, we wanted it that way. We assumed this would work, but then in 1947 our neighboring planets began to make themselves known to the world.

Because of Roswell and the mysteries of Area 51, we came to realize that if we made known our race to the world then it would be total chaos. We decided to stay hidden until it was our time to shine. But something happened that I didn't expect. I met and fell in-love with a pilot in the military. He was so wonderful and so...human."

Yes Chris, that's right. If you aren't catching on now, my mother was from another planet and my father was a human from Earth. Keep reading, I know you think it's crazy, but trust me, it's true.

"At first, your grandfather didn't approve. He said it wasn't safe. But when they met, it was an instant bond just like it was for him and I. Our life became a perfect resemblance of a perfect American life: hard working family, love, and happiness. We were at peace in our life, though it was just our little family, it was what your grandfather had always wanted.

We lived on a farm at the time, and your father and grandfather would work all day and in the evenings fly planes around the property. And of course everything had to happen for a reason.

One day while your father was cleaning out a stable, something unbeknownst caused a horse to kick your father in his rear end. As comical as it was, he busted through the wall and landed on top of our shuttle. We thought it was the end then and there, but instead of your father running to the media and the authorities he ran to your grandfather. Because of their bond and the trust they had in each other, your grandfather told him everything as I am telling you now. None of it scared him away or changed any way that he acted around us. In fact, he took it all in as his family also. Which in a couple of years after that we were married.

Being a part of the family, he painted our symbol on his airplane and had a patch designed for his jacket. That was how he showed his love and respect for us. And only we knew what it meant. And then, I became pregnant with Becky. We were afraid that she would come out like US, *but nope. She came out like her father and part human. And obviously years later so did you.*

We didn't tell you kids about it because we didn't know what would happen if the world found out. Your grandfather did predict that one day the colony would come looking for us, and he was right. U.F.O.s- as the world called them- were spotted multiple times. It was then your grandfather knew his predictions were true.

And even your father and his partner Private Spooks were called to investigate a sighting. Your father made the first contact and when he did he saw the family emblem underneath the saucer and knew who he was dealing with. He was authorized to shoot and kill and he did just that, but one of them escaped unharmed.

Back on base, they were sworn to secrecy not to mention this to anyone. The mission did not happen, so to speak. But your father knew it was far from over and asked an oath from Spooks that if anything was to happen to him, that Spooks would keep his jacket. And etched inside was a journal that your father kept of files and logs and the secrets that all of which added up to one reason- to find us."

Sure enough Chris, the book was stitched inside and buried deep in the padding. End of Entry #2.

Entry #6
Mom's dead. I don't know what happened, but she's dead. These last nights at my grandparent's old farm have been

too peaceful. Though the place was abandoned, it was still calm. The last I saw of mom, she stood from Grandma's rocker, walked outside and screamed. Her screams were cut short by a flash of green light. Gone. And I'm alone. End of entry #6.

Entry #15
Chris, you won't believe the things they've got hidden here at Area 51. I know now why it's such a high security facility. My mom was right, the aliens are here. My relatives are here in the world. End of entry #15.

Entry #2013
This is the last entry that I can give you. If I haven't been caught already, both the government and our colony are close on my tail. Before it's too late, I'm going to do all I can to protect you and Michael and your wives from any harm. All they want is to get to me and erase anything and everything about me.

I need you to go to the Christy County Library Archives and look behind section H8/14. End of entry #2013.

<u>Chapter Forty-Nine</u>

"Hello? Hey Chris, what's up?" Michael asked, his cell phone to his ear as he leaned against the counter at Dunzy's Coffee Shop. "Yeah he's here...no, no that shouldn't be a problem. I'm sure it's okay...okay, see you in a few."

Michelle looked at Michael with unease. "Was that Chris? You ain't leaving me are you?"

"You'll be okay- Detective Marshall is here, he'll keep you safe. I won't be gone long I promise, I'll just be at the library. That's not far is it?"

"No, I guess not." She still didn't seem too happy. "Just don't be gone *too* long, I can't stand to be alone right now."

"I promise I won't be." Michael kissed her before heading out.

...

"Hey quit it!" Detective Acuff yelled out, more frustrated with Emilee than dealing with the children.

"What? I'm not doing anything."

"Yes you are, stop it!" Another paper wad hit him in the head. "I'm warning you! Stop it!"

"But what?" Chris and Michael walked in through the door. Emilee continued, "Ooh you're in-trouble now

Detective."

"Christopher Wilson! Control your wife." Acuff pleaded.

"Uh oh, what's she done now?"

"Hey, I am doing nothing, he-he."

Michael looked down at the army of paper balls scattered around Acuff. "Hey, you kind of missed the trashcan there, Buddy."

"Those aren't-!"

"Shh, this is a library," Emilee cut in.

Acuff grunted, sitting back down.

Chris walked up to Emilee and winked. He knew that his wife was up to no good and he loved that about her. "Hey, you got a minute?"

"For you, I've got all of the time in the world." Emilee walked around the desk and pointed to Acuff, "Stay boy!"

"You were right, that guy is a jerk." Emilee said as she closed the Archives door behind her.

"I told you so." Chris pulled out David's journal from his shoulder bag and turned to the very last page written. "Can you find me this section? H8/14."

"Oh sure, that's right over...here." Emilee pulled out the book. She noticed something laying behind the book. "Hey, what's this?"

She reached in between the books and pulled out a ragged journal.

"That's it! That's what I'm looking for!" Chris was almost excited as a kid in a candy store.

"What is this? We didn't put this here, there's no info tag or anything."

Michael cut in. "Did you really call me from work over a journal?"

"It's David's father's journal." Chris said and carefully took hold of the journal and opened to the first page.

"Umm Chris, you know we aren't supposed to have anything to do with David; we've got wives to think about now. Not ourselves."

"I know Michael, and I haven't…sort of. Here," Chris handed him David's journal. "Take a look at this. He left it in my desk."

"He was in our house?!"

"Yeah sweetheart, but if what he says is true about his father's journal then he's innocent."

"Can you possibly believe that though? I mean even to me, this journal seems a little farfetched." Michael skimmed through the pages.

"I don't know. Anything *is* possible." He turned to Emilee. "I don't want to keep you working, but can those computers get internet or just newspaper archives?"

"It can get the internet. Chris, I trust you and I support you in anything you do, but I've got to ask- what are you getting us into? This seems pretty serious to me."

Chris made his way over to the computers in the corner, "Sweetheart, I'll never let anything bad happen to you. I promise that; it's my duty as your husband to keep you protected, but yes this is pretty serious. I-umm…huh."

"What?" Emilee asked.

"This is really weird. Either the internet is down, or David is right, and the government is erasing what I search. It always comes back with '0' Matches Found'. It's almost as if every single website, or rather, information about aliens have vanished- like they've never existed at all."

"It's almost as if we are made to forget about what an alien is. Try looking up movies such as *E.T.* or *X-Files,* or *Aliens* something like that." Michael suggested.

"It's worth a shot." Chris added. Typed up the information and hit send. "Nope, nothing."

"Wow. Creepy." Emilee whispered. "Be right back."

"Wait!" Chris stopped her.

She jumped. "What?"

"Please don't say 'be right back' at a time like this. You know horror movies have made it very clear that anyone who says 'be right back' will certainly not be right back."

"Okay, umm, I'm going to check something out?" Emilee shuttered, "No wait. That's bad too, especially with someone checking out a weird sound. I've got it: I'm going to check out a few books."

Michael waited until the door was closed, "Chris? This is all true isn't it? If so, and if the government really is on it, there's nothing we can do. I hate to imagine what steps they'd take in formally and informally keeping secret about people like us whom know about the situation. We aren't getting off easy as it will seem when this is all over. Even if it really will be all over."

"Believe me, I've thought about that. Best I can concur is we put our trust in the Lord. His will be done."

"And here's a wild thought. What if our wives are these so-called aliens? Wouldn't it be obvious though? They did coincidentally show up out of nowhere and did know who you were down to the letter. And also, at the same time as the drifters came through town, not to mention David popping up. I don't know what I'm thinking, but I am a little suspicious right now."

"Of the girls though? Come on, be rational. They love us. And look at how sweet they are. There's nobody like them. They're perfect."

"A little too perfect. Don't get me wrong, I love them both also, it's just they seem to be too perfect. It just so happened that two women are 100% compatible for both of us and shows up at the exact time. How is that not odd? You know what we've been through in life, nothing that good ever happens. Well to me at least."

"I'm sorry Mickey, but I don't mean to contradict you. Yes, nothing like that does seem to happen, but think about the wedding. We both didn't plan on proposing at the same time, but it happened. I just think that everything happens for a reason and that God surely works in mysterious ways.

This may be foolish of me, but I have faith in the wives that they aren't from another planet."

"Yeah, maybe."

"Come on man, don't start questioning the wives now."

"I wouldn't be if it wasn't for this-" He dropped the journal back on the table.

"You aren't going to believe this." Emilee busted in through the door, large encyclopedias in her hands. "So I checked our book directories and searched the state wide book library directory and not one book of U.F.O's or aliens in the system. Period. And I called around at some used book stores, and they have been reported missing as well. But this is even more strange-"

Emilee opened each encyclopedia to where any information would be. Michael glanced over her shoulder and said, "They've been all crossed out with a black marker."

"That is really creepy." Chris said. He looked up at Emilee's face. The color had drained from her skin. "Are you okay sweetheart?"

She shook her head. "No, this is all really weird. Almost something you'd expect from a movie or a book or something. I don't even know what's going on. Chris, I think you and Michael need to tell Michelle and I what in the world happened when you all were kids."

Chapter Fifty

Michael peered through the window blinds at the Detective's cruiser across the street sitting silently and motionless. From reading through both journals more than once in the past few hours, he lost more trust in the law enforcement even more than he already had. It was little moments as such that got him to reminisce on Barry and even Angela at times, as he felt more could've been done. That more *should have* been done. He did not know if something like this could ever stop hurting.

"Michael, hey Mikey!" Chris interrupted his daydream. "You okay buddy?"

"Yeah, sorry. I kind of dazed out there for a moment." He turned around from the couch and felt Michelle's hand grab a hold of his. With just her touch it brought him back to the present with his wonderful wife by his side forever. And not to add that also with her touch, he felt total guilt for ever doubting her humanity to being an alien. He was just caught up with emotions at the moment.

"It's okay, man. Dinner's ready."

"Okay, we'll be there in a second."

"Take your time."

Michael turned to Michelle with tears in his eyes.

"Honey, are you okay?" Michelle asked with a concerned look on her face.

"Yeah, I've just been thinking a lot since today- mostly

about my past and what I've been through. It's made it even harder for me to trust someone, but I just want you to know that I do trust you. And this is something you don't hear every day, but sweetheart I trust that you aren't an alien."

Michelle burst out laughing.

"What's so funny?"

"I'm sorry for laughing, it's just you are right- that is something I don't hear every day. I know you are being serious, but that caught me off guard. I'm sorry. And I'm glad that you trust me, sweetie, because no, I'm not, nor will I ever be an alien."

"Good. I'm glad, because I don't want my brains sucked out today. Well, not just yet anyway. Or even probed for that matter."

"Ha-ha-ha, I promise you that's not going to happen. And thank you, I needed that laugh. Oh, and by the way, you need a brain for them to suck out. Now come on my silly man, let's eat."

"Mmm, hamburgers from the stove, my favorite." Michael said with a grin.

"Hey if you want to re-cook yours on the grill in the cold, be my guest." Chris implied.

"Umm, no thanks. I'll settle with these."

"That's what I thought."

"Yeah, yeah, yeah. So, seriously though, we know why we are here- to explain to our gals about David Lowery and why the jerk detectives are now watching over us...again.

Chris, would you like to begin? This all started with you and David in the first place."

"Well, I guess I can do that. Let's see, umm, I first met David in a computer store. We ended up talking about horror movies which sparked our friendship. I'll admit, he intimidated me at first because of his 'Gothic' attire, but once I got to know him I realized how quickly people can judge one another. He turned out to be a really nice guy, and religious I shall add.

And as it turned out, David and I lived right next door to each other. Their house had been vacant for so long, I didn't even notice them move in. Then I met his mother and older sister, Becky. Michael and I weren't on good terms at all because of a girl, so I spent most of my time with David and Becky.

Sometime later, that girl Michael was so in-like with committed suicide and that's when Detective Marshall and Acuff came into the picture. Gosh we had to have been what 16? Maybe even 17 at the time? Way too young to be dealing with all of that, but we made it through it. And Michael and I eventually rekindled our friendship."

"Then that's when things got really weird." Michael cut in. "Well they weren't *that* weird, but with everything going on now, there must have been something. I had started hanging out with Chris and all of them, and both my brother Barry and I had weird vibes around them- not Chris, but David and Becky. Maybe it was the black clothes, but I don't know."

Michael looked at Chris and Emilee whom both work

black and thought to himself *oops,* but then continued. "After Angela's suicide, the girl I liked, things were like a chain reaction. Becky left Chris and moved away, then Barry moved away also. I started having nightmares. And then-"

"What Mickey?" Chris asked. They all stared at the frightened look on Michael's face.

Dropping his burger, Michael asked. "Where are those journals?"

"Still in my shoulder bag. Why?"

Michael ran from the room leaving Chris, Michelle, and Emilee all to wait in silence.

"That's part of what I kept seeing in my nightmares! Right there!" Michael pointed to a page from the journals where David's father drew their family emblem.

"The emblem? What about it?" Chris asked.

"I don't know, all I can remember is that it was on the walls, and it had something to do with green lights. Only vivid dreams I can remember of back then are of Angela's ghost. And those didn't really stop until after Barry's death."

"When did your brother die?" Emilee asked.

"Huh, funny, but I don't remember if it was before or after the old Spook's farm burned to the ground."

"And that was the night the detectives showed up again because of David and going on about how we were all the cause of the fire." Chris added.

"Which we didn't start that fire." Michael insisted. "All we did was just break into it. Or rather, Chris and David did. They wanted to search an abandoned house, but of course I was just too chicken to go in. I was appointed the guard."

"And David found a flight jacket and pictures of his father. It didn't make any sense of why until now though."

"But he disappeared after that, and we didn't hear from David nor the detectives since then."

"Until now." Chris stated.

"Yep, until now."

"So that's it? That's what the detectives had us all worried about? Yes, I'll admit the whole alien ordeal is pretty creepy, but what you went through as kids sounds normal. Sure it was mature for your age, but normal none the less." Emilee said.

"You're not mad that we brought you into all of this?" Chris asked, confused.

"What's there to be mad about? You didn't bring us into anything. All the detectives want is that David guy, not y'all. All we can really do is wait."

"But what about the alien stuff? The books and everything else." Michelle added in. "I saw the lights too ya know? What if there *was* a war between aliens going on? At least I think that's what I read correctly."

"It has nothing to do with us though. All this is a matter of coincidence. No need to worry anymore." Chris said.

"I'm not so sure about that. I've got a really funny feeling that *something* isn't right. *Something* isn't adding up to me." Michelle admitted.

Chapter Fifty-One

All Michael could do was lay and stare up at the ceiling. His wife lay on her side with her back facing him. There was an unquenchable tension in the room, heavy in the air.

"Sweetheart, are you awake?" Michael asked. Softly, he rubbed his finger against her back.

"Kind of." She whispered.

"Are you okay? Upset any that we didn't tell you all what happened in our past?"

"No...well, maybe a little, just because I wish I would've known that about you before we married. It wouldn't have changed anything between us don't get me wrong, just would have gave me a heads up what I'm getting myself into."

"I'm really sorry. You have no idea how bad I feel. We honestly thought it was said and done. The detectives coming back are all but a shock to us also."

Michelle rolled over. "Mikey, that's okay, really. I'm only worried about what's going to happen. Like I said at dinner, something isn't right. I just can't put my finger on it."

"Nothing is going to happen, I promise."

"I really hope you are right. It's getting late, let's get some sleep. Good night, I love you."

"Good night, I love you too." They were both out in just minutes.

...

2:35 A.M. Michael awoke from a deep sleep with his mouth dry. He glanced at the clock while he pulled himself up out of the bed.

Downstairs, the house was quiet. He peeked through the blinds at the detectives across the street, and made sure the front and back doors were locked. They were. Before he could blink, a bright white light illuminated the house. Michael tripped over a coffee table and landed on the floor. On his back, he couldn't see anything in front of him, nor could he see the hands that pulled him up.

"Michael, you've got to listen to me."

He knew that voice from anywhere. "Angela? What-?"

"No time to explain Mikey. They're coming. They're coming and you've got to fight."

"Fight what though?"

"The aliens. David was right. I'm warning you now. They. Are. Coming."

"This has got to be a joke. Michelle, is that you?"

"Does this look like Michelle?" Angela's face zoomed closer into his. Her white hair swayed back and forth.

"Oh cra-" He fell over the couch. "You're real! You're real! But you're…you're…dead."

"That's right, I'm dead. I'm your angel, and as your angel I'm here to warn you."

"Okay, okay. I got it. They're coming."

"Michael, take me seriously. They killed me, and I

297

know you saw me that night. You saw me when I guided you to the Aurora Borealis."

"That really was you!"

"Yes, and the aliens were in the Borealis. They were watching. Waiting. For now."

"But if all of this was real, why us? Why now?"

"Because God knew you, Michelle, Emilee, and Chris all together can defeat them. Everything in your lives has led to this very moment. It's God's plan for y'all. I'm sorry, but I have to go now Mikey."

"Angela wait! Wait!"

...

"Wait!" Michael yelled. He woke himself up as well as Michelle.

"Michael, what is it?"

He sat up in a cold sweat and glanced over at the alarm clock. "I believe you now. I believe you."

"Well you should, the wife is always right."

Chapter Fifty-Two

"Hey wake up." Security officer Rydell insisted. He nudged his partner's chair with his foot. In his hand were two cups of coffee from Dunzy's Coffee Shop.

Security officer Morgan jumped from his sleep and smacked himself awake. "Oh geez, how long was you gone? I didn't mean to doze off."

"Not long at all. Here's you some coffee."

Morgan rubbed his eyes, gladly took the coffee. "Mmm, thanks. What time is it?"

He looked at the clock above the security monitors that of which he was *supposed* to be watching.

"Geez, it's only 7:44." Morgan continued. "This is going to be a long day. I can't seem to wake up. Why do they have us working all the way out here in Christy for? I thought this was a nothing town."

"Apparently there has been a lot of break-ins lately, and not to mention patients have been escaping. I'm guessing they just want extra security and eyes."

"Well we are posted at a hospital, where could all the cops be?"

"Small town, one sheriff. Just precautions is all. Hey, be thankful you're getting the extra overtime."

"Not on behalf of my dog, Booger. He kept me up half the night barking at the sky. Whatever he was seeing or smelling he didn't like."

"That's odd. My neighbor's dogs were doing the same thi-" Rydell was interrupted by a loud bang. Coffee spilled down his uniform as he continued. "What in the world was that?"

"Computers are frozen, nothing's moving on the monitors. I can't bring up any alarms." Morgan leaned forward and picked up the desk phone. "That's odd. Phone's dead too."

"So is my cell phone service. Nothing is working."

"This is too weird."

"My service is out too, but it's a hospital- cell phone service is terrible as is. Plus we are out in the middle of nowhere."

"I'm not so sure that's the just of it."

"What do you mean?"

"I think you need to see this, Morgan."

Morgan checked one last time at the computer monitors-still froze. The digital clock was stuck on 7:47.

"What are you wanting me to see?" Morgan asked as he made his way around the desk to Rydell.

Rydell gazed out of the window up at the sky. Total fright covered his face.

"What in the world?!" Morgan yelled out. He ran for the exit, but smacked right into the glass doors and passed out before he hit the floor. A power outage caused the doors to lock at that very second.

...

The power outage didn't just affect the hospital, it affected the entire town of Christy, Tennessee.

Cars were completely stopped in the middle of the streets, the drivers and passengers were unable to get out. Everyone's clocks and watches stopped at 7:47. With the cell phone services down, batteries went dead only seconds later. Kids on skateboards, bikes, and rollerblades were thrown to the ground as their wheels locked up. Birds, dogs, cats, and any animal around became silent and hid from the outside world.

Like a domino effect, it started with Christy and spread from one county to the next. Eventually the so call 'time freeze' was all over the world. Panic was inevitable, as every single door was locked shut. Any human being inside a building or even inside a room or bathroom stall were locked in. On the outside nobody knew what was going on, nor did anybody even know what to do. All there was to do was run and find safety or even shelter. Whatever that could be.

The sky turned a dark gray with storm clouds covering the world. Only the lightening was green- a bright neon green. It certainly didn't help to the chaos.

...

"I told you! I told you! I told you! I told you! I-." Mental patient Dillingham yelled out consistently. He was strapped to his bed in a straightjacket, but could still see the sky from his window.

There was an unusual silence that covered the world on Floor 13 of the Christy Hospital. Each patient stood at the windows, fingers raised and pointed to the sky. All were in unison chanting, "They're here. They're here. They're here."

Chapter Fifty-Three

"Chris! Chris! Wake up!" Emilee yelled. She shook him as hard as she could. When he slept, he slept hard.

"Flip-flopping-snicker-diddly-doo!" Chris said as he sat up real fast.

"What?"

"What?"

"What did you say?"

"I...what?"

"Never mind. Just look out the window. It's 7:47 A.M. and someone is shooting fireworks off."

"Fireworks? You've got to be kidding me. It's way too-." He ran to the window and pulled back the curtains. Glaring down towards Farmer Johnson's farm he said, "Oh no...those aren't fireworks."

Chris rushed and ran down the hall and kicked Michael awake. "Mikey come on let's go! Ted's going crazy with a gun."

"Chris wait!" Emilee pleaded. "Don't go, I really don't like this."

"It's okay, really. He's not after us. I just want you girls to stay right here on the porch no matter what. Promise?"

"I promise, I've just got a bad feeling about this. A very bad feeling."

"Everything's going to be okay, we'll be home safe." Chris kissed her on the forehead. "I love you."

"I love you too."

He smiled, looked down at Michael still sleeping and gave him a harder but swifter kick. "Michael up!"

"I'm up! Gosh!"

"Let's go, come on."

"Go where?" Michael groggily said.

"I just told you, Ted's. He's going crazy with a gun."

"Pssh, it's storming outside. Forget that."

"Michael, that isn't a storm."

"What...Oh...Snap!"

...

Ted glanced up to see Chris and Michael running toward him. He stopped shooting and stepped into his barn.

"Boys, thank goodness you are here. You're gonna need these." He tossed two rifles at the guys. They caught the guns and never even shot a rifle before.

"Ted...umm what's going on? Why are you shooting the sky?" Chris asked, now unsure why he even dragged Michael out there. He should've thought this through before making a sudden judgment.

"Ha-ha no son, I'm not just shooting the sky, I'm shooting those varmint aliens. I know those space creatures are here, and I'll be making sure they don't take this farm of mine. No sir." Ted raised his rifle and aimed. "Come on men, be men and shoot like men. Don't fright, kill these boogers with all your might."

All three heads turn to the sounds of screeching tires around the block. A cruiser chased after a man at full speed. The man ran with his life on the line.

"David?" Chris asked out loud.

One foot after the other down the gravel path, David yelled out frantically, "They're here!! It's happening!!"

Fires rang out from inside the unmarked cruiser. Detective Marshall and Acuff hung out the windows with guns locked on David. Ten Johnson took fire at the aliens in the sky once more.

Reverend Brown watched the entire moment from the church window. His hands clutched onto his Bible. The tips of his fingers turned white. "God be with us. Bless us in our times of trouble dear Lord."

A single bright green light flashed with a bang- much louder than thunder.

Farmer Johnson froze in the moment during a shot, smoke and blast from his barrel hung in the air. David- as he was being shot in the back when the flash was hit- stood frozen in mid-step as green blood splattered in the air. The detectives still hung out of the windows, blasts frozen from their guns.

The earth was in complete silence- silence besides a hum of U.F.O.s hovering in the clouds.

Chapter Fifty-Four

"What are you doing? How can you possibly write at a time like this?" Emilee asked as she paced back and forth in the living room. Chris sat on the couch with Michael and Michelle huddled up on the love seat across the room.

"I have to document this. Finish David's journal. Something is really wrong here in Christy."

...

From the final pages of David Lowery's journal.

We stood there, in total shock. Time had been frozen before our eyes. What in the world is happening? David is practically dead on his feet, as they say. He hangs in the air, blood motionlessly splattered before him.

The last words he said to us- before shot to death- was, 'They're here!!! It's happening!!!'

We stood and watching, nothing. Literally nothing. Everything was silent except for a metallic hum from inside a wall of clouds above us.

"This is weird. This is really weird." Michael said.

"Let's get out of here...now." I said as we ran back to my house.

Our wives were screaming from the porch as we ran, "What's going on?!"

"I have no clue, I just feel safer…inside, away from here."

I locked the door behind us. We all stood by the living room window and stared out waiting for something to happen. Anything. But nothing happened and though everything was only a few minutes it felt like hours.

"Hey, my phone's not working." I said while I tried to call Sheriff Boston. Of course I really didn't think there was anything he could've done at the moment.

Everyone checked their phones at the same time, all dead.

"TV's not working either." Michael added.

"Interesting." I whispered to myself. "Is there any electronic devices in this house that does work?"

We all scattered and checked, but just like the phones, nothing worked.

Michelle stepped in, "I wonder if it's like this all over town?"

"Well…we could go outside and find out… At least I don't think anything would happen due to the fact everything is practically frozen." I suggested.

"Yes and no, I mean what are those humming sounds coming from the sky? And what about the green lightening? I don't like this at all. To be honest, I never thought I'd say this, but I believe David. I believe he was right and we are under attack…by aliens." Michael said.

Michelle twitched, and cold chills ran down her spine. "I've got to agree with my husband on this one."

"What has changed your mind?" I asked Michael.

"My dream last night...about Angela."

We all sat down to listen.

"At first," Michael continued. "I thought my Angela dreams were all stress- especially becoming sober, and of guilt because of her death. Now I think she was just warning me, warning us. She told me in last night's dream that we're going to be attacked and that God wants us to fight them to save the world."

Emilee burst out in hysterical laughter. "I'm sorry, I'm sorry, but are you all playing a trick on me? You know, funny ha-ha? Listen to yourselves."

She turned to me and continued, "Chris, baby, I love you, but all of this sounds like something you'd write. It's just one thing after another that has me believing this is all made up. Come on, stop pulling my leg."

"Sweetheart, none of this is made up. I know it seems that way, but I'm serious. Go look out the window and tell me David isn't still being shot on his feet. Tell me Farmer Johnson isn't blazing the sky. And the sky- tell me the sky isn't flashing green lightening as we speak. My books may be a tiny bit farfetched, but all of this...I certainly couldn't make up."

The smile on her face faded just as quick as she let it appear. Emilee jolted to the window and peered out. Admitting defeat, her head fell as she turned to us and sighed. "So what do we do now? If God wants us to fight, how do we even approach this? I don't understand why He chose us out of the entire world. We aren't exactly the most fit...or rather sane bunch of country folk there is. You know what I mean?"

"Well who was that kid in the bible that took down a giant?" Michael asked.

"Oddly enough, David. And the giant was Goliath." I answered Michael. Suddenly I could see where he was getting at with this.

"I'm no prophet or anything, but what if these aliens was David's Goliath? Our David not THE David. And because David put his trust into us, God gave us the task instead. Maybe God sees something in us that we can't. After all, God does know everything."

"Michael, I do believe you are right." Michelle added in, "God does have a reason for everything and all of us coming together probably wasn't just a coincidence. My best guess is we pray about it, be patient, and wait on God to show us the way to His will for us."

And we did just that.

...

We patiently waited and waited for some kind of answer. Possibly even a sign. Not that any of us were terrified, we just did not know what to do. Nobody said anything for what seemed liked the longest time. All that day seemed like a dreary rainy day. Only there wasn't any rain, but the mist never did dissipate, nor did the green lightening. It felt as if the day was covered by a continuous thunderstorm, and here we were cozy by a fire. And me of course in my office.

"Knock, knock." Emilee said as she entered in.

"Hey sweetheart." I sat up from having my nose in David's journal.

"What are you up to?"

"Just trying to figure all of this out. Figure out what we are all supposed to do. I guess I'm just waiting on God's sign. When He's ready to answer our prayer, He'll surely let us know."

"I think it all just takes patience. After all we aren't really certain that God wants us to fight. We're putting our trust in human conditions. Well, except for that David guy, I'm not so sure if he was human or not, but still."

I closed the book.

"You're right, it's all really up to God what we do."

We walked into the living room, Michael and Michelle watched out the window from their knees like little kids waiting on snow.

"Boo!" I yelled. Michael screamed and fell backwards off the couch.

Laying on his back, he looked up at me with frightened eyes, "Dude-Wha-what was that all about?"

"I don't know, tension breaker I guess." I turned to my wife whom had a smile on her face. Gosh I love her. "Sweetheart, could you get me a pot of water and coffee and creamer?"

"Yes master, yes." She replied with laughter.

"Are you seriously thinking of coffee at a time like

this? Umm have you forgotten that the power is out? Explain to me how you are even going to make it?"

"Simmer down my child. I plan on rocking this coffee the old school way, yo,- boiling water over the fire. Word."

I placed a log into the fire and glanced over at Michelle. A part of her seemed to want to relax, but another was still terrified. "Michelle, it's okay to relax. Loosen up. And that goes for you too Mikey. We're all terrified and confused and none of us knows what in the world is going on. So the way I see it, it's best we live life and be happy until we know what the Lord wants from us. And even then we should be happy also. It's His way or no way."

"I don't know, it just doesn't seem that easy."

"I agree with my wife," Michael said. He pulled himself up and wrapped his arms around Michelle's leg. "I don't see it being possible to just let all worries go. Especially at a time like this- when literally evil awaits right outside the door."

"I can't just be pessimistic right now and give up hope and faith that God will be our strengths. After all the bible does say to leave all of our burdens and worries upon Him and He will give us rest."

Emilee walked in with coffee and supplies in her hands.

"Something tells me not to give up..." I continued, "On my belief that in while we are patiently waiting, God's answer WILL come. Not meaning in the sense that it'll come regardless, but that it'll come basically when we least expect it. Just have faith in me, for a little while at least. And let's live for the moment with no regards to those boogers outside."

"Shew that was a workout." Emilee said as she dropped the supplies by the fireplace. "What did I miss? And there you go my dear, have at it."

"I think I'm trying to bring the faith out of these two peoples. Or at least convince them of their faith."

"You mean like in Hebrew chapter 11 verse 1? Faith is being sure of what we hope for and certain of what we don't see."

"Exactly! And thank you my dear for bringing me my medicines."

"It's not that we don't have faith, we just don't see how we can have 'fun' knowing what's outside." Michelle added in.

"But do we actually know if we, as in us four, are under attack? Maybe we are safe in here and they don't know we are even here..."

"Emilee," I chimed in, "I'm pretty sure they do know that we are, but as of how safe we are that I'm not so sure. David was coming especially for us, so yeah I'm sure they know. I'm not meaning to add fuel to the fire- I apologize for that-, but look guys, we can't keep worrying ourselves with 'what if's'. That's where we need to put our full trust in the Lord."

They knew I was right and that we had the least bit of control to the situation. All we had was the moment and the time together.

"Okay, so let's just say we put all of this off and just have our minds on us right now; what are we possibly going to do? No cable, no tv, no electronics. We now be back in the olden days, yes sir. I'm at a loss." Michael mentioned.

I poured everyone a cup of coffee. "Well first off, we enjoy our coffee. It's not Dunzy's quality coffee, but it'll do. After that, we'd just have to see."

I won't lie, it was a bit difficult at first accepting total silence, besides the crackling of the fire. After being accustomed to the modern day technologies, breaking free was a bit torturous. Though as it left us with nothing but our thoughts to keep our minds occupied, I realized what good could come out of the situation.

Our poison filled minds of the world could be renewed to a sense of purity. It could give us a chance to really just slow down, rest, pray, and grow our hearts stronger to one another and to the Lord Almighty as well.

...

"Hey Chris?"

"Hmm?" I asked, deep in thought of my next move. Michael and I had an intense game of Battleship going on.

"Who is this in this picture?" Michelle curiously asked, focused on the pictures on the wall. "I've walked by these plenty of times, but I never stopped to actually look."

"Umm." I glanced up from laying on my belly in the living room floor. "That's a picture of your dear husband, the famous Angela, and myself at a school concert."

"THE Angela?"

"Yep, that's the one."

"Dude...I can't believe you still have that. Well a picture of her I mean." Michael was shocked.

"That photo was taken just a couple of hours before 'the trouble' began and our friendship was beginning to be in a turmoil."

"I really don't see what you two seen in her. She isn't that attractive. You can just tell from her smile and how she has her arm around both of you that there's something shady about her. I'm sorry to say that, but it's true."

"No baby, you are right though. That girl was just more trouble than she was taken for. We were just teenagers with way more hormones than we could muster." Michael turned to me and asked. "And what do you mean that was the night the troubles began?"

"Because the entire night before that she flirted back and forth between us. It was like she was trying to decide which guy she wanted to be with. At the time, you had the looks and charm, and I was the good guy- best friend type. She led us on and set us up.

Though our teenager adolescent minds really believed she wanted us, we kept giving in to her. So then after the picture was taken, she chose you. After all, you were the bad kid. You have to admit that you were. And then I walked in on you two making-out on the picnic tables."

"So that must be where the tension between us began."

"Yep. To beat it all, she and I went to the movies the next day. Oh yeah, that didn't make the matter any less confusing. She seemed to have a good time. Though Monday came along and then she acted like nothing had ever happened, and take a wild guess who she was with?"

"Me?"

"Yeah, which it hurt, but I stuck around at first. I thought maybe I could handle it and eventually someone would come along for me."

"But no one did."

"Nope. And I got tired of being the third wheel all of the time, so I stopped coming around. Then there was David and you know what happened after that."

"Man, I'm sorry. I didn't realize how much that was affecting us then. I know when it did break us apart, you and I hated each other. But looking back on it, we were just kids. That just seemed like too much pressure for us to be having."

"It's all steps to where we are now in little odd ways. We wouldn't be here if not."

"Oddly enough, yeah that's right."

"Your high school years sounded like a soap opera." Michelle laughed.

"Sweetheart, unfortunately, that's how it really was. High school was a pain. You didn't go through any drama?"

"No. Emilee and I weren't the most popular kids. We just stuck to ourselves in the library and read and kept to our studies. That's all we really knew. And it was a way *that God kept us from the temptations and troubles."*

"Which speaking of keeping to yourselves, my wife has been in the restroom awhile now. I better go check on her." I pulled myself up to my knees. "Oh and Mickey, by the way, B-6."

"B-6? Dang it! You sunk my Battleship!"

"You're welcome."

"Sweetheart," I knocked on the bathroom door. "Is everything okay?"

"Yeah...umm, can you come in here a minute?"

"Of course."

Not sure what I was going to walk into, I entered to see Emilee gripping the sink. Perspiration was on her forehead. I kissed her on the back of the neck. A single candle flame radiated somewhat of the restroom.

"Chris, you may want to sit down for what I'm about to tell you."

Chapter Fifty-Five

Journal entry continued…

Emilee and I walked out of the restroom and each of us had tears in our eyes. God really has a plan for everything. No matter what, He always has a blessing through any circumstances.

We sat down on the couch beside Michelle and Mickey whom set up themselves a game of Battleship. Which by the way, what is it with us and battles?

"Y'all okay?" Michelle asked.

"Yes everything is just fine…just fine." Emilee answered.

"Very good, very good."

I so wanted to talk to everyone about what my wife and I talked about in the restroom, but I felt that it should be between us at the moment. Instead, I turned to Michelle. "So Michelle, before I left the room, you were talking about how you and Emilee were different from everybody and just stuck to yourselves. What did you do outside of school?"

"I don't mean to interrupt, but does anyone see the irony in all of this?" Michael began. "I mean, here we are waiting patiently on the Lord, when the world could be ending outside and yet we're opening doors that should be

closed. What's the point in all of this? I mean seriously? I'm sure this is all fun and games, but my dreams...David's journal...everything? Aren't we supposed to fight? Don't get me wrong, but I can't see how anyone can't see how obvious it is. We must fight."

"That was so random Mickey, and yet it does make perfect sense. It's all very strange to me too. From the talk that Chris and I just had, I believe there could possibly be more to the story we don't know yet. Which maybe these conversations will lead to something that God is going to open our eyes up to. I understand where you are getting at though Mikey, I really do."

"Well, then why aren't we fighting just yet? But carry on then."

"We really didn't do much," Michelle began. "We had our church groups if we weren't at book stores and or volunteering. I know it doesn't sound exciting, but to us it was. It kept us out of trouble, and we met a lot of good people along the way. What about you guys?"

"Video games and movies for the most part. Before girls came along."

"And not to mention my drug and alcohol problems." Michael added.

"Oh and the occasional Shovel Rock game."

"Ha, ha, ha, I totally forgot about Shovel Rock. Wow, good times. Good times."

"Umm, what's Shovel Rock?" Michelle curiously asked.

"It's in a way like baseball, only you use a shovel instead of a bat and a-" a sudden chill and peace came over me. All worries and fears of the morning…(or afternoon…or even…I don't know what time of day it is. Stupid aliens for stopping the time.) was suddenly completely gone.

"A rock instead of baseball." Michael finished my sentence. "Did you blank out old man?"

Even this brought a smile to Michael's face.

"You guys had way too much time on your hands." my wife added. "Although, it brings out the creative side in Chris' novels."

"Chris? Earth to Chris." Michael snapped his fingers in front of my eyes. "Hey Chrissy Poo, come home."

"Whoa, hey sorry." I came to. "I just had an epiphany."

"Sounds like something I'd have after a business meeting in the restroom." Michael said.

"Michael!" Michelle burst out.

"What? I just had a sudden flashback of my teenage ways. Scary."

"No, no keep that. It's a good thing. We're going to need it. It brings you a certain sense of energy- an energy we had when we were kids. Do you remember when it was okay to just have fun and not have a worry ever?"

"Okay then, Chris, what are we supposed to do then? I mean what are we doing?"

"Mikey, I think it's time for a much needed game of Shovel Rock."

"Shovel-! You can't be serious right now? You are aren't you? There's no way we could-" Michael stopped himself and sighed. "This is so stupid, but dadgum I know you're right."

"No, no, no, no, no. This is just crazy. There's got to be another way. I understand what you are getting at, but how do you expect to stop an alien invasion with shovels and rocks?"

"Michelle's right, Chris. I'm going to have to side with her on this one. Given the circumstances- and you know what I'm talking about- I don't think that's the safest way to go. Or the smartest."

"Oh I know, it SOUNDS that way, and I don't like it either. In all honesty though, doesn't it say that David defeated Goliath with only stones? We all know that faith is confidence in hope and assurance of what we can't see. I feel this is what God wants us to do."

"But Chris, you are talking about going against aliens with rocks-"

"And a shovel."

"Yes, and a shovel, when they could have laser guns, or, or, or bombs, or I don't know- anything that goes boom. Look, they've already got the ability to stop time and our electronic devices all-together, who knows what other types of weaponry they have on board their saucers." Michael said.

"That's exactly my point, we DON'T know what they have. Shoot, they could have weaponry that consists of squirt guns, sling-shots that fires grapes, and that are harmless for all we know. Hey, they may not even have anything at all except mind control. We'd be the ones scaring them away."

"Very unlikely Chris. Very unlikely." Michelle said. The room went silent.

Michael paced back and forth along the hallway and took quick glances at the photo of Angela, himself, and I. His arms were crossed and tears swelled in his eyes.

"Michael? Sweetie, what's wrong?" Michelle asked. Concerned, she made her way towards him and wrapped her arms around his neck.

He laid his head on her shoulder and let out the tears. "I'm just scared. So very scared. I really don't want this, but guys I know Chris is right. We have to do this. There's just been so much that's gone on here lately, I just don't want to lose you Michelle. You are my wife and you've made me the happiest man I've ever been. I'm just not ready to give up on that."

"Mickey, I promise you, you will never lose me. Okay? As much as I hate to admit it, Chris might just be right. This may be the only way, but with it being God's will, God will get you through it. You and Chris both. God wouldn't put us together and marry us just to take it all away just as fast as we met."

"Okay. Okay, I believe you." Michael looked toward my way before squeezing Michelle tight against him. "Chris, I really hope you are right about this."

"Thanks man, I'm behind God 100% on this." I turned to Emilee. She did not look too happy. Though, honestly, I don't blame her. It's not every day we fight against aliens. "Sweetheart, are you okay? What's your thought about all of this?"

"I hate it. I hate it with a passion, only because of what you and I talked about earlier. But I have to agree with Michelle on that God will keep us safe and free from any harm. We are all in this together."

"No."

"What? What do you mean no?"

"Not you all, just Michael and I. I don't want the women fighting, given that of the conversation we had. Not until we know for sure. Michael and I will protect our wives, as well as the rest of humanity, but still. I want you two to stay in here. Michael do you agree?"

"Honestly, yes I do. I think that's a good idea."

"Okay good. Good." I took a deep breath. "Well, shall we get on with it?"

Michael slumped down, "Ugh, fine. I guess now is as good a time as any."

"Wait! Wait!" Michelle stopped us. "I feel safer if we prayed before y'all went. It's the right thing to do."

And we did. Spent time kissing and holding our tearful wives close as if we were leaving for a long day's work. All of us were unsure of what was to happen next, only that we keep one foot in front of the other.

Michael and I exited through the side door through the dining room and into the garage. We grabbed the shovels from beside a tool shelf and then headed toward another side door that led outside.

"Chris wait a second." Michael stopped me. "Look, just in case something happens in the next little bit that we *don't get another chance to talk, I think I know why you wouldn't let the wives fight along beside us. If it's what I think, then I'm proud of you. I love you man, thanks for everything you've done for me. You've never given up no matter what, and stuck by my side since we were kids. You're a great man."*

"Thanks man, I appreciate that. I can't say what we talked about, I promised my wife that I wouldn't tell. But if you think you know, then thank you. And Mikey, I love you too. You've always been my best friend and always will be. This is not the end of us, so don't you even worry about that. We're gonna come home to our wives and live happy every after."

"Well I don't know about happy ever after. We are married you know. Ha-ha."

"That's true, there will be those ups and downs, but we'll make the best of it with love and care."

"Yeah man."

We both knew it was time.

"Okay, let's do this."

<u>Chapter Fifty-Six</u>

Journal entry continued: As told by Emilee Wilson.

My husband is the writer in the family, so I apologize from here on out if my entry isn't as exciting as his was, or as well written. But I'll do my best and continue with the story while the boys play. And I promise you, as Michelle and I sit by the window that everything you have read is true and that everything you are about to read is true. None of this is fiction.

I can only imagine that whomever does pick up this journal to read that they are wondering, 'how can they just sit there so calmly watching their men fight before their eyes?' Well trust me, we aren't calm. We are both nervous wrecks and being hyped up on coffee doesn't help. What does help is writing in this journal. For some reason getting my thoughts out and down on paper is relaxing me some.

But any who. I wonder what's taking the men so long in the garage? I can only imagine the macho talk that's going on between them right now when us ladies aren't around. Probably going a little something like this, 'Yeah man lets do this thang! Let's kick some alien booty!' and then grunt, cheer, and scratch their own behinds. You know how men are.

There they are. I see them, walking so casual around to the front yard, shovels in their hands. They look so tough, but Mikey is shaking so badly. It's obvious how scared he is.

Nothing is happening. The guys look at each other and shrug their shoulders, unsure of how to make contact. Chris waves his hands in the air, "Hellloooo, aliens we're down here. We're ready to fight. Come on come get us."

My husband, I swear. But still, nothing.

"Oh Lord, did my husband just-?" Michelle asked in total shock.

Yep, Mikey did just pull down his pants and moon the aliens. And yet, nothing. Having just the slightest thought that we were wrong, that the aliens weren't here to attack, these guys turn to walk back toward the house. It was then that the first U.F.O. made its move- swooping down out of the clouds like a bat. There was a simple shape to it, like a skinny football. And it was shiny with no markings on it except for

...on the bottom. Green lights circled around the outer edge. A blacked-out dome sat on the top leaving no view of the creature that lurked inside.

Just as fast as it made its appearance known, it was

taken down by our men with garden tools. The creature had made a shot at the men with a green laser beam, that of which on reflex, Chris instinctively swung the shovel around him. The beam ricocheted and blasted against the saucer. It exploded on contact and shook our house. Debris and shrapnel flew every which way. Awesome.

And to beat it all, it was the blast that started the war. Our men were laughing. Apparently, they thought the explosion was awesome as well and were having a good time out there. Having fun while facing death with shots being fired at them and to have saucers exploding every which way, all the while we were nervous inside the house. Men.

Boom. Boom. Boom.

Left and right they exploded. Chris and Michael swung every which way, having a game out of the battle. Grown men looking like kids playing a video game- a virtual 3D video game, I might add. I couldn't even tell you how many they have destroyed in such a very short time. Knock on wood, we might just have this battle in the bag and save the world after all.

Though I believe I spoke too soon. Everything just stopped. Dead silence. No flashing lights. No humming. Nothing. The men didn't loosen up and let their guard down. It couldn't be that easy of a win. Could it? Something's not right, regardless of the entire battle not being right. But something's not right.

Michael mouthed the words, 'Is that it? Did we do it?'

"Whoa, is that an earthquake?" Michelle asked.

Vibrations began to shake the house.

"I don't think so." My eyes never left the men, they felt it too.

Their eyes were locked to the sky. Each step they took backwards I saw what they were gazing at. A U.F.O. more than double the size of the fighter saucers lowered itself to the ground. Underneath, landing pads form while the green triangular emblem spins and picking up speed so fast that it was nothing but a bright green blur. Out from the light opens a hatch, just shy of landing in the middle of the street.

The men stand up, raising their swor...shovels at high, ready for come what may.

Figures walk down the hatch in tune at the same pace. People? Aliens? Only an outline of whomever...or whatever, could be seen over the glare of the light. Michelle leaned in closer, and I believe we were both expecting to hear the famous, 'We come in peace.'

Once the gathering of bodies descended from the U.F.O., the light faded but the hatch remained open leaving a black darkness into the abyss. Each body's eyes were closed with pale skin almost transparent. Not one of their hair styles nor fashions were alike. Each were from a different time and era.

"Is that old man Spooks...Eric...the boys from Halloween night? Oh man, it's everyone who became missing over the years. The...the...the aliens got 'em!" Chris yelled out.

"And there's..." Michael dropped his shovel. The color

from his face drained to the same color as the pale bodies. "Barry."

"Mikey be careful. I don't think that's Barry. I'm not so sure the aliens would let them free, you know?"

"Oh, come on, Chris! Don't you see, they are right there! Right in front of us! Haven't you ever seen an alien movie before? All they do is experiment and let them go. That's all they are doing now."

"Mikey...I-"

"Shut up Chris! Just shut up for once! Stop trying to be all high and mighty. You can't always be right all the time. This is about my brother! MY brother! Just-! Forget it!"

Michael ran, screaming to Barry that he was coming. The body's eyes open, bright green lights shine from their empty eye sockets. Faces emotionless. Michael came to a dead stop and fell to his knees.

His head turned to Chris, drained from his emotions. "I'm so sorry Chris. I love you. Lord please forgive me for all I've done."

The last ounce of fight Michael had in him was gone. He had nothing left. Seeing Barry, or what was portrayed to be Barry, suddenly all the pain and anger he held deep down for many years came rushing back in. All he could do was all he knew to do: pray and pray for forgiveness.

It all happened in a flash. Couldn't have even been seconds, but merely instantly. Both at the same moment Chris and Michelle yelled in unison, "Michael no!!!"

And then he was gone. One blast from the mother ship, Michael's life was taken from him. All that left was a charred body on the ground. I tried to stop her, but Michelle broke free from my grip and ran towards the door. The green lights from the body's eye sockets shot lasers at Chris. He was fast to react, knocking each shot back at the bodies. Michelle zoomed past, charging toward the ship through the bodies with her eyes dead straight ahead.

Chris did not run. He courageously stood his ground until the last body fell. Something then told him to get cover. We could only imagine WHAT was going on inside the mother ship once Michelle had made her way inside through the open hatch.

All I know is I need my husband. The End.

Chapter Fifty-Seven

Journal entry finale: As told by Chris Wilson.

When the jerks killed Michael, I knew it was all survival from then on out. Instinct kicked in to keep going, there was no time to mourn. I knew that Michael was in a far better off place now, being welcomed by Jesus and Barry at the pearly gates in heaven above. It was my job to protect my wife and Michelle now.

Though, now with Michelle, that caught me off guard. I didn't expect her nor anybody to run past me at that moment, especially straight through a war zone and straight into enemy territory. My guess is a wife's rage of losing the love of her life, murdered right in front of her eyes would cause her to react with vengeance. And vengeance she did well proclaim.

I kept on fighting, it was all I could do. As the last body fell, I waited for a more exuberant army to come, but the way the mother ship shook side to side and then began to rise, I had a feeling that I just needed to get away from there. My fight was over. So I ran for cover behind the willow tree in our backyard. Do I know what all went on inside the ship? No, but Lord I wish I did.

My wife burst out from the front door and practically leaped from the porch to get to me. She wrapped her arms around me as tightly as she possibly could and in an odd romantic way we watched the fireworks together under the willow tree.

The ship rose into the sky swaying out of control before exploding in a massive mushroom cloud of green light. The fog and clouds floated away to let in a beautiful sunrise shining down on us. Life was back to normal, time started back up. Morning birds chirping, flying into the sky to get the day started with.

"Is it over?"

"Yeah, yeah it's over." I said and kissed Emilee on the forehead. We both cried and prayed at the same time.

But I was wrong, so wrong that it was over. Gun shots began blaring and men were screaming. I completely forgot all about Farmer Johnson and David being gunned down by the detectives.

We started to run that way, but Emilee dead stopped. I saw why but kept going.

The blasting was over by the time I made my way to the farm. Farmer Johnson lowered his rifle and emptied his shells with his eyes never leaving me as I ran past him to David. David now laid face down in a puddle of green blood. Somehow he still had a pulse.

"Ch-Chris?"

"Yeah David, it's me. Don't move, let it come easy." We both knew what was coming.

"I know Chris...this...is...it...for...me. I saw...the...flash...thank yo-" David took his last breath and died right there in Farmer Johnson's field.

I looked over to see shadows moving close to us, feet

squishing on the morning grass.

"Mr. Wilson? What happened?" Detective Acuff asked. Both detectives had no color to their faces what so ever. Both were in shock and shaking.

"What you don't know?" I stood up. "I believe you've got a murder on your hands."

I started to walk to Ted whom was casually making his way up toward us also.

"Mr. Wilson?" Detective Marshall now asked.

"Yeah, detective?"

"Did we- Did we-?"

"Yeah you did. Do you not remember chasing him down and shooting profusely at him?"

"No, we got a hotel room last night and the last I remember was falling asleep in bed and then waking with my gun in my hand just now."

"Huh, I guess they did have mind control devices after all."

"Who's they?"

"You're looking at him."

I met with Ted halfway down the hill. "They were, here weren't they?"

"Yes they were, Ted."

"I saw 'em and I shot 'em. They were here only for just a second, but I saw them. I told you I'd get those boogers."

"Thank you Ted, you did get them. I can vouch for that. It's over now."

Like I had said before, we don't know what happened

inside the mother ship, but what we do know is that Michelle is alive. We found her laying on the ground, unconscious. Somehow she made it out before the explosion. It was a miracle to say the least.

Emilee sat beside her. "I called Dr. Cravens and he said there was an uproar at the hospital, but he's sending out an ambulance. And I called Sheriff Boston, he's on his way also."

"Okay. Good. Thank you sweetheart." I fell down beside my wife and took her hand. We both stared up at the clear sunny sky.

"Chris, what are we going to tell everyone about what happened?"

"We don't...well, not yet anyway. I'm going to write all of this down, and finish up the journal. As of now, I'll put it away for a rainy day. I don't what to say about Michael, but with David the detectives have not a clue as to what they did. The Feds will do with them what they will, but as for us, only we and God knows what happened today. And God will see to that."

And by this is how I will end this journal entry. What David's father had started many years ago is now complete. Truth be told, I don't know how to really end this. A lot more went on this past week that caused a large amount of confusion to the people.

For one, is that Michelle is doing just fine. Dr. Stalls says because of the detective's double murder of David Lowery and Michael Gable, she suffered a mental breakdown, but is recovering slowly. Which I don't blame her for breaking down, and that she nor the town remembers much about that very morning. Once time began again, it begin right where it left off. Everybody in the entire world suffered a split second power surge along with an extreme feeling of déjà vu, or so that's what the papers and news stations are saying.

After three days, nobody seemed to care anymore. The only thing that was really paid attention to was Michael's funeral. Can't you blame them?

So, I'm going to leave this final note about David. When his body was found, it was believed that the detectives shot him with acid filled bullets which was the cause of his death. Answers unknown as to why they could've caused this to happen. David was laid to rest by his father's grave in the mountains of Tennessee. Together, now their truth has been told, the world has been saved, and their work (this journal), is done.

END OF ENTRY.

Chapter Fifty-Eight

7 years later.

Emilee put on her pajama bottoms and a long sleeved shirt getting ready for bed. She heard laughter coming from the bedroom down the hall- laughter that should have died down minutes ago. Though she knew when it came to the two guys in her life, they were inseparable from one another.

She eased her way down the hall, glanced at the picture frames on the walls. The frames before she came along were once of Chris and Michael, but now seven years later they are filled with not only of pictures of her and him, and of pictures of their son Michael.

It was hard to believe how fast seven years has flown by. Just yesterday it seemed like she and Chris were meeting for the first time at the Christy County Halloween bonfire and now their son was in the 2nd grade. Life has certainly been a blessing.

"Knock, knock," Emilee said. She entered into Michael's bedroom. Chris was on the bed beside his son, both of them looking through a photo album.

"Hey sweetheart, you ready for bed?" Chris asked as he glanced up to Emilee.

Michael held onto his favorite stuffed animal- a tiny tiger that of which he named Tiger. "Hi mommy."

"Mikey, what are you doing up?" She turned to Chris, "And yes I'm ready for bed, but SOMEBODY is keeping a little boy awake that has school in the morning."

"Awe mom." Both boys sighed.

"Can't we just finish this one page? Daddy was just telling me about him and Uncle Michael."

"Well, just one more picture. And then it's nighty night for you mister."

"Okay! Yay!" He leaned over and locked his eyes on the album. "Let's see…what happened in this one?"

Chris smiled at the picture. "That was when your uncle and I were at a high school football game and he was being pushed into the bushes."

"Why would he do that daddy?"

"Because…he loved the attention. He loved to make a fool of himself just to impress girls. He was a wild one, that man."

"Is that why you named me after him? Because he was wild and funny?"

"No, because he was a good man despite all of that. He was loyal to his friends and a really nice guy when he was older."

"I wish I could've met him. He seems like he would've liked me."

"He would've loved you and treated you like his own brother. And you will meet him someday, not any time soon, but someday. Do you know why?"

"Because of heaven?"

"That's exactly right. Good job, son." Chris closed the

album. "Okay, time for bed Stinker."

Both Chris and Emilee tucked him into bed. They kissed him good night and turned on his dinosaur night light.

"Good night buddy, we love you."

"Good night mommy, good night daddy." They were almost out the door. "Hey daddy, when are the aliens coming back?"

Chris and Emilee gave each other a confused glare. "Umm, what do you mean aliens, son?"

"The aliens you and Uncle Michael fought before I was born. You did fight aliens, didn't you?"

"No we didn't. Where did you hear that from?"

Emilee grabbed his hand. Seven years ago after the attack, they made it to where their names nor Michael's and Michelle's names weren't even mentioned in any newspaper or news segment. Not even the town knew about what really went on that very morning. All except Farmer Johnson. He was the only source.

"Uncle Michael does. He visits my dreams sometimes. He says one day they will come back, that he will keep me safe. Is that true daddy?"

"No buddy, that's not true. It's only a dream. Dreams are only dreams. They aren't real okay?"

"Okay daddy. Good night." Michael rolled over on his side. They eased the bedroom door shut.

Emilee made it to the bedroom before she let out her tears.

"Gah, I really hate lying to him. I know it's for the best

that he doesn't know about that, but still."

"I thought this was all over Chris. Why is this happening to us? Why now? Why with our baby?"

"I don't know sweetheart, I really don't know. It's just got to be over. It must be, we saw *it* blow up didn't we? We saw it happen."

Chris held onto his wife.

"We did, but I don't want them to hurt my baby. They killed Michael, they killed all those people. Why can't they leave us alone?"

"Maybe it's all just dreams. Maybe we don't have anything to worry about."

"But can you honestly believe that though?"

"Lord willing I must, otherwise the 'what ifs' will destroy me. I have to protect my family regardless."

...

He swung back and forth on a swing. A cool autumn breeze gave him the feeling as if he was flying high in the sky. Being an only child, his imagination ran wild. No other kids were on the playground, only him and mommy whom was on a bench reading one of daddy's new books.

Up high he went and back down with a swoosh of air. Up again, and down, but...where's mommy? Her book lays on its back, pages turned in the wind.

"Mommy? Mommy where are you?"

No answer.

Michael knew not to leave the playground, that was

for certain. He knew to stay in one spot if he lost his mommy or daddy. He took a seat on the bench, hoping she would come back. When she didn't after what seemed like forever, he wanted to run for help. But who could he run to?

There was nobody else on the street. Nobody on the sidewalks, nor any kids or their parents at the playground. He really was all alone. But wait, there was Mr. Dunzy at the coffee shop behind him. Mr. Dunzy could help. He always gave Michael a free hot chocolate every time he seen him. That would really warm him up. Only one problem, he wasn't supposed to leave the playground-especially by himself.

That plan was ruined. Now what? It looked like rain, but not just rain: a heavy storm. A once sunny sky was now being covered by a dark, dark, black cloud.

Thunder. Pow! Green lightening.

Michael screamed and ran towards Dunzy's Coffee Shop. Stuck in the middle of the street, he couldn't move any farther. He'd kick his legs as fast as he could, but never moved an inch.

"Michael…" A woman's voice whispered to him. The voice echoed in his ears. "Michael…"

He turned his head to see a woman floating in the air. Black hair with bright green streaks floated with the wind along with the black dress she wore. Her eyes were green lights and she smiled a smiled with sharp jagged teeth.

"Tell your daddy we are coming. We are coming and the world will be ours."

"Who…who are you?"

"You just tell him!"

Lightening flashed. The woman was gone but left a trail of green smoke in the shape of…

…

"Daddy! Daddy!" Michael screamed as he woke from his nightmare.

Chris and Emilee burst into the bedroom. "What is it buddy? I'm here."

He was hysterical. Tears rolled down his cheeks. He wrapped his arms around his daddy's neck. "I had a dream, a very bad dream. A woman said- she said she was coming to get you. And that- and that- the world was hers."

"Buddy there's nobody coming to get me, I promise. I'm not going anywhere."

"Please don't, her green eyes were just scary." His tears flowed from his eyes.

"It's okay, it was only a dream. Daddy will take care of it." Chris said, his eyes on Emilee's. They both knew without even saying it that the battle will happen again. This time though, over the sake of their son. It wouldn't be pretty. They will end it when the day comes. They will protect Michael.

Chapter Fifty-Nine

Chris and Emilee stayed with Michael through the rest of the night. He slept soundlessly with not one more nightmare. They contemplated whether to keep him out of school the next morning. Yes it was only a dream, but after everything they've been through it could be real. Could it?

In the end, they decided against simple paranoia and dropped him off at school. A normal day as any day. At first, no he didn't want to go, but once he saw his friends all memories of the dreams were gone. A happy, carefree boy once again.

...

The atmosphere in Dunzy's Coffee Shop had changed in the past seven years. With both Michael and Michelle gone it has been less cheerful and even more gloomy. Chris still visited out of respect to Mr. Dunzy and Dunzy was still his friend. He sat in his normal spot with his laptop open in front of him. He picked up his phone and dialed Emilee.

"Hey sweetheart, how are you doing?"

"I'm doing okay, sitting behind the desk reading, trying to keep my mind form wandering back to…you know."

"Trust me, I know exactly how you are feeling." Chris

took a sip of coffee and stared out the window at the park across the street. Kids laughed and played with no worry in the world.

"Why is this happening to us? Why again? Why now?"

"I really can't answer that. All I know is that if we do go through it again, it won't be pretty. Shovel Rock wouldn't be an option. I will take an even more drastic measure to end it once and for all."

"Not you, but we. We will end it. You didn't want me to fight before because I was pregnant, but now that Michael is born and older, I will do my duty as a mother to protect him. He's OUR son."

A mischievous grin came across Chris' face. "You are very right sweetheart, we definitely are in this together. I didn't plan on stopping you this time, because Mikey and I couldn't finish the job together. It just has to take a woman to come in and do a man's job."

Emilee laughed out hysterically. "Ha-ha, that's so funny and true. Gosh I love you, thank you for that. I needed a good laugh." She paused for a second. "Ugh, I've got to go, I have customers...or really wouldn't I say readers? I really love you."

"I really love you too, bye-bye."

Chris ended the call, put his phone into his pocket. For reasons unbeknownst to him, Farmer Johnson popped into his mind. He felt as if he needed to see him.

As he pulled up to the farm land, he noticed how much of the land had over grown. Farmer Johnson's age caught up with him with exhaustion kicking in.

"Good morning, Ted." Chris greeted him as Ted sat in his porch rocking chair. Gray hair stuck out from underneath his straw hat.

"Welll, good morning Mr. Wilson. Have you a seat." Ted raised his feeble hand to motion Chris to the empty chair beside him. "What brings you around these parts?"

"Haven't come by in a while, you've been on my mind today. My son sees you more than I do."

"Mighty fine boy you have there, Chris. Hard worker. Real polite."

"You are talking about my boy right? How do you do it? He just loves to help you out around here."

"Ah ha, well now you see, I shouldn't reveal my secrets, but a root beer float will go a long way."

Chris burst out laughing. "Bribery, I should've known."

"If you had one of mine you wouldn't be laughing. Would you like one? I don't mind to make it."

"No thanks, it's a bit early for me."

"Okay then, you'll say that now, but when this next summer comes around you'll be back."

"I'll take your word for it." Chris stared out at the growing grass. As many times he saw it, he never noticed it was in the same spot that of which David was shot. "Hey Ted, let me ask you something. How come you're letting the grass go yonder ways?"

"Because Chris, every time I even have to look over there, I see in my mind that boy's death. How he was innocently shot up, unarmed and in the back while running no less. It just sickens me that our hard earned money is spent to support those cold blooded murderers."

"Ted, you are right. It very well was dishonorable, but did you know that he was an alien? The same creature that you yourself were shooting at that very same time."

"Your point? That still doesn't give them any right. Granted, yes they were trespassing, that's why I took fire. Though you have to admit, if we as humans were to invade another planet and they were to shoot us there would be a flat out war."

"But yes, Ted, there was a war. What people don't know is that in that split second of déjà vu, time had stopped and Michael and I fought them. And won."

"Oh I know there was Chris, I may be old, but not senile. I'm sorry we lost Mr. Gable though- that was a shame. War is evil like that."

"Unfortunately, yes that's very true. I hope I never have to go through that again."

...

"Hi good morning." Emilee greeted her first customer with joy. "How can I help you today?"

"I'd just like to return these." A boy no older than 12 placed a stack of books on top of the counter.

"Well let's see what we have here?" A cold chill ran down the back of her neck. She shuttered and glanced at each book. Though they were only children's books, they were that of the extraterrestrials.

"Ma'am, are you okay? Can I go now?"

"Yes. Yes. Have. A. Good. Day."

The boy left Emilee sitting and staring at the books. It was the first time in seven years that she had even set eyes on anything extraterrestrial and it struck a nerve. She remembered the section where the books were supposed to be. Each day she'd return to that empty section, hoping that the books would mysteriously return and that what happened seven years ago was only just a dream. And in that dream everything would be okay- only it never did happen that way...until today.

All of the books were back and back in their original spaces. She about fainted with both excitement and curiosity kicking in. Frantically she ran from one end of the library to the other just searching. Encyclopedias, magazines, archives, all and every bit of alien phenomena was back on file.

"Chris baby, I'm sorry to interrupt, but-"

Chris cut her off as he answered his phone. "Whoa, whoa sweetheart calm down. Slow down, breathe. What's wrong?"

"Something weird is going on. Is Michael there with you? Is he still working at Dunzy's Coffee Shop?"

"No baby, Michael has been dead the past seven years. I'm sitting with Farmer Johnson right now. What's going on?"

"Ohhh you remember how all of the alien paraphernalia just vanished out of thin air? Well it's back- all of it, every single bit of it."

"Oh wow, that's interesting." This caught him off guard.

"No kidding. Chris, what could this mean?"

"I don't know, maybe a warning to really dig deep on research and, Lord willing, find a clue on how to destroy them. Just in case of course."

"I'm scared Chris, but I don't want to jump to conclusions that easy. This was just a weird coincidence. I don't want there to be any just 'in cases'. I don't want there to be anything."

"And neither do I, At all."

"I think I'm going to see Michelle after work and see how she's doing."

"Okay sweetheart, that's completely fine."

"Okay, I'll be home sometime. I'm going to jump off here and get some coffee and relax myself. I love you."

"I love you too."

Chris hung up the phone.

"Mr. Wilson, is there something going on that I don't know about?"

"I'm not really sure. Here, let me explain." Chris went through details of his son's dreams lately and with the reappearance of alien files.

"Lord, Chris."

"What?"

"Why didn't you say something before? Is that why you visited me out of nowhere? To warn me? You don't have to do that, I know they are coming. I can feel it in my bones. I've got nothing left. I-" Ted rose from his chair and limped with his cane to the porch railing. He gripped the rail so tight that the whites of his old knuckles were shown through.

"Ted what's the matter?"

"We have to make ready…and now."

"What makes you so sure?"

"There's a storm coming in the distance."

"It's just a storm, we've been through worse."

"Maybe, but maybe not. I don't trust storms. Storms bring clouds, and in the clouds THEY wait. I'm not taking any chances. If I were you Chris I wouldn't either. Get your family to safety- before you regret it."

He left Chris to himself and limped inside the house. The screen door slammed shut behind him.

…

"Hey! What are you guys doing here?" Emilee asked. She was shocked to see Chris and Michael walk through the door and hugged them both.

"Daddy came and got me early from school today."

"He did? Well how come?"

Michael shrugged his shoulders. "Umm…I don't know. To take me for ice-cream maybe?"

"I figured with Farmer Johnson getting ready for some guests that he believes are going to be in town here soon that I should take Michael here out for quality time."

"See I told you ice-cream!" Michael cheered.

"You better bring me back some. And does Farmer Johnson feel that we should get together with his guests? Have us a little neighborhood reunion?"

"Yes he very well believes that."

"Well okay then." Emilee tried her best to keep calm, for Michael's sake. "I think that can be arranged. You two go have a good time. I'm going to get back to work."

"Okay, I love you mommy." Michael hugged her tight.

"I love you too sweetheart."

Emilee locked the library doors as she left the library that afternoon. She checked out every alien book and stuffed them in her backpack on her shoulders.

The sky was gray and cloudy. No rain has yet to fall, but a cool breeze blew through her hair. Autumn was surely here. She made her way down the empty sidewalk to the Christy County Hospital. The streets were deserted from the storm to come.

She checked in with the security guards in the main lobby and left her backpack with them before she jumped on the elevator to the psychiatric level.

Michelle turned from the window that of which she was watching out of to a familiar knock at her door. She didn't have a smile on her face or a single sign of life in her eyes.

"Hey Michelle, how are you doing today?"

...

Ted Johnson wasn't going to take any chances. Coincidence or no coincidence he knew the aliens would return one day. A part of him thought he was crazy to believe in the fact that the creatures were once here before, but the other part was a knowing in the pit of his stomach.

It was his land he had to protect. Protect not for himself, but for the honor of his relatives. Form generations to generations, his land was passed down from one son to the next. Now in his name- the last of his family- he swore not to let it go without his good name.

He walked through the house and made sure everything was neat and tidy. The floors were clean, and shelves dusted only a couple days before. All at the same he had a rifle in his hand and a cane in the other. He set the rifle down only to tighten the straps on his overalls and throw his father's suit jacket over top and then stepped out onto the front porch.

His eyes glowed green from the lights glaring around the outer rim of the U.F.O. parked on his front lawn. "I knew you'd be back. May God have mercy on your souls'."

Ted cocked his rifle, raised it to the saucer and fired. Only two shots were heard: one from the rifle and the other was a single PEW from the U.F.O. Farmer Ted Johnson's last sight was a green laser heading toward his face.

Chapter Sixty

Rain poured down right after a loud crash of thunder that shook the hospital. Michelle turned from the window and asked, "How do you think I'm doing Emilee?"

"I hope you are doing okay."

"Look where I'm at, do you think I'm okay? You saw that lightening right? It was green. GREEN! Do you remember what happened the last time lightening was green? And you have the audacity to ask me how I'm doing. Pssh."

"Michelle I- I'm sorry. I just wanted to see how you were."

"Riiight, when was the last time you came and 'checked on me'? I'm not stupid or mentally incompatible. I do know why you are here. Now out of all times- you want to know if I believe the aliens are coming again, to see if I've had some sort of *vision* or *sign*. Well guess what? Nothing! The only sign I'd know they were coming back was that alien woman kicking me out of the U.F.O. and flying away. I just knew one day she'd be back for revenge."

"I'm- I'm sorry. I didn't know. Are you sure they are coming?"

"Isn't it obvious? And no, you didn't know. How could you? You all left here, left me to believe I had a nervous breakdown...again. My husband was charred right before my eyes, of course I was going to have one!"

"We really thought that you did, it seemed very reasonable. It's what the doctors told us. I'm really sorry. All this time they said you were slowly recovering. I wanted to see you, I really did."

"Yeah well, it's too late for that now. Take a look outside, they are here...again. And don't think I'm just going to let my guard down just because you are here and relax from my anger. I have every right to be this mad...this angry."

Emilee didn't know what to say. Her eyes stared out the window past Michelle, frightened at how true her words hit. And not to mention, frightened because of how black the sky was turning. One by one the power of each building down below flickered out with green lightening following in the sky.

"I told you they were coming! Didn't I? Didn't?!"

"Yes Michelle, you did. And so did my son. He dreamed it"

"And you didn't come to me sooner?"

"We just thought it was just a coincidence at first and didn't want to jump to conclusions."

"Well it's concluded, they're here and obviously darker than before. There's no convincing now, let's get out of here."

...

"Daddy?" Michael asked as he watched daddy lick on

his ice-cream and looking out the window at the sky.

"Yeah, son?"

"What are you thinking about?"

"Just that those clouds are looking pretty nasty with this rain."

"Will the aliens come with them?"

"What makes you think that? Or that aliens even exist?"

"Because Uncle Michael told me so. In my dreams. He comes to me and talks to me. He's an angel."

"How long have you been dreaming of Uncle Michael?"

"Just on and off. He doesn't want me to worry anymore or be scared about the aliens. He says you and mommy will take care of me."

Chris looked at him with his eyes open wide.

"And he also says that he's finally with Barry again. Who's Barry?"

"Barry was his older brother. He died in a car wreck a very long time ago."

"No he didn't. He was ab...ab...abducted and was believed to have died in a crash. Michael told me so."

"Umm."

"It's okay daddy, I know you didn't tell me because you didn't want me to be scared. But I'm okay, really."

"Wow son, you are growing up so fast. You are pretty mature for your age."

"Hey what can I say, I get it from my amazing parents."

"Welll, you are right about that." Chris threw a paper wad out of a napkin dispenser at Michael. He returned the blow with a paper wad himself. An all-out paper wad war had begun.

An explosion boomed out so loud that it shook the windows and silverware.

"Daddy was that thunder?"

"I-I'm not sure." Chris didn't like the sound of that. He wanted to believe it was thunder, but with a gut feeling it was different.

"Umm daddy, I think we need to go." Michael pointed out the window at the power going out of every streetlight heading their way like dominoes.

Chris grabbed up Michael and made it outside just as the power went out in the diner. There was an eerie silence besides the pouring rain.

"Daddy I don't like this!"

"Neither do I. Let's -" He glanced in the diner; everyone was frozen. *Oh no*, he thought to himself. "Let's go get mommy."

...

As they ran down through the stairwells, Michelle thought of the frozen orderly. How they dodged in an out of them like in an obscure statue maze. "Was people like that...you know, before?"

"They may have been." Emilee answered. "Though I'm not really sure. All we saw was the incident in Farmer

Johnson's field."

"Well you know what, if so that would explain more why we are meant to kill these aliens then- why God put us all together in the first place. Which honestly, the first time I didn't really fully believe it. But now seeing how everyone's time has stopped and we aren't, I'm more convinced than ever that it's our destiny.

Yes I'll admit that I'm more angry at the murder of Michael, and I'm wanting my revenge. Eye for an eye, but I have a faith stirring in me that I have lost since his death to do God's will. To fight in His name. I'm so ready for this."

They exited the stairwell, in through the main lobby. With the main doors locked, Michelle picked up a chair and heaved it at the glass.

Chapter Sixty-One

'Say not thou, I will recompense evil; but wait on the Lord, and he shall save thee.' -Proverbs 20:22

Chris slid his car to a stop at the Christy County Hospital entrance doors just as a chair smashed through the glass and sailed over his head.

"Whoa!" Chris yelled out. Michelle and Emilee ran to the car, both jumped in the back seat. "Well hey sweetheart. And Michelle...wait, Michelle? How did you-"

"Just drive!" Both women yelled out in unison as they jumped in the car.

"Yes dears."

Michael turned around in his seat. "Hi mommy, are you okay?"

"Yes baby, I'm okay. Thank heavens you are alright. Mommy was worried about you."

"I'm okay, I've got three people watching me: God, daddy, and Uncle Michael."

Michelle, whom was in a paranoid state was frantically looking through each window and stopped with Michael's response. "Michael? What's the boy talking about?"

"Sweetheart, what do you mean?" Emilee asked.

"He's my guardian angel and comes to me in my dreams." Michael looked over at Michelle. "You must be

Michelle, I have a message for you. He's told me a lot about you and says that he's waiting for you when it's your time to come home."

"I-I-I-" Michelle turned to Emilee caught off guard.

"Michelle, meet my son- Michael."

Chris made a U-turn in the street to head back toward their home.

"Chris! What are you doing?!" Emilee yelled.

"I don't know- the car just died." He tried and tried to start it with no avail.

"They've got us." Michelle whispered.

"What?" Emilee asked.

"They've shut off our power. We have to find shelter, and quick."

"The library is right there, let's go." Emilee suggested. She ran from the car and fumbled her keys to get the door unlocked. Over the rain, a distinct vibrating hum hovered over them.

Once they were all inside, Emilee locked the doors behind her. Green lightening from outside gave an eerie green glow to the library.

"Okay, so what now? What are we supposed to do in a library? Read them to death?" Michael asked. He shocked everyone how much control he was taking and a maturity in his voice with only being 7 years old.

"He's got a point." Michelle added. Through the paranoia, her strength was coming back.

"Let's not rush anything and pray about it. God's going to keep us safe, we know that. Let's just be patient and-"

Chris began.

"No you listen here, if God's keeping us safe, why is my husband dead? Patience my behind, if God wants us to kill them and protect his creations, then let's not lollygag around and do what we are meant to do. I'm not going to sit around in a mental ward another seven years waiting for these aliens to return. No, no it's time to take some action. And to add to that, you've got your son to protect now. As a parent that's your duty to do everything you can to keep your family safe."

"Okay, okay. You're right Michelle. We just need to have patience and figure out a plan then. Of course I'm going to protect my family, there's not a question there. So we need to sit down and figure out SOMETHING. Obviously Shovel Rock wouldn't work now, and didn't fully work before either."

"What's Shovel Rock?" Michael asked interested.

"It's a game that daddy and Uncle Michael played when they were growing up. We'll have to show you after all of this is over." Emilee said.

Michelle sat down at a table. "Okay Mr. Patience Man, lets brainstorm the far out of this battle plan."

The mahogany entrance doors blew into pieces. Fog rushed in with a bright green light.

"So much for that." Michelle added.

Both Chris and Emilee held Michael close to them as a figure emerged from the light towards the group. "Let's all not just stand here," Michael said. "We've got to run and get out of here."

Michelle glanced around the library and moved to the desk. She searched for anything that could be used as a weapon. "He's right. Y'all get him out of here. I've got this. Go, now!"

"Nobody's going anywhere." A voice said through the fog, just steps from where Chris, Emilee, and Michael stood.

Everyone turned to see Becky with an evil grin upon her face. Her eyes glowed green underneath her old wrinkled rotten body as if it were a sweater taken out of a closet tucked away for the winter. Though she was dressed in a black dress over a long sleeved fishnet shirt.

"Well hello Chris, long time no see. How have you been?" Becky asked, the grin never leaving her face revealing sharp teeth.

Emilee whispered in Chris' ear. "Old girlfriend?"

"You can say that." He replied, his eyes with rage toward Becky.

"Cat got your tongue?" She stared a moment in awkward silence. "Anyways, so this must be little Michael, huh? Do you prefer Michael or Mikey?"

"Stay. Away. From. My. Son."

"Well then, he finally speaks." She walked around the family and sat down casually at a round table. "Come, come lets all take a seat. We're all adults here. Let's talk like adults."

Nobody moved.

"Okay..." Becky continued. "I'm trying to be sensible here, but if you all want to be this way then I will take affirmative action. Is that clear? Now be good humans and kindly take a seat.

The lighting is a little dark in here isn't it? Not suitable for a decent conversation I wouldn't think."

She pointed to the ceiling only lighting a chandelier in the middle of the room.

Michelle snickered, "A decent conversation huh? That's so hard to believe considering the people you have killed and the wars you have started. And people, I'm meaning my husband and brother-in-law."

"Yes my dear, I am only desiring a conversation. You all seem to have me all wrong. Hey, I had to retaliate to his and Chris' actions, now didn't I? Just like you plan on making an attempt to harm me this very evening."

"Oh I don't plan on making an attempt, I'm going to flat out take your life. How about that?"

"Well now that's a bit cruel isn't it? I'm doing no harm right now am I? Just merely sitting here. Now come on and sit, sit before we do get in a heated argument. That surely wouldn't go over too well."

Michelle sighed. "Alright, we'll play it your way. Come on fellas, let's have us a sit down."

They all sat as seated: Michelle, Emilee, Michael, and Chris.

"What exactly are you wanting?" Chris spoke up, anxious to get this situation over with. Of course they all were.

"Geez, why all the hostility?"

"Umm hellooo?" Emilee cut in, "You've practically got

us and the entire world held against our own will."

"Oh no, no, you've got me all wrong. You all can walk out of here as you please. Though you wouldn't have the opportunity to hear my proposition."

"Yeah right, I don't believe that one bit. If so, why such a *bang* of an entrance? There's something we humans call knocking. And thanks for that by the way, my insurance agent is going to love my explanation on how the doors exploded."

"Just to get your all's abiding attention. But no I'm serious, you can walk out right now. All I'm wanting is to talk. You've all got my family and I all wrong of why we are on Earth. I just want to get my point across before someone else gets unnecessarily hurt. Which like I said, you all killed my cousins, and I killed Michael. Eye for an eye as you say."

"And how are we wrong?" Chris asked. "David said you've all been here for many years as is, but that you want to start a war and take over our bodies."

"David always took everything wrong. Yes, we have been here hiding and there still are many more of us hiding in the world. Do we want to take over? Not at all. Just want to be accepted. With the way your government is and how they lie about us, it's hard to get our word out and make our presence known. And that is where you come in Chris. I want you to write a book about us, tell the world. Make us known with the full truth, and not the secrecies the government portrays. Will you do that for us?"

He was stunned.

"Don't do it Chris, it's too risky. Something isn't right about it. Too good to be true." Michelle cut in.

"Yeah sweetheart, I agree with Michelle. It's too fishy." Emilee added.

Chris looked down at Michael. "Buddy, you had nightmares over all of this. Your nightmares didn't seem this nice did they?"

"No, not at all daddy. She's an evil, scary woman. I don't like her."

"Thank you son." Chris turned back to Becky, "No, I won't do it. My son's opinion is more important than anybody's...besides my wife's of course."

"Good save, hubby." Emilee said

"Thank you, sweetheart."

The grin from Becky's face faced. "That was the wrong choice to make Chris."

"Hey, what can I say? This whole time I kept my patience and waited on the Lord to answer. What better answer than from a child of God. Plus come to think about it, in the scripture it does say not to put my trust in any man, only in God. You technically are not a man, considering the skin you wear is a human's, but evil underneath. And that of which where could you have gotten the skin in the first place without killing someone for it. I remember your little army of missing persons. I-"

Becky cut him off. "Fine then. If you believe that to be true then I'm going to just have to take you all with me and make you write it the hard way."

"Oh sure, you can go right ahead and take my husband, but he won't die so easily, and he'll definitely annoy you. Husbands are good at that at times. And you certainly wouldn't get any book out of him. So you are just wasting your time." Emilee said.

"What?" Becky, Chris, and Michael all said at the same time.

With all eyes on Emilee, Michelle ran around the table and stabbed a pencil through the side of Becky's head into her brain. Becky screamed and jumped from her seat, pulled and pulled on the pencil that would not budge. In only seconds, Becky exploded in a bright green light.

Michelle looked over at Emilee, "Thanks for the distraction."

"Huh, I guess the pen is mightier than the word." Chris said. "Thank the Lord it's finally over."

"No." Michelle said from the window. They all knew what she meant. The green lightening still lit up the black sky. "It's not. There's still one more thing to do."

She headed toward the hole of an entrance. Wood chips crunched under her feet.

"Michelle, wait. You don't have to do this." Chris pleaded. "There must be some other way."

"But you see, Chris, there isn't. With everything that has seemed bad, God has made good. He took Michael home to watch over little Michael. I survived to kill that creature, now I can self-destruct the U.F.O. to take me home to God and my husband. Now all that's left is for you to expose the aliens to the world. Write, write, write all about the truth. The world needs to know about the evil that has lurked within us in the crowds of humans.

As it says in the book of Ruth, 'Where thou goest I will go,' so don't mourn for me leaving. I'm going to a better place and will see you all again someday. I know you want to stop me, but I'm happy about what I've got to do. May God bless you."

"Michelle, wait!" Emilee yelled, but she was gone and disappeared in the fog.

In mere seconds, one explosion after another banged out in the sky like a blast of fireworks. Only in the end there was one final explosion that followed- an explosion so loud and strong that the entire library shook. Every book fell from the shelves to the floor.

The rain disappeared along with the clouds. A bright sunset shinned through the windows along with each light turning on as time came back to life. "That's it?" Michael asked.

"That's it." Chris smiled.

"Okay, great. Now please let me go, I can't breathe."

They all had a good laugh, a laugh to ease the pain, stress, and just to enjoy the moment. A moment together alive in God's grace.

Chapter Sixty-Two

Still laughing, Chris stood up and helped Michael and Emilee to their feet.

"Come on, lets clean up this mess." Emilee smiled. She wanted to cry, she wanted to just breakdown, but she knew that the truth was that Michelle WAS in a better place. Her life was in God's hands.

Chris' cell phone began to ring.

"Hello? Hey, Sheriff Boston, what's up? What kind of bad news? Do you mean Michelle escaped from the mental ward? Oh never mind then, it's a long story...oh...thanks for letting me know. Good-bye."

Chris hung up.

"What's wrong?" Emilee asked.

"Ted Johnson's farm apparently burned to the ground and Ted was in the house when it happened. He's gone."

...

It was a sad morning for the town of Christy, Tennessee. Reverend Brown gave a eulogy for both Ted Johnson and Michelle Gable. Closing a tearful service, Chris, Emilee, and Michael stayed behind.

Chris stood over Michael and Michelle's joining graves. He was silent and dazed off completely. Emilee took a hold of his hand. "What are you thinking about, sweetheart?"

"How funny life is, how that growing up with Michael it was him, Barry, and I. We were three. And now in the end, it's three still with Michael, you, and I. Everything seemed to somehow go into a cycle, while things just seem to always change. Not that I'm complaining, I'm just saying it's a funny thing about life."

He got down on his knee and looked Michael in the eye. "Son, I want you to stop and really listen to me right now, okay? You are still our baby and this is going to be hard for you to understand, but I want to explain something to you. Look around you, this is your life. Life is short so never take it for granted. Each day you are alive is a blessing and never let the perils of life get you down. Always be happy, give as much love as possible and always remember that God is real and in you right now.

The only thing that matters, the answer to life, is to live each day believing in God with all your heart, loving Him and loving one another. And one day, when you grow up, you will meet the right woman for you, marry her and spend every second you can with her as one. You have witnessed how fast life can change in just a split second, so that's why I'm telling you to never take it for granted. Have patience and take life slow, no matter what everything will take care of itself. Remember that son, and mommy and daddy both love you very much. We always will no matter what."

"I love you too daddy. And I'll remember I promise." Michael embraced Chris in a hug. "Can we go home now?"

"Yes we can go home now." Emilee said.

Epilogue

Chris spent the rest of the day playing catch with both Emilee and Michael in the backyard while the weather was sunny and nice. They grilled out that evening, and ate out under the stars. That night they made popcorn and cuddled up on the couch laughing at home movies from mommy's and daddy's childhoods. Michael fell asleep and daddy carried him to bed as both him and mommy tucked him in and kissed him good night.

By the time Chris and Emilee laid down themselves, they were out as their head hit the pillows. Later on into the night, Chris woke up and couldn't go back to sleep. He eased down the hall to his office and closed the door behind him quietly not to wake his family. He turned on the desk lamp, and started up a pot of coffee. This was going to be a long night.

As his laptop loaded up, he opened the top desk drawer and pulled out both David's and his journal. Both colors had faded over the years and collected dust. Chris bowed his head to pray. It was now time to tell the world the truth, that aliens do well exist. And the aliens live among each and every one of us. We may not see them, but they are there, among us.

Author's Note

The idea of this book first came about back in 2008, which took 11 years to complete. It's been a long journey to finish this book; I put it down and picked it back up more than once and had many rewrites and editing sessions. It's a novel that I meant to entertain and to also show that God does exist. And that God is with us no matter what.

Do I believe in aliens? Of course. And I hope you as the reader enjoyed this work of fiction and will read my next work of literary art. This is only the beginning.

ABOUT THE AUTHOR

R. E. Henderson is a Christian author from Knoxville, Tennessee along with his wife and painter, Rachel Henderson. They live with their daughter and 4 crazy dogs.

www.r-e-henderson.com

Among Us

Other books by R. E Henderson:

Expect the Unexpected
Seek
Lessons of an Old Fashioned Life
Confused: Greatest Hits
Dunzy's Coffee Shop